FREE RANCH

A novel

by

Paul Wallem

Main Point Press
Los Angeles • Chicago

FREE RANCH

Print ISBN: 978-0-9977543-8-4

Cover and interior designs and illustrations
by Stephen Wallem.

You can contact the author via the publisher, Main Point Press, at
(312) 912-8639
or via email: mainpointpress@gmail.com

DEDICATION

To present-day ranchers who struggle to maintain conventional lifestyles and beef herds in the face of a changing society and diets.

ABOUT THIS BOOK

As a kid growing up on an Illinois dairy farm, I always wanted to live on a ranch instead.

Every Christmas, I hoped for a pony, but he never showed up.

Years later, after visiting a friend's Wyoming ranch for 19 years straight, those experiences led to this fictional story. Mark Willand represents my long desire to own a ranch. Like me, he has owned several businesses through the years, and he uses those experiences to manage Halestone Ranch.

He treats his employees well. He could be a role model to influence new business owners.

Saddle up and spend some time on Halestone Ranch!

Paul Wallem

Halestone Ranch
Upton, Wyoming

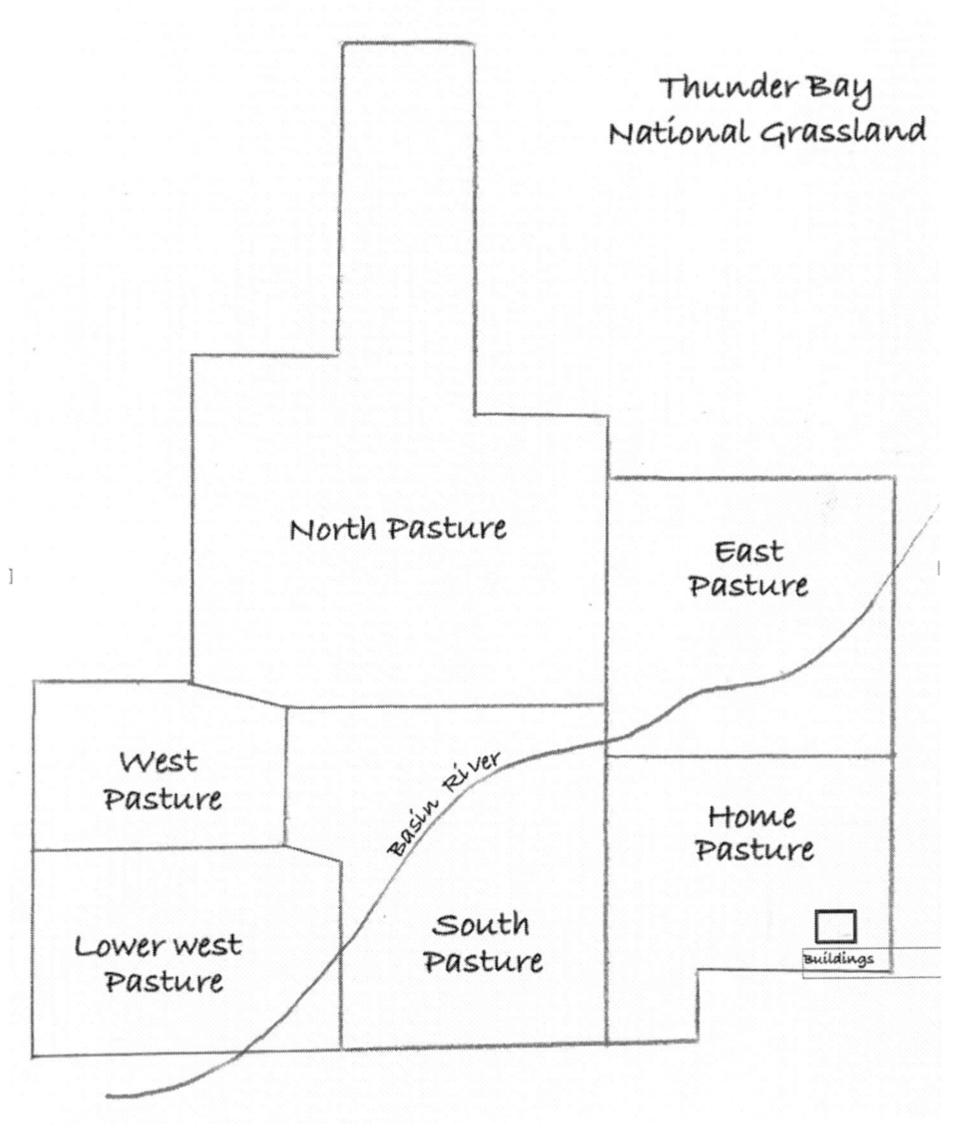

A FAVORITE SPOT

From Chapter 20

Zach had told me that the highest point on the ranch was in the South Pasture. It adjoined the ranch house, and was easy walking distance. It had always been called "The Hump." I headed there on foot with hopes of seeing the sunrise.

Daybreak is a magical time of day. The wildlife are coming alive. A mourning dove first with its gentle and rhythmic "coo, coo-coo," then the bellows of cattle complaining about some thing or another.

I climbed to the high point of The Hump just before 6:40 and, right on cue, the sun blazed over the eastern horizon.

The surrounding hills take on brilliant colors of pink and violet, which last only moments before vanishing in the daytime brightness.

CHAPTER ONE

Rockford, Illinois
September 18
7:20 p.m.

My wife, Barbara, and I were settled in front of the TV for an episode of *Shark Tank*. "Mr. Wonderful" appeared ready to make an offer on a squirrel-proof bird feeder when my cell phone vibrated. Not a number I recognized, no name ID, so I ignore it. Another robocall, no doubt. Those are mostly the calls I get, two or three a day, despite the "Do Not Call" list I am supposedly on. The beep indicated a voice mail, which was odd for a robocall — most don't leave messages — so I listened.

An unfamiliar voice said, "Mr. Willand, this is Alan Creston calling. I'm an attorney and my office is in Newcastle, Wyoming. The reason for my call is in the will of one of my clients who died early this month. He named you as the beneficiary of property he owned in Weston County, Wyoming, near the town of Upton. Please call me."

He left a phone number and disconnected.

My mental scam-o-meter reacted immediately and the needle started pegging in the red zone, but as I thought about it, something about this call seemed different. It wasn't some automaton telling me that I'd qualified for a lower rate on my credit card, or that I was in serious jeopardy with the IRS if I didn't return the call within two hours. Listening to it again, hearing his calm and professional tone of voice, I decided to sleep on it and call him the next morning.

September 19
9 a.m.

"Mr. Creston, it's Mark Willand in Rockford. You called me yesterday. What about?"

"Good morning, Mr. Willand. Thank you for returning my call. The deceased client I referred to in my message named you as the beneficiary of property he owned. He also gave me specific instructions to ask you three questions that would clarify if I had the right person. Can I ask you to respond to these questions?"

The scam-o-meter was moving toward the red again as I thought about whether I should answer any of his questions or provide any personal information.

"Do you have your own law office, Mr. Creston?"

He said yes.

"Do you have a website?"

He said he did.

"Are you in your office now?"

He said he was.

I told him I would call him back in 15 minutes and clicked off the call. I brought up his website and it indicated he was a sole practitioner who concentrates on estate planning with emphasis on rural clients. Same phone number he had given me.

By now, I'm starting to feel that Alan Creston is legitimate. I decided to proceed with caution.

I called back and told him to ask the first question, and if I was comfortable with it I would answer.

"Fair enough. Were you ever in the military?"

My LinkedIn bio states that, so it's no secret. I answered yes.

"What branch of service?"

That's also on the LinkedIn page. I answered Army.

"Last question, Mr. Willand. Where and how long at each?"

I thought about this and remembered that it wasn't on LinkedIn, but I had included it in one chapter of a book I had written a few years back. Someone could have found it there and it wasn't exactly a state secret, so I decided to find out where this was leading.

"Fort Knox and Schofield Barracks. Six months at Fort Knox and 18 months at Schofield Barracks."

"Wonderful, Mr. Willand. These are the answers my client gave me to confirm you are the man he wanted me to find. Now let me explain what this is all about."

Rewind 40 years to July 1978

It was a Sunday afternoon at Schofield Barracks, 25th Infantry Division, Oahu, Hawaii. My job for the past six months had been Detachment Commander, Military Police. We rotate the duty of OD (Officer of the Day) and today was my turn. I stopped in at the automotive hobby shop garage, a section of the motor pool where soldiers could work on their own cars while off duty.

In one bay, a car could be driven over the top of a five-foot deep pit, and the mechanic could walk down a stairwell and be able to stand as he reached up to work on the vehicle.

Just as I walked in for a routine inspection, someone yelled "FIRE!" The sergeant on duty grabbed an extinguisher. Down in the pit, there was a soldier with his clothes on fire, trying to find the stairway to climb out. Thick, black smoke had filled the pit, and he couldn't find his way to the steps. On my belly, leaning over the edge of the pit, I called for him to follow my voice and come to me, and when he was close enough, I grabbed his shoulder and guided him to the stairs. The sergeant in charge had extinguished the pit fire, but the soldier's clothing was burning till we wrapped him in a fire blanket.

He had suffered only minor burns, but was in the base hospital for a few days. I went to see him the day after the fire. He was grateful, and I felt good that we had helped him.

A week later, he came to my office and thanked me again for saving his life. We talked about the fire.

"What went wrong?" I asked.

"Aw, it was just stupidity on my part. I was replacing my muffler, and without even thinking about it, I lit a cigarette while I was loosening the U-bolts. It fell out of my mouth and with all the oil and gasoline that was on the floor, there was fire all around me before I knew it."

He continued, "You know, when the smoke blinded me and I was starting to choke, I had a flashback to when I was a little kid. I had gotten in over my head in a pond, and thought I was drowning. My dad reached down and pulled me out, just as you reached down and led me to the stairs. You saved my life."

"Well, I'm just glad I was in the right place at the right time. Anybody in my shoes would have done the same thing."

He said he was going to quit smoking. I never saw him again; don't know if he did.

Forward 40 years to the present

"Mr. Willand," continued attorney Creston, "now that I know you are the intended beneficiary, I'll describe your benefactor. Private Jack Hale was installing a muffler on his old car at the Schofield Barracks Hobby Shop in Hawaii. The year was 1978.

"A fire broke out in the pit below the car. You were there, weren't you?"

"Yes. I remember the kid screaming. That was a long time ago."

"Jack said he would wake up from nightmares for years afterward feeling that his clothes were on fire, that he was blinded and choked by oil smoke. Then he felt a hand, your hand, grabbing his shoulder and leading him to safety."

"I was surprised that his burns weren't worse. His clothes were burning off of him."

"Mr. Willand, Jack Hale believed till his death that you saved him that day. All these years, he had saved an article in the 25th Infantry Division newspaper about the heroism medal you received for helping him that day."

I remembered the article. The 25th Infantry Division is known as the Tropical Lightning Division. About a month after the incident, this article appeared in the base newspaper.

HAWAII-LIGHTNING NEWS

USARHAW / 25TH INF. DIV., Schofield Barracks, T.H.

Vol. 4., No. 13
July 10, 1978

TWO SOLDIERS AWARDED COMMENDATION RIBBONS

Two members of Army Hawaii have been awarded the Commendation Ribbon with Metal Pendant for heroism.

The two, Capt. Mark Willand of Hq.Co. 25th Infantry Division and Sergeant Kevin Johnson of Army Garrison Detachment, Schofield Barracks received the awards for their action during a spontaneous fire at the Schofield Barracks Automotive Hobby Shop.

Part of the citation credits the soldiers for their use of the highest qualities of a United States Soldier, to wit: "(Their) quick thinking, resourcefulness, and disregard for their own safety saved a young boy from serious injury, disfigurement and death...displaying sound judgment, initiative, and fortitude in the finest tradition of the United States Army, their exemplary action reflects great credit upon themselves and the military service."

Capt. Willand and Sgt. Johnson braved the flames issuing from a pit of burning gasoline to wrap the victim in field jackets and smother the flames which were eating away at the victim's clothing and flesh.

"After his two years in the Army ended, Jack returned to the ranch here northwest of the town of Upton, Wyoming, that his grandfather had started, and his dad then owned. He worked on the ranch with his dad until 1988, when a truck accident killed his father. Jack was 34 at the time, an only child, and took over running the ranch with his mother. She died 12 years later, and the ranch became his alone.

"Jack was a good rancher. He understood the land, the weather, and the animals. He knew how to survive in the lean years, and how to thrive in the good ones. Gradually, he expanded the operation by buying neighboring acreage whenever he could. Usually, it was land ranchers had worked until they got old and couldn't, or until they went broke. In both cases, they knew their land would be in good hands with Jack. Eventually, the Halestone Ranch exceeded 11,000 acres, plus he had leases for additional BLM grazing land."

"It sounds like he did well in life."

"Yes, but two years ago, he was diagnosed with ALS, commonly known as Lou Gehrig's disease."

I let out a soft groan.

"It sounds as if you know about ALS."

"I do."

"Then you know its cruelty and finality. It attacks and weakens the muscles needed to move, speak, eat and breathe. Nearly everything shuts down, except the senses. Patients are aware of every failure; they have to watch themselves deteriorate.

"The disease weakened Jack, and he was bedridden during his final year. He continued to live on the ranch and hired a foreman to run the operation. Jack never married, and hired a local woman to take care of him and the household. He had never had much contact with his few relatives, and none lived in Wyoming.

"Before the accident, Jack's dad had told him many times that the ranch was never to be sold or split up. Jack's dad had heard the same from his dad."

Attorney Creston continued with his story. Needless to say, he had my full attention.

"Before his illness, Jack had stayed true to his father's and grandfather's wishes and never considered selling the ranch. When he was told his days were numbered, and with no heirs, Jack knew he had to come up with a plan. As he lay in bed, he realized that the ranch might have to go to a new owner who might split it up. Only a year earlier, a neighboring ranch was forced to sell to avoid foreclosure. The new owners sold off parts of it to reduce the loan. That's what Jack wanted to avoid. Could he find a new owner that would keep the ranch intact? He called a long-time realtor friend and was told it would be hard to prevent a new owner from selling off parcels. Even if they agreed to the stipulation, there'd be no one around to enforce it.

"He knew his employees could not buy it, and as he searched for an answer, his mind, for some reason, returned to that day in the pit 40 years ago. He dug out that newspaper article, went on LinkedIn and found your name as well as your biography. He saw you had been a successful businessman. Just maybe, you would be the one to keep the ranch in one piece."

"Well, I ..." I started.

"Please let me finish, Mr. Willand, and then I'll answer all of your questions. Jack called me to the ranch, and designated in his will that you receive the ranch — provided you maintain sole ownership for at least five years. He felt that by that time, you might see the value in keeping the property in one piece permanently. The ranch is in a trust, and if you attempt to sell it or any part of it within those five years, a named charity would become owner."

Creston stopped talking. My mind raced, trying to corral everything I'd just heard. I was not ready to make any comment. I kind of felt like a lottery winner, except for the conditions tied to the prize. Plus, I'm retired! I like my life! Why would I want to own and operate a Wyoming ranch, and have to do it for at least five years? If I were 40 years younger, I would be on top of the world with this news. But this is now, not then. I'm past 60. Why would I take this challenge on in what should be my "golden years?"

After a long silence, Creston said, "Are you still there?"

I said I was, and asked him if anyone other than he and I knew what was in the will. He said he had drawn it up himself on his laptop, and no one but the two of us knew the contents. I told him I would call him the following day with questions. We set 3 p.m. to talk again.

The instant I hung up, questions started to flood my brain: Is the place debt-free, or is it burdened with mortgages, short term loans, machinery payments, etc.? How many cattle? How many employees? How big was the payroll? I wondered what brand the ranch was known by. There are thousands of registered brands. Those would be the first things I would ask tomorrow.

I was familiar with Wyoming and had a pretty good idea of where Upton was, but checked a map anyway. It's near the South Dakota border in far northeastern Wyoming, on the northern edge of the Thunder Basin National Grassland. That's over 800 miles from my home in Rockford.

I knew about Wyoming because for 19 years, I flew my Cessna 210 to a friend's ranch in eastern Wyoming. He had a landing strip right there on the ranch. We spent great weekends moving his herd to summer pasture. I looked forward to these trips every year, because it was as close as I was going to get to my boyhood dream of being a rancher and a cowboy. But those visits were for only a few days, not to own and be responsible for the place.

Before retirement, I had owned and sold three different businesses. My long-time attorney and friend Dave Enfield always said to call him when I had doubts about anything financial or business related. Surely this is one of those times. I made an appointment for the next morning at eight.

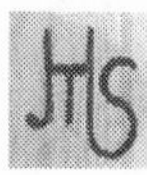

CHAPTER TWO

Newcastle, Wyoming
Six Months Earlier
March 10

Randy Gotch, a Newcastle CPA, does the tax returns and payroll for Halestone Ranch. Gotch has ranch manager Judd Turner to thank for that. The two had met in a bar shortly after Judd was hired by Jack. Right away, Randy started plotting how he could get Judd to help him get the ranch's business, even though Jack, and his dad before him, had a longtime friend as their CPA. Randy considered such loyalty admirable, unless it got in his way.

One afternoon, after Gotch had met with clients in Upton, he stopped for a beer at the Buckskin Bar before driving the half-hour down Highway 16 home to Newcastle. He and the bartender had been friends for years. The bartender knew Randy had Jack as a client and asked him if he knew Judd. Randy said he did.

"You know, I sure have a lot of respect for Jack Hale, and I hope Turner doesn't try to steal from the ranch."

"Why do you think he would?" Randy asked.

Leaning over the bar, he lowered his voice. "I hear a lot of things in here. One night, Judd was sitting right where you are, and after several shots of tequila he was feeling pretty sorry for himself. Told me he sure wanted to find an easier way to make money than running a ranch. With Jack getting sicker, I wondered if he saw a chance to take advantage of him."

Randy put on the appropriate face and feigned his disgust at such a prospect, but secretly, he made a point of getting to know the ranch foreman a little better. He liked the idea that Judd was hungry, and might be willing to ignore the law if there was profit to be made.

Gotch, himself, had rarely missed an opportunity to operate in the shadows where ethics don't reside. In recent years, he found what seemed to be a foolproof way to skim from his clients' accounts. When he could convince them to name him as trustee, he would find ways to transfer small, unnoticeable amounts from their accounts to his account. He used these funds to upgrade his office, create an image of success, and start obtaining ever larger businesses as clients.

That wasn't enough for Gotch, though. He had become acquainted with a Gillette CPA whose value system seemed even more defective than his. He moonlighted as a drug dealer. Randy sensed an opportunity because some of his oil field executive clients had made it known at various social gatherings that they enjoyed the occasional nose candy, and wanted a reliable supplier. He had also heard rumors that oil field workers combatted long stretches of job boredom with drugs.

Randy would never touch the stuff, but was more than happy to arrange for them to get cocaine and other drugs from his Gillette buddy, who rewarded Randy handsomely.

As Jack's health deteriorated, Randy was making plans for the biggest score of his career. But he'd need help from Judd Turner. He called Judd and asked him to come by the office.

At the appointed time, Judd walked into the offices of Randall Gotch, CPA, Inc. It was his first visit. Before being summoned today, he'd always met Randy in a bar or cafe. Judd was blown away as he looked around the large reception area. There was a large, overstuffed cowhide sofa and matching armchairs parked around a coffee table with deer antlers holding up the glass top. In a corner was a bar with a top made out of a 10-foot length of a log ripped lengthwise and lacquered to a fine sheen. The bar stools were made out of old saddles, with bases made from used horseshoes welded together. Some kind of fancy coffee contraption sat atop one end of the bar, with a bowl of fresh fruit — as fresh as fruit can be in the middle of Wyoming — and snacks next to it. The walls were decorated with expensive-looking Western paintings, and a few deer and antelope head and antler trophies. *Randy must be doing better than I am,* thought Judd. Overhead in the middle of the room was a 'cowboy chandelier': a wagon wheel with lights attached, hanging flat on chains.

Randy's assistant ushered Judd into Randy's office, where a huge head of a bison was mounted on the wall behind Randy's desk and seemed to be overlooking everything that transpired. Judd removed his Stetson and sat down in another plush leather chair across from Randy's huge, hand-carved desk. It was the cleanest desktop Judd had ever seen. No stacks of files or papers, no cups holding pens, nothing except a shiny brass plate reading "Randall C. Gotch, Certified Public Accountant." Right next to it, a coiled prairie rattlesnake, set by a taxidermist in mid-strike, mouth open wide, fangs facing right at Judd. *Appropriate choice for a mascot.* Behind it was Randy, head down, working on his laptop, not acknowledging Judd's presence. He sat in a large, executive chair that looked as if a Hereford had been skinned and the chair was covered with it. *A lot of cattle gave their lives for this office.*

Finally, Judd tired of waiting. "What's on your mind, Randy?"

Randy made a show of finishing whatever he was working on before looking up and smiling.

"Are you happy, Judd?"

"Uh, well, I suppose so. Whaddya mean?"

"Well, you've worked really hard for Jack and have done a great job not only just keeping things running, but running well."

Not sure where this was headed because he knew how Randy worked and there had to be a string attached, Judd responded with a tentative, "Thank you. I'm doing my best."

"And, frankly, I'm not sure Jack has adequately compensated you for that hard work."

Judd gave him a slow nod of cautious agreement.

Then Randy dangled the bait. "You deserve to be rewarded, and I have plans to own the Halestone Ranch after Jack's death. How would you like to be part owner?"

A grin slowly grew on Judd's face as the words sunk in. He told Randy he would do "almost anything" to get some ownership in the ranch. He was tired of scratching out a living and wanted to make some big money.

Randy explained that he had arranged for an LLC to be prepared by a western Wyoming attorney, in which a charity would own the ranch after Jack's death and keep it in one piece. He was sure he could get Jack to agree to it.

"Here's the kicker, though, Judd. The charity is really me, but I'm sure Jack is too sick to read it. He'll just sign it.

"So, Judd, I can sign over 10% of the ranch to you after Jack's death. Interested?"

Judd leaned forward. "I'll do whatever it takes."

"That's what I was hoping to hear."

Randy continued, "I'm helping a drug dealer in Gillette expand. He wants to build a market here in Newcastle. If you can find a spot on the ranch where a small plane can land and take off unnoticed, he will have someone local take delivery and distribute. I'll give you a $5000 credit for every delivery. Once you have built up $100,000 in credits, I'll be ready to sign over 10% ownership in Halestone Ranch as soon as Jack dies. That won't be long. He's not expected to live another year."

Judd was quick to respond. "At the north tip of the ranch out of sight of the buildings, there's a strip of land we don't use that's probably a half mile or more long. It's pretty level, but rough. I can probably clear the rocks and clean it up enough so a plane could land there. Is that long enough?"

Randy thought it would work. He told Judd to get to work clearing it.

Judd got up to leave, then stopped.

"One more thing, Randy. I know you own the used car lot at the west edge of town. Can I get a good deal on a Ford pickup? I've got some cash saved up to put into one."

"Sure, go see Mario Bianchi. He runs the lot. Tell him I sent you. He can set up financing for you."

After Judd left, Gotch thought back to when he first hired Bianchi. It was about ten years earlier. Randy had an old used car salesman running the lot, and Bianchi had stopped in looking for a job washing cars. Barely out of his teens, Bianchi told Randy he had been accused of beating a man to death in Brooklyn during a liquor store robbery. He used the cash to buy a bus ticket to California, wanting to get as far away from the cops as possible. When he got off the bus at Newcastle to stretch his legs, the town looked pretty good to him.

Randy told him he would give him a job and tell nobody about the Brooklyn robbery if Bianchi would do whatever Gotch told him to do. Bianchi agreed. From that moment on, Gotch owned him. After six years working at the car lot, Randy made Bianchi the manager. He had done a good job ever since on and off the lot. If Randy wanted other things done, Bianchi would respond without question.

Jack Hale's Funeral
September 1

Patti Malik sat in Jack Hale's memorial service, wondering if he had considered her in his will.

Fifteen years earlier, Patti and her husband moved to Upton when he got a job driving a truck at the coal mine. They often rode his Harley together and en route home from Sturgis one year, he lost control. Patti suffered a broken knee, and even after several procedures it continued to hurt. After their divorce, she worked as a waitress. Being on her feet all day made her knees ache even worse.

Tylenol helped for awhile, but when that stopped working, her doctor gave her Vicodin, which was much more effective. But after a time, Patti couldn't get her doctor, or any other doctor in town, to continue her prescription. A co-worker, another waitress, let her try oxycodone, and that really wiped out the pain. She felt great till it wore off, but she couldn't get prescriptions for that, either. She started buying it from other sources, at a high price. Patti also realized she had become hooked on it. Even when the knee wasn't hurting, she needed it.

Around this time, Jack Hale started coming into her restaurant for breakfast once a week. He was a successful rancher, always polite and a good tipper. They became friendly, and she would sit with him while he finished eating. She had heard that he had never married, and lived alone on the ranch after his father died.

One day during breakfast, he told her he had been diagnosed with ALS. She knew just enough about the disease to realize it was serious. He said he probably wouldn't be coming in as often. Some days were not good.

A month had passed before Jack stopped in again. He asked Patti if she would consider taking care of his house and cooking for him. He offered her a lot better income than she was getting, so she started working at the ranch. She would drive out every day, cook his meals, wash his clothes and do his housework. The nine-mile drive was no problem. Best of all was the extra money that she now had to afford her black market oxycodone.

Jack's condition steadily worsened, the disease robbing him of his strength and vitality everyday. After about a year, Patti started staying longer after her day's work was done to keep him company. They became closer, but never with any intimacy. She liked him, felt bad about his failing health, and wondered about the future of the ranch after he was gone. They never talked about that. She also wondered about her future once the job, and the income, stopped. Patti started wondering if he might name her in his will.

About six months before Jack hired Patti, he had realized he couldn't continue to manage the ranch and be his own foreman, as he always had. He left word around town that he was looking for a foreman. When Judd Turner came to the ranch to apply, he brought along a list of references. Jack didn't take time to call them. He made a decision on the spot to hire Judd. It wouldn't have made any difference if Jack had called the references; they were false. Judd had talked two old friends into taking the reference calls and recommending him.

As Patti waited for the service to begin, Judd Turner walked in and took a seat in the row ahead of her. Her thoughts went back to an afternoon some months back. As she was about to leave the ranch, she found an envelope under her windshield wiper. It had a 50-dollar bill in it. Besides Jack and Judd, Zach Talty was the only other one on the ranch. Zach had worked on the ranch for quite a few years. Patti was curious, but gladly took the money and drove home.

A month later, another envelope appeared on her windshield with another fifty inside. This time, she asked Judd if he knew anything about it.

"Yes, ma'am," Judd smiled. "I put it there. The one last month, as well."

"Why? What's it for?"

"It's just a token of my appreciation for all you're doing to help Jack. I know it can't be easy."

"Well, it has its challenges, but I've really grown quite fond of him, and I'm happy to be able to help."

"That's good, that's good. I've been a little concerned about your knee pain, though. I hope you've been able to manage that."

Patti had confided to Judd that she had a problem affording the oxy and wondered if he knew where she could get it cheaper.

"Well, you know, some days are better than others."

"Look, Patti, there's something you need to know. Some 'irregularities' might be going on around the ranch, and it would sure help me out if you could, well, overlook what you see, and not mention it to Jack, either."

A few weeks earlier, as she was leaving the ranch right after dark, she heard a low-flying plane. It was too dark to see it, but it was a surprise, because no airports were anywhere near the ranch.

"Was that plane I heard a while back one of the 'irregularities?'"

Judd smirked, nodded and added, "All you need to do is look the other way and keep your mouth zipped and you'll keep getting an envelope each month."

Patti knew Jack would not be alive much longer, and decided she could overlook whatever Judd was talking about in order to get the money. It would help her buy oxy.

"OK, Judd," she said. "No problem".

After the service, Judd spotted Alan Creston mingling among

the mourners. Judd had seen Creston at the ranch often during the past month, and knew he was an attorney. They hadn't formally met.

"Mr. Creston," Judd said as he approached and stuck out his hand, "Judd Turner, Mr. Hale's foreman."

"Oh, of course, Judd. Jack spoke highly of you. I'm sorry to meet under such sad circumstances."

"Yes sir, and I'm sorry to bring this up at this time and place, but do you know whether I still have a job?

Creston assured him he did and explained that his law firm was the executor of the estate, and he would keep Judd informed. He said Judd's paycheck would continue for the time being.

"Will the ranch be sold?" Judd asked.

"Well, that has yet to be determined. I've got some paperwork to clean up with Jack's estate, and we'll know what's next in due time."

The two shook hands and parted.

Judd looked around for Randy Gotch, who was heading for the parking lot.

"Randy, can we talk?"

"Come to my office tomorrow morning." Randy got in his car and drove off, appearing reluctant to be seen in public with Judd.

Moments later, Patti approached Alan and asked if she was still expected to come to the ranch daily. She had been continuing to cook for Judd and Zach, and maintain the house. Creston told her to continue for the time being, and her check would be continuing.

She, too, asked about the future of the ranch. Attorney Creston repeated that nothing had yet been resolved.

I bet he knows if I'm in the will. Patti resisted the urge to ask at that moment.

Rockford, Illinois
Six months later
September 20

As planned, I walked into the offices of my long-time friend and attorney Dave Enfield for our eight o'clock meeting. Over the past 30 years, he's steered me away from some mistakes and encouraged me when the direction was good. He never bills me for a discussion where he approves my action without needing research. If he thinks I should slow down and look more closely at a project, I happily pay for his advice. Often, he has uncovered reasons to not go forward.

"So," began Dave, "a free ranch, eh?"

"With strings," I quickly added.

"Well, I'd tend to think this one falls into the 'too good to be true' category, but let's take a close look at what we have and move accordingly."

I agreed, and we went to work on a series of questions for attorney Alan Creston:

1. Is the ranch incorporated, or in a trust, or single ownership?
2. Has an appraisal been made regarding value of the ranch?
3. Is there a mortgage? Loans outstanding? Any judgments? Any easements?
4. How many employees? Who does the weekly payroll?
5. How much cash on hand?
6. Is there an employee pension plan? What's the ranch participation?

Dave also wanted Creston to again confirm that no one but he and I are aware of the conditions of the will. This would allow me to visit the community and learn more about the ranch before accepting ownership. He suggested that if all goes well and I end up with the property, I could consider having Alan Creston continue as attorney for the ranch.

Eighteen months earlier
Judd Turner

Judd was raised in Missoula, Montana. Son of strict parents, he chafed under their constant supervision during his teen years. From an early age he looked for ways to get around their rules. Missoula has long been a headquarters for smoke-jumpers, going all the way back to 1939. These free spirits love to push the limits, and Judd started hanging around them as a teenager. Some of them lived for the adrenalin rush that came out of a jump into a forest fire. Judd couldn't do that, but he loved hearing about their risky experiences.

Judd found his thrill with shoplifting and the rush of avoiding being caught.

He got a part-time job during high school at a gas station. He started stealing six-packs while on duty, not considering that the owner took occasional inventories and would know beer was missing. Finally, the numbers caught up with him and he was fired.

Judd's father decided a change of scenery would be good for Judd and imposed on a friend with a ranch between Missoula and Hamilton to hire him as a gopher. Judd took well to the work, found a thrill in learning how the ranch worked, and how to handle horses and work cattle. He stayed on for several years, eventually moving up to ranch foreman.

Judd liked the work and was good at it, but it wasn't long before he got the itch for more excitement. A drinking buddy drove a cattle truck for a custom hauler, and after a couple six packs one night, they decided Judd's ranch wouldn't miss a few steers.

A week later on a clear, moonlit night, their plan went into action. His friend borrowed a Kenworth and cattle trailer, and Judd had loaded two saddled horses in his own trailer. They met at the far end of the ranch where the herd was summer pastured. After cutting a dozen head out of the herd, they loaded them in the big trailer and hauled the load over the border into Idaho where Judd had found out about a cattle buyer who was willing to ignore brands. They delivered the load to him, received an envelope full of cash, and hurried home.

The thrill was back. Judd craved more, and the rustling continued. Rumors started flying about a cattle hauler traveling without lights late at night.

But Judd remembered how the beer shortage caught up with him at the gas station, and he started worrying that the rustled cattle would be discovered at the ranch's upcoming roundup. He decided to tell his boss he had a new job in Nebraska, and quit.

He packed up and drove east to see what he could find.

After three days of rambling through Bozeman, Billings, and into Wyoming, he drove through Gillette and south till he stumbled on Upton in late afternoon. He liked the looks of a motel with a restaurant and stayed overnight.

Breakfast was good and the waitress treated him like an old friend. She asked if he worked on a nearby ranch.

"No, I've been in Montana all my life ranching, finally quit and drove over here to see what Wyoming is like."

"It's 'Big Wonderful Wyoming' according to the tourist ads," she smiled. "Upton is surrounded by good ranches. An experienced ranch hand shouldn't have any trouble finding work."

Judd's Ford pickup was getting old and tired, but he had kept it up. Getting the oil changed at the local garage, everyone seemed friendly, just like the waitress, so he decided to focus on getting a ranching job there. He still had $1200 cash remaining from his last paycheck and the stolen cattle. He wanted to get a job before he used it up.

The Open Range Steakhouse was just down the street from his motel. That night at the bar, he told the bartender he liked the people he'd met in town, and wanted to find a job close by. He repeated the story that he'd just left his job as a ranch foreman in Montana to see what Wyoming was like.

The bartender leaned his elbows on the bar. "I might just have something for you. The Halestone Ranch is owned by a nice guy named Jack Hale. He used to stop in for a drink when he was in town, but I don't see him anymore. Someone told me he's got ALS and from what I know of that disease, you aren't going to get out of it alive. You get weaker until you are gone. I know his ranch hand, Zach Talty, and he doesn't want to run the place. You might go see Jack, because I think he really needs to hire someone to be foreman."

Judd thanked him and got directions to the ranch.

The next morning, he drove to the ranch. Pulling into the yard, he saw the buildings were well-kept and his first impression was good.

The man sitting at the door of the machine shed looked like he had spent his life outdoors, and also looked tired and worn out.

The old Ford's door groaned as Judd opened it and stepped out to walk toward the man.

"Hi! My name is Judd Turner. I'm looking for a job. The folks in Upton have been nice, and the bartender at the Open Range Steakhouse suggested I come out here and see Jack Hale. Would you be him?

"I would be," Jack said, giving the stranger a head-to-toe once over. "What kind of work are you looking for?"

Judd repeated the somewhat truthful story that he had just quit a seven-year job as a ranch foreman in Montana, and wanted to find another job like that.

Still sizing him up, Jack asked, "Why'd you quit?"

Judd had prepared himself with an answer. He said he had always been in Montana, was born and raised there, liked his old ranch, but wanted to see other parts of the country. He had never married, so he just packed up one day, got in his pickup, and hit the road.

Hale saw a good-looking man with a confident appearance, dressed like a rancher, driving a tired pickup like most ranch foremen had. Judd Turner had no way of knowing that he had arrived at precisely the right time. Jack was sitting there wondering what he was going to do. He had a good ranch hand, but needed a foreman.

Jack had spent his life being careful, just like his dad and grandfather. He had always checked references before hiring a ranch hand. Yet, sitting here today, he felt that maybe God was giving him a break, sending this man to ask for a job doing what Jack could no longer do.

"Judd, this ranch was started by my grandfather. My dad ran it with him, and after Dad died in a car accident, I took over. Eleven thousand acres here, with 3000 acres of BLM lease land for more grazing. We've got some good hay ground, it's irrigated and we bale enough for ourselves and sell the rest to other ranches. We run 300 head of cattle. Up till last year, I only needed one man to help. Now I can't do much, and my man doesn't want to run the place."

He continued, "Tell me about yourself. How you were raised? How you managed the help at that ranch you just left, and how much drinking you do."

Judd told his story, some of it true.

Jack liked enough of what he heard that he said Judd could start immediately on a 90-day trial basis. If things worked out, he would have a permanent job. Jack made no mention of what permanent meant.

CHAPTER THREE

Rockford, Illinois
September 19
3 p.m.

Dialing the office number for attorney Creston in Newcastle, I wondered if, even with all of the right answers to the questions Enfield and I had put together, it would be enough for me to say yes; to agree to honor Jack Hale's last wishes.

"Alan Creston speaking."

"Alan, it's Mark Willand. What kind of day are you having?"

"Well, hello there, Mark. I've been expecting your call. My day? It's been a good one, thanks for asking. I began it as I do as often as I can: in the air. I've got a Cessna Skylane and there's nothing I love more than cruising over Northern Wyoming."

That made me like Creston even more. "I'm a pilot, too, Alan, and I always enjoy comparing notes with others. Where are you based?"

"It's nice to be part of the same club with you, Mark. I've got a hangar at Mondell Field here in Newcastle. I got bit by the flying bug when I was a teenager, and I've never missed an opportunity to be up there. How about you? What do you have?"

"That Skylane is a great plane, isn't it? I had one for several years, but I needed one with a little more room. Right now I've got a 210T, and for each of the past 20 years, I've flown it to a friend's ranch south of Newcastle, land right on the ranch, and spend a weekend moving cattle. The ranch is probably within 30 miles of Upton, so I already have a good feeling about this part of Wyoming."

"Well that makes Jack's choice of you make even more sense. And those Centurions do have the extra power. I hope to see yours one day."

"Well, I'm sure you will if this free ranch deal becomes reality. Which is why I called: My local attorney and friend Dave Enfield helped me put together a list of questions for you. I've started and sold three different businesses throughout the years. I've had my share of financial headaches, and I don't want to inherit another one. As soon as you can assemble answers for me I'll take a position on the inheritance."

I read through the questions for Alan. He didn't indicate that he'd be reluctant to answer them.

"I can have answers for you two days from now, on Friday, Mark, but I'd really prefer to give them to you in person." He added that he always looks for an excuse to fly his 182 for business purposes, and would fly to see me that day, weather permitting, if I wanted to share the fuel cost. He felt he could provide a much clearer financial picture of the ranch if we met in person.

I gave him the identifier for Poplar Grove Airport, (C77) where I've based my plane for many years.

"Give me a call when you're on the ground, Alan, and I will pick you up at the flight office."

"It's a deal. See you Friday, Mark."

After the call ended, I sat for several minutes thinking about this whole crazy development, not having any idea what would come of all this, but already thinking about my flight path from Rockford to Upton. I saw that Upton has a small municipal airport, which would get me close to the ranch. My 210T would get there in five hours, with a fuel stop at Ainsworth, Nebraska.

But my thoughts always went back to whether I really need this at this point in my life. The internal debate was growing louder, and it seemed as if the part of me who loved a challenge had a slight edge.

Creston's answers on Friday will decide what comes next.

Friday, September 21

Alan Creston's Cessna landed at Poplar Grove just before noon, right on time for lunch at the Boone County Family Restaurant. A few miles north of the airport, it has been my second office for many years.

As we slid into a booth, I was in no rush to talk about the ranch. I wanted to find out more about Creston, and get a read on what kind of person he was. I decided the best way to do that was to find out what kind of pilot he was.

"Let's talk about flying for a bit," I said. "I'm always eager to hear other pilots' experiences. I usually learn something."

"Yes sir, I agree with that. One old-timer who shares space in the hangar I use, told me that when I think I know it all, it's time to park the plane and walk away."

"Wise man, wise man. Are you IFR rated?"

"I'm working on it. It hasn't been much of an issue for me as I generally stay pretty close to home and avoid flying in sketchy weather. VFR only for me. Flying here was my longest trip and I wouldn't be sitting here if the forecast hadn't been clear. I'm no daredevil. No offense to you, but there's no place I absolutely have to be."

"Words to live by!"

"Ha! Yes. I have completed the written test, though."

"How'd that go?"

"I passed, but, oh boy, it was one of the hardest exams I'd ever taken, and that includes everything they threw at me in law school."

"Well I didn't go to law school, but I agree the IFR test is difficult. I'll guarantee you this, though: Earning that instrument rating is one of the most challenging, rewarding, and fun projects a pilot takes on during a lifetime in aviation. How many IFR hours do you have?"

"That's going slowly, Mark. There's basically one authorized instructor at our little airport, and getting our schedules coordinated has been difficult. I've only got about six hours in, and most of that has been under a hood, but I'll get there."

"I have no doubt you will. Having that rating in your back pocket won't mean you'll be looking for storms to fly into, but it's sure nice to have."

"Yes sir, that's how I look at it. Kind of an insurance policy."

The waitress came and took our orders. Linda already knew

what I would order, as I had never strayed from the "cold turkey on light rye, hold the mayo, fruit instead of chips, coffee and a water" in all the years she'd been waiting on me.

"What can I get you?" she asked Alan. He ordered a BLT and coffee.

I'm impressed with Alan's passion for detail, and his deliberate approach to flying. Whether or not I end up taking his free ranch offer, I like him, and have a feeling we'd be good friends.

As we ate, we talked about his law practice. Now 51, he had worked for a Newcastle law firm for 12 years, then went out on his own. Born and raised on a ranch in the area, he concentrated on developing a client base of ranchers, and now did work for them all over northern Wyoming. His dad had bought hay from Jack Hale's dad, which is how Alan got acquainted with Jack. When Hale, Sr., died, Jack hired Alan to handle his inheritance and future affairs. That was eight years ago.

After Jack's diagnosis with ALS, Alan made a monthly trip to the ranch to help him prepare a will.

"The ranch is in a trust and has very little debt," Creston explained. First State Bank in Newcastle has extended a $500,000 line of credit to the ranch for many years. Currently, $75,000 is drawn against the line.

"Machinery is modern and Jack updated most of the equipment when CaseIH and other manufacturers offered interest-free programs. The estate appraisal will be concluded over the next 90 days and the machinery value will probably come in at about $700,000.

"The corporate checking account, as of yesterday, showed a balance of $320,000. All current bills have been paid.

"There are no short-term obligations. There are no mortgages on the property. Wells Fargo last made an appraisal in 2017 when the credit line was renewed. At that time, the per-acre land value was stated at $550. At $550 times 11,000 acres, that's a total of $6,050,000. There has not been an appraisal of buildings for many years.

"There are no assignments, judgments or easements pertaining to the ranch.

"You asked about an employee pension plan, Mark?"

"Yes, and what the ranch's contribution is."

"There is no employee pension plan. There are two employees. Judd Turner is ranch foreman. Zach Talty is a ranch hand that's been with the ranch for over 20 years. He was first hired by Jack's dad, was close to both Jack and his dad. Never wanted to be foreman, however. Just wanted to do the work. In his own words, he always wanted to "be a doer, not a thinker."

"That's honest and admirable. Good for him."

"Over the past year, Jack has had to hire a woman to help him with housework, and drive him to the clinic. Before Jack got sick, he cooked meals for himself and his two men. Since he hired Patti Malik, she has been cooking breakfast and lunch."

I had to admit that it all sounded good. A solid operation. A thriving ranch. But I knew there was more to Alan's story.

"Now, let's talk about the conditions Jack imposed. A stipulation in the will is that you must agree to retain ownership for at least five years, and you cannot sell any part of the ranch during that period." He explained, "Jack felt you would never sell it or break it up if you got familiar with the place over that amount of time. He thought you would ultimately feel obligated to keep it and carry out his wishes."

With that, Alan Creston closed his file and sat quietly. He had answered the questions I had given him Wednesday. He looked around the restaurant, caught Linda's eyes and asked for more coffee, and left me alone with my thoughts.

So, I thought. There go a lot of my reasons for walking away from this gift. I woke up last night at three hoping I would learn from Alan that the ranch was so buried in debt that I could easily say no, and carry on with my uncomplicated life. Since I sold my financial planning office, I've had few worries. I've sold my first book, an aviation story, and am in process of selling my second one involving the dismantling of International Harvester Company in the '80s. Writing and book signing has been fun.

But now, with this information that Creston flew in with, how can I turn my back on a huge windfall? This is a major asset. My children and grandchildren will benefit, and I can even establish an education trust for future great-grandchildren!

Looks like I'm about to become a ranch owner, at least for five years. But there are still questions.

"Alan, what do you know about Judd Turner?"

He considered the question for a moment. "I know very little. I met him a few times this past year after Jack hired him. He appears to be experienced, capable and is pleasant. Jack was so desperate for help with the day-to-day ranching, he gave him the job on the spot when he first came to the ranch, didn't check any references. I thought Jack should have checked into Judd's background, but he was already on the job when I first met him. That day, I tried to make conversation by asking him where he had come from. All he said was 'the Missoula area.'"

I also asked about Jack's CPA. Alan said Randy Gotch in Newcastle had started doing the ranch tax returns within the past year. He said Jack had switched from the ranch's longtime CPA after Judd convinced him a more modern office and approach would be beneficial. Then when Jack became ill, Gotch also took over the ranch payroll.

Alan was quiet for a moment, and then added, "Once, about a month ago when Jack was still able to speak, he commented something about an LLC that involved Gotch. I asked him for details and he couldn't recall anything. At this point, his attention span had diminished greatly. A week later, I asked about it again, and he had no recollection about it."

I wondered about that. Is there something in that information I should be concerned about, or am I just looking for something that would make me walk away from the deal?

We talked about the next week.

"Alan, I plan to fly to Newcastle on Monday, rent a car and spend some time in the Upton area. I'll stay there Monday night and maybe even Tuesday night, I'll see how it goes. I plan to say that I'm considering buying property, so I can ask about the ranches in the area without tipping anybody off. Then I'll go to Newcastle to meet the CPA, and after that, get together with you."

I took him to the airport and bid him a safe flight. The forecast was good, so I was sure he'd be fine. On my way home, I found the internal tug of war between getting into the ranching business, or running away from it, was stronger than ever.

One voice had grown louder. *Are you really going to go ahead with this, you old fool? Start running a ranch at your age? And what about this Judd Turner fella who didn't want to talk about his past? And the LLC that Jack couldn't recall? Run, Mark, run!*

The slightly more dominant voice, though, reminded me of my lifelong dream of being a rancher. *He's giving you a ranch! Try it for awhile and see what happens. What could possibly go wrong?*

Plenty, I suppose, and I can still say no.

But I'm pretty sure I won't.

CHAPTER FOUR

Zach Talty
Halestone ranchhand

Zach was born and raised in Upton. His dad worked long hours for the BLM. His mother worked at the phone company. He had one sister, 12 years younger. In later years, she married and moved to Cheyenne. Zach had very little contact with her after that.

Zach was big for his age as a teenager. By the time he was a junior he was over six feet and almost 200 pounds. By that time, he was working part-time at nearby ranches, and felt more at home there than at high school. He never got involved in sports; he much preferred working with ranch horses. By the time he was out of high school, he was breaking yearlings for the saddle.

A brief marriage to an old classmate ended in divorce and he vowed he wouldn't do that again. He was fairly good-looking, and was always courteous, but his relationships with women were never very romantic. After the divorce, he lived in bunkhouses wherever he worked.

He enlisted in the Army with a ranch friend and spent two years there. The military found out he was good with machinery and he spent most of his time in motor pools. When his two years were up, he was encouraged to stay in, but he missed ranch life and returned to Upton.

It was easy for him to get back to ranch work. Through the years, he had built a good name for himself. He was reliable, good with horses and machinery, and extremely loyal. He was never critical of his bosses. Zach was gentle-mannered, except when someone wanted to pick a fight. His size (now 230 pounds and 6' 2") made him someone to be left alone. He was slow to anger, but when he did get mad, folks tended to get out of his way.

During his Army years, he had enjoyed physical fitness training, and it became a habit that he decided to continue back home. Zach ran every day and drank little, not typical for ranch hands.

Breaking horses was easier for him than most because he was in such good physical shape, but also because he just had a way with them.

Twenty years earlier

Jack Hale and his dad had done most of the work on Halestone Ranch through the years. They hired part-time help for branding, baling and roundup, but did the rest themselves.

When Jack's dad started suffering from a bad hip and couldn't ride any longer, they agreed to hire a permanent ranch hand. Soon after that, Jack was in the hardware store and ran into Zach.

He had known Zach for a long time, thought highly of him, and had even hired him a few times during busy seasons. He knew that Zach had worked part-time jobs at several ranches, and the rest of the time he had worked for a horse breeder.

After the normal hellos and chitchat, Jack got to the point.

"Zach, Dad's hip is bothering him a lot. He can't ride much any more. We're thinking about hiring a full-time hand. Would you be interested?"

Zach smiled. "I sure would be. I wouldn't mind having a steady job instead of jumping from one ranch to another."

"I'm happy to hear that. Come out and talk to Dad and me. Let's see if we can work something out."

The next day Zach was hired full-time.

Twenty years later Zach is still there. Now 42 years old, he considers the ranch his home.

Rockford, Illinois
Monday, September 24

It's 7 a.m. at Poplar Grove Airport (C77). The hangar door goes up and I start pre-flight for the trip to Wyoming.

It's a beautiful day to fly. The weather report shows VFR all the way to Newcastle. The Cessna 210T is ideal for this kind of trip. At 160 knots, the time to the Ainsworth, Nebraska, fuel stop is under four hours. Ainsworth to Newcastle is just over an hour.

Both gas tanks are full. Oil is OK. After pulling it out of the hangar, pre-flight includes flaps and aileron check, pitot tube, wing tips, tire inflation, prop tips, antennas, clean windshield, stabilizer and rudder. Then the inside cockpit check list, taxi to runway 30 and depart. I opened the VFR flight plan in the air.

At 6,500 feet, the gentle roll of the Iowa farmland stretches as far as I can see. Crops are just starting to turn brown. Wind farms are showing up in increasing numbers every year.

There is nothing quite like a clear day, with smooth air in a good airplane.

As I made my way west, passing just south of Waterloo, Fort Dodge and Sioux City, I saw a familiar landmark on the horizon. It's always interesting to descend over the cattle yards east of Ainsworth Regional Airport (ANW). Some years, the feedlots are full. Some years, there are only a small number of cattle on feed.

After landing, I taxi up to the gas pump, swipe my credit card, fill up and depart, without seeing anyone. The airport is unmanned, but there's a pop machine and a clean restroom. Both are important.

This is almost the same trip I've taken over the years to visit my friends' ranch southwest of Newcastle. Yesterday, I looked up the distance between it and the town of Upton. Just 37 miles. That tells me the topography of Halestone Ranch will be similar.

Back in the air and cruising toward Newcastle, I think about the work ahead of me. This is going to be an interesting trip, to say the least!

By picking up an hour as I crossed into the Mountain Time Zone, I'm on the ground at Mondell Field Airport (ECS) before noon. A few years ago, while on one of my annual ranch visits, a hailstorm dropped golf ball-sized hail. If those hit a Cessna's aluminum body, the damage would be incredible. So yesterday, I called Tuff Air, the FBO (Fixed Base Operator) and reserved room to put my 210 inside.

After they refueled it and towed it inside, it was time for me to refuel. I got a rental car and stopped at McDonald's. Chewing on a Big Mac, I wondered what I was going to do first when I got to Upton. I decided to figure that out when I got there.

Twenty miles later, I was there. A small strip mall at the edge of town had a sign on one of the storefronts, advertising Davig Real Estate. I decided this was as good a place as any to start asking questions.

It was a one-desk office. A friendly-looking, well-fed fellow stood, hitched up his pants, and welcomed me with an extended hand. With his jeans and boots, he looked like he was more at home outdoors than in an office. I was also wearing jeans and a snap-button shirt, the same uniform I had used on all my Wyoming trips.

"My name is Todd Davig. This big real estate operation is all mine! Can I help you?"

"I'm Mark Willand. I come here to eastern Wyoming every couple years to spend time with a friend who ranches south of here. I sold my business back in Illinois recently, and I decided to wander up this way, maybe see if there's any property on the market that would make a good investment."

"Are you thinking about a residence or a business?"

"Not a home. Our life, friends and family are back in Illinois. Maybe a small ranch that had potential to appreciate in value? It would need to have good people in place already, folks that are running it well. I would only be there occasionally to oversee the operation."

Davig smiled and pointed to a chair. "It's a quiet Monday here, and you look like you're in no hurry. Sit down and let's talk."

He sat across from me behind his desk and reached for a file.

"This is good ranch country, and most of the outfits have been here a long time. I've been here all my life, know most of the operators. There aren't any small operations near here. Most of them in Weston County are six or seven thousand acres, or more. They all have some BLM leases for grazing, run at least 250 head of cows and sell off calves in the fall. A few breed horses. Most of them have antelope and whitetail deer, and hunters visit each fall. That brings in some extra income."

I asked if he thought most of them operate at a profit. He said yes, most did. The weaker operations had been bought out through the years, and became part of neighboring spreads.

He paused and looked down at the file in his hand. "There is one interesting development here in the county," he continued. "The Halestone Ranch, about nine miles out of town, has been a successful outfit for many years. Jack Hale's grandfather, Robert, bought it a long time ago, during the Depression in the '30s. His son, Luke continued with it, and added a bunch of BLM grazing leases. Luke had only one child, Jack. After Jack came back from the Army, he worked with his dad, and when Luke died about fifteen years ago, Jack continued running it with his mother. When she passed, he inherited the ranch."

"I see, and what's the interesting development?"

"I was just getting to that. Jack was diagnosed with ALS a couple years ago. He and his long-time ranch hand, a fella named Zach Talty, continued doing it all till Jack got too weak. He tried to talk Zach into running the ranch and hiring some help, but Zach just wants to do the work, not manage anything. So Jack hired a ranch foreman. That was about a year and a half ago.

"Less than three weeks ago, Jack Hale died. A real shame. He was liked and respected as a good rancher, and also as just a good guy. He had no children and no heirs that anyone knows of. His executor is a Newcastle attorney, and at this point, no one knows what's going to become of Halestone Ranch."

So far, what I've learned from Davig coincides with what Alan Creston told me.

"Mr. Davig, how big is that ranch?"

Checking the file, he said it was 11,000 acres of deeded property, plus BLM grazing leases.

"You mentioned the ranch hand, Zach. He sounds like a valuable hand. What about the ranch foreman?"

Davig looked out the window, as if he was trying to decide how to phrase what he was going to say.

"Judd Turner came to town a stranger from Montana and remains a bit of a mystery. He apparently was an experienced ranch foreman, at least that's what he told Jack. I've seen Jack a few times since, and he was satisfied with the way Judd was handling the job.

"I've know Zach all my life, and I run into him often. He never talks bad about anybody. All he says is that Judd never talks about Montana or where he worked before he came here."

"Is there anyone else working at the ranch?"

He briefly described the job that Patti Malik had been doing. He didn't know if she was still working there since Jack's death.

After a half hour with Davig, I had been able to confirm much of what Alan Creston had said. I also learned more about Zach, and everyone seems to think a lot of him.

And once again, I heard that Judd Turner keeps his past hidden. If I do go forward with the ranch ownership, I'm going to have to know a lot more about him before I decide to keep him as the foreman.

I liked Davig. He didn't ask if I would be interested in the ranch, which made me respect him because he didn't have the listing. Seemed to me that he could become a friend down the road.

I asked him where he thought I should stay, and he recommended the Weston Inn Motel.

I called and made a reservation.

CHAPTER FIVE

Law office of Alan Creston
Monday, September 24

Alan sits at his desk thinking about Mark Willand's arrival today in Newcastle, and his visit to Upton.

Who is he going to talk to?

What does he want to find out?

Surely he will decide to take the ranch. No one walks away from a windfall like this. But what if he decides the five-year restriction ties him down too much?

What do I do with the place if he decides to walk away?

After roaming around the internet, Alan can find no similar situation described, and no information regarding his legal responsibilities if the beneficiary rejects the inheritance. He knows there is precedent for this, he'll just have to dig deeper. In law school, one professor said everything an attorney faces in his lifetime is covered by some rule.

He decides to put it out of his mind till Wednesday, when Willand promised he will say what he's going to do.

The phone rings, and it is Willand on the line.

"Alan, I'm in Upton and still plan to be in your office Wednesday morning. In the meantime, will you get me the GPS boundaries of the Halestone Ranch? If you could do that by tomorrow morning, I plan to look at the ranch from the air. I flew my 210 to Newcastle, and would like to do that tomorrow afternoon."

"Yes, I'll be glad to get that for you. I have another thought for you to consider. Last week, an Upton realtor called me, said he had heard I was executor for the ranch. He said he has been in that area all his life and offered to help. I told him I wasn't interested in listing it at this time, but would pay him to show me the property from the air, if he was familiar enough with the ranch to do that. He said he knows the area well enough. We agreed on $500 if I wanted to do it.

"Mark, I think it would be difficult for you to pinpoint the property with GPS and at the same time look down and observe the layout while also flying the plane at a fairly low altitude. I think you'd have your hands full doing all three. His name is Todd Davig, if you are interested. Instead of me going, you can take him up on his offer if you like."

"I've met him, Alan. I stopped in when I saw his realtor sign, and he told me about Jack Hale's death and that the ranch would probably be on the market soon. I'm still in Upton, so I'll stop back at his office, tell him about this conversation, and see if he wants to fly with me tomorrow. I won't need the GPS information if this works out."

Back in the office of Davig Real Estate, I told my new friend Todd that I had stopped in at a Newcastle law firm to inquire about property in the area, and had met Alan Creston.

"He said the two of you had talked about a ranch that you would fly over with him and point out the boundaries and features. The one he is executor for."

"Yep, that's that Halestone Ranch I had mentioned to you. The one whose owner just died. Like I said, though, it isn't for sale, yet, and I'm not sure if and when it will be. I get the sense that the estate may be tied up because of some complication."

"Well, he suggested I fly over the property with you, so maybe things are about to change. I'll be happy to pay you to fly with me in my plane. How about it?"

We agreed to meet in the morning at the Mondell airport.

There's not much more I can do here in Upton without disclosing my reason for the visit. I called the CPA in Newcastle that Creston told me about, Randy Gotch. I gave him the story about looking for ranch property, and that Creston had suggested I call him, as he had a lot of ranching clients. I made an appointment for 8 a.m. tomorrow.

The Weston Inn Motel wasn't a Westin, but it was clean and in good condition. Friendly folks and a nice enough place. I'll stay another night here before returning home Wednesday.

Newcastle, Wyoming
Tuesday morning

In researching the area, I discovered via Google that Newcastle calls itself the "Energy Capital of the Nation." It is centrally located in an area involved with the development of large quantities of coal, oil and cabled methane gas. The town is not large, yet the downtown area has several modern office buildings. Energy money.

It's the county seat of Weston County. It's busy and prosperous.

From the looks of his office, Randy Gotch must be busy and prosperous. It's on the second floor of one of those modern office buildings. Everything in it looks expensive. It had the look of a corporate officer's office, not a CPA for ranchers. I wondered if he had coal and oil companies as clients, too. Certainly his ranch clients wouldn't provide this kind of income, would they? His receptionist was expecting me.

I had thought a lot about what I should tell him. Obviously he had known Jack Hale well, and I had no idea what Jack might have told him about the will and trust.

Randy was about 45, well-dressed, friendly, and no doubt curious about my visit. He didn't show any sign of recognizing my name.

"Randy, my name is Mark Willand. My home is in Illinois, but I've come to Wyoming regularly over the past 20 years to spend time with a rancher southwest of Newcastle. He's located near Rochelle Hills, was a close friend back in Illinois till he relocated out here."

"Yes sir, Rochelle Hills is down in the bottom portion of the Thunder Basin National Grassland. I know the area."

"I expected you would. I've heard about Jack Hale's death, and Alan Creston said you've been doing work for his ranch for quite a while. Would you be willing to tell me a little about the place?"

"Mr. Willand, may I ask what your interest is?"

"Fair question. I've sold my financial planning business, and have thought about investing in Wyoming ranch property."

Gotch reached for an overstuffed file. If it is the ranch folder, he obviously has done a lot of work for the place.

"The ranch has always been in the Hale family, for three generations. I've done tax work for them for the last year or so, and then Jack asked me to do his payroll last year when he couldn't do it any longer. Jack became a close friend as well as my client. I sure hated to see him destroyed by that disease."

I asked him if, since he did the payroll, he could give me his opinion of the employees.

"Well, sir, I don't know them real well. Even though it's only about a half-hour from here to the ranch, I have to admit I did most of my work right here at my desk. The ranch foreman, Judd Turner, is fairly new. Jack hired him not long before I started doing the taxes. I'd seen him around now and then, and I must have made a good impression because Judd suggested that Jack hire me. There is a long-time ranch hand that Jack thought a lot of, and a woman from Upton has been cooking and doing housework. They are all still working."

He clearly didn't want to say more. Everything he told me was common knowledge, at least to Alan Creston and Todd Davig. I had the feeling that, where both of them wanted to help me with information about the ranch, this man Gotch wanted to tell me as little as possible.

Another thought came to mind as I sat there: the LLC Alan had mentioned that Gotch had something to do with. This wasn't the time to ask about that, and since I wasn't going to get any more information out of him, I thanked him and left.

Driving to the airport to meet Davig for our fly-over, I couldn't help but wondering what Gotch wasn't telling me. I wondered if he wanted to own the ranch himself.

CHAPTER SIX

Newcastle Airport
Tuesday, September 24
9:30 a.m.

Todd Davig showed up on time. I like the guy, he seems straight-forward, and if I end up in Upton more often, I will be glad to have him as a friend. I'm sure he hopes our interactions will lead to him being involved in the sale of Halestorm Ranch, but he seems genuine.

As we sat in the Mondell Field lounge, drinking free coffee, he opened his briefcase and took out a Google Earth photo.

Pointing at a multi-sided parcel, he said, "This is the ranch, and I've outlined the boundaries that I got from the plat book. Eleven thousand acres are registered under the Hale Trust.

"Most of the acreage, at least 9,000 acres, is positioned in a fairly square block, with indentations that are probably BLM leases. It looks like all the irrigated hay ground is scattered in this block, as well as the ranch buildings."

"What's this area up at the top?" I pointed.

"That finger of land is the remaining couple thousand acres. As you can see, it is long and narrow, and it is rougher terrain than the rest. Probably too rough to graze cattle. You wouldn't be able to get them out.

"Jack told me years ago that his grandfather, Robert, bought that part of the ranch sight unseen because there were no roads or trails to get into it. The price was so low he bought it anyway, thinking that hunters might want to go in for antelope, and he could charge a fee."

I looked closely at the photo, and tried to memorize the boundaries. Everything looks different from the air, and I was glad I had Davig along to show me the way.

The 210 had been pulled from the hangar and was parked out front. I told the Tuff manager I would be staying again tonight. I loaded

Todd into the right seat, completed a pre-flight, and got clearance to depart. Todd had suggested I track Highway 16, as the ranch is near the highway, to the northwest.

Before taking off, I had looked at the Cheyenne Sectional Aeronautical Chart to find the elevation at Upton Airport. It is 4,290 feet and the ranch is nearby, so I'll use 5,300 feet for the fly-over.

Davig had also marked on the Google photo the boundaries of Thunder Bay National Grassland. It's a huge piece of federally-owned land, and borders Halestone Ranch to the east. We both assumed that much of the BLM grazing leases the ranch has are on this grassland.

Highway 16 was taking us on a 300 degree heading. After a few minutes, he directed me to change the heading a bit, so I altered it to 285 degrees. A few minutes later, he pointed off the nose and said the north finger of land on the ranch diagram was directly ahead.

"That's the finger of the ranch land I was talking about. The 'sight unseen' parcel? See how rough and rocky it is? No wonder it's not fit to graze."

Looks to me like this north piece amounts to about 2000 acres, about three sections.

Pilots are, or should be, always on the lookout for a place to set down in case of an emergency, especially over rough terrain. I noticed one narrow and fairly flat area on this piece of ground that could possibly be a spot to touch down. Looked to be maybe a half-mile long. Nearby, a barely noticeable lane looks to be what hunters probably use. There are a lot of trees, rocks and deep ravines showing in every direction.

Todd is pointing ahead at the eastern border of the ranch. I've put in 20 degrees of flaps and throttled back to about 85 knots so we will have more time to look at the area. He pointed out the ranch buildings and the house. They all looked in good repair, at least from 1,000 feet above the ground. West of the buildings, the irrigated hay looks to be on level ground. It's a big field, and having the sprinklers has to be a real bonus in an area that only has 12 inches of annual rainfall.

The road leading to the buildings looks in good shape. Todd says the county maintains that road.

We took another pass and climbed another 700 feet to get a broader view. To the east, the Thunder Basin National Grassland showed rougher terrain than that of most of the ranch.

It was all pretty impressive. This flight had really given me a sense of what the ranch is like. Now it was time for flaps up and throttle in as we headed back for Newcastle.

At the airport, I asked the folks in the Tuff office to again hangar the plane, and told them that I'd be leaving the following afternoon.

To my guide, I said, "Todd, thanks for doing this. You obviously know the area around Upton very well."

"You're quite welcome, Mr. Willand. And do you mind if I stick my nose in your business and make a suggestion?"

"Please do."

"It does appear that you are interested in the ranch. Earlier, I told you I've known Zach Talty all my life. He's straight as an arrow. I don't think he could lie if his life depended on it. Now that Jack is gone, Zach knows more about that ranch than anyone alive.

"My suggestion is to let me call him and arrange for you to meet and talk. I'll tell him you asked me about the ranch, and might be interested in it, and that he could tell you more about it than anyone."

"Good idea. But at this point I don't want to meet Judd, the foreman, yet. Will Zach talk to me without Judd knowing?"

"Yes. I think he would agree to that, and I think he should come up here to Newcastle to meet you and not meet in Upton, where everybody's into everybody else's business."

I told him to make the call, and suggested that Zach meet me at the Weston and I'll buy his dinner. "Let him set the time."

Todd punched some numbers into his phone and went outside to talk. After a few minutes, he came back in.

"Zach'll meet you at six at the motel. He'll be easy to spot. He's a big, good-looking guy. Looks like a rancher. You should know that he is very concerned about his future at the ranch and is eager to talk to you."

"I appreciate the suggestion, Todd, and thanks again for the tour of the ranch. If I'm ever back in Upton, I'll stop and say hello."

After he left, I sat in the pilot's lounge and thought about the last couple of days. I decided to return to the hotel and sort out my thoughts. Tomorrow's meeting with Alan Creston is coming up fast. It's almost decision time.

First, though, I want to hear what Zach Talty has to say.

CHAPTER SEVEN

Halestone Ranch
Tuesday, September 24
Noon

Just after Judd saw the plane flying low and circling the ranch, he pulled out his cell phone and punched in Randy Gotch's number.

"What's going on, Judd?" answered Randy.

"That's what I'm wondering! There's a plane buzzing the ranch. Is that one of yours?"

Silence. Finally, Gotch said, "Come to my office."

"I can't right now. We've got hay to move. I can't get there until next week. Just tell me what's going on, Randy."

"Don't worry, don't worry, I've got it under control. Have you heard anything more from Creston?"

"Nothing since the funeral. Why?"

"He wanted me to let you know that I'll be continuing to issue paychecks until further notice. Just get here when you can." And he clicked off.

Judd didn't like it. Something was off. He told Zach that they needed to finish loading the sold bales that afternoon, and he needed to be gone a few days.

Zach nodded and said he'd deliver the bales the next day, and check the wells in all the pastures when he got back. Ever since the funeral, Judd and Zach had avoided talking about anything other than delivering hay they had sold to a neighboring ranch.

Patti Malik heard the plane, too. It was the wrong time of day for the "irregularities." As she cleaned up the ranch kitchen after lunch, her mind wandered, again, to the ranch's future, and more precisely, to her future.

One decision she made on her own was the length of her workday.

She told Judd and Zach, "You guys don't need me for three meals," she said. "From now on, I'll be here to fix breakfast and lunch, and I'll leave you something for supper."

The Weston Inn
6 p.m.

Exactly at 6 p.m., a tall, well-built man walked into the lobby of the Weston Inn. He was dressed like a rancher. Looked like a friendly guy. I guessed his age at 40-45. He walked directly toward me so I assumed Todd Davig had given him a description of me.

"Mr. Willand, I'm Zach Talty. Todd Davig thought I should come up to meet you."

"Zach, I'm glad you came, and let me tell you a story. A long time ago, someone wiser than me said there are only three choices you can make when it comes to an appointment. You can be early, be late or be on time. You walked in exactly at six. That same guy must have talked to you!"

"Sounds like my dad. He thought that way. I try to remember it." As we walked next door to dinner, I asked him about himself.

"Well, sir, all my life I've been around Upton, except for two years in the U.S. Army. Grew up here, got married and divorced here, and did a lot of part-time work till Luke and Jack Hale hired me to work for them full-time. I've been there ever since, about 20 years now."

"Do you have family here?"

"Just my mom. Dad died some years back. He worked for the BLM a lot of years. My sister is quite a bit younger, she married a fellow from Cheyenne and they've lived there ever since."

During dinner, we talked about farm machinery, land and cattle prices in Weston County, and weather. When dessert came, I told him I was an Illinois farm boy, had worked for International Harvester and then became a dealer. When IH became CaseIH, I sold out and started a financial planning office.

I also told him about my summer ranch trips, how I got acquainted with Wyoming and how much I like it.

"Zach, I'm interested in Halestone Ranch. I'm told you are the only person who's been around long enough to know where that name came from?"

"Sure. Luke told me the story. He said right after his dad bought the place back in the '30s, a nasty hail storm pelted the ranch, with stones so big some cattle were injured. Everybody talked about that storm for a long time. Robert decided to personalize a new name for the ranch and called it Halestone Ranch."

"What was Jack like? Was he a good boss?"

He nodded. "Yes sir, I really respected both him and his dad. After Luke died, Jack and I did everything on the ranch. I hated to see Jack's health fail. He could do any job before that happened."

"How did you and Jack split up the jobs?"

"In the Army, I spent my time in the motor pool. Really liked working with machinery. On the ranch, I handled the irrigation equipment, as well as cutting and baling. Jack watched over the herd, handled the calving and whatever vet jobs he could do. I helped him whenever he needed me. I don't mind working cattle, he just did it better."

"And how do you and Judd divide the work?

"He decides."

"What's your work schedule" How many days a week?"

"Judd has me work five days. He thought I would enjoy more time off. I always worked six days before he came. Now my wages are less, and my mom needs help with her prescription bills, so I work Saturday nights as a security guard to make up the loss."

"How do you feel about that?"

"Doesn't matter how I feel. That's the way it is."

"I'm told Jack asked you to foreman the ranch before he hired Judd, but you said no. Why?"

"Both Luke, and later Jack, knew all about the herd, the right feed, the best bulls to buy, how to use the pasture so it would last longer, and I didn't know any of that. I was scared to take on the responsibility for all of it. I figured Jack had enough worries with his health problem, and I was afraid I would mess up the job."

"Are you happy with the arrangement the way it now is?"

Zach looked down at his hands, and I could see he was trying to decide how to answer.

"Nothing is the same with Jack gone. But it's a job. We have a good cook. And I love that ranch."

I walked with him to a Ford F-150 pickup in the parking lot. It was spotless, not a dent anywhere. Probably 15 years old.

"You know how to take care of a truck, Zach. It looks like new."

"Thanks. It's a 2001 with 160,000 miles on it. I can't afford to trade very often, so I take care of what I've got. You'd really be impressed with Judd's new truck. It's an F-250 four-wheel-drive with all the extras."

I thanked him for coming to see me. As he drove away, I thought about Judd's Ford pickup. Probably $60,000 new. I wondered how he could spend that kind of money on a ranch foreman's salary. I also remembered Todd Davig's comment that Zach Talty never said anything bad about anybody. He sure avoided any criticism of Judd during our time together tonight.

My impression of Zach after spending time with him? That he's quite a man.

Weston Inn
Room 108

Back in my room, with my meeting with Alan Creston just hours away, it's time for the yellow pad.

Through the years, I developed the habit of using a yellow legal pad to make decisions when I'm at a crossroads. Two columns, one pro and one con. Five points on each side.

About a half-hour later, this is what I'd written:

Pro

1. Unexpected windfall
2. Favorite state
3. Ideal timing
4. I've had various business experiences.
5. I've got some ranch knowledge.

Con

1. Potential liability
2. A sidetrack if my health fails
3. Employee turnover
4. Time commitment
5. Market and weather risks

I stared at the ten points for a moment, decided that those were the right words in the right places, and put the pad aside. I turned on the TV for a while before falling asleep.

Weston Inn
Room 108
3 a.m.

Why is it that when I face a significant decision, I wake up at three?

3:30 a.m.

Decision made.

CHAPTER EIGHT

Law office of Alan Creston
Wednesday, September 25

"Good morning, Mr. Willand." Alan Creston's receptionist, who I assume is also a paralegal, welcomes me to the office. It's in a modern one-story office building that houses other businesses as well. The office is stark compared to Randy Gotch's, but it looks the way I expect a small town lawyer's office should look.

After our phone calls and his visit to Illinois, I like this guy. Every indication is that he is up-front, serious and does his job well. I'm comfortable with him.

Alan comes out, offers me coffee, and we sit down at his conference room table.

"I suspect you've had a busy couple of days, Mark."

"I sure have, and thank you for suggesting I take Todd with me for the flyover of the ranch. He knows the area very well."

"I'm glad to hear that. Todd is a solid guy."

I'm the one that set up this appointment, so I proceeded to describe what I've been doing and who I've met since I arrived, including my meetings with Zach and Randy.

"Alan, because the ranch is in trust, I expect that the public need never know that I received this ranch as a gift. Am I correct?"

"Yes."

"If I retain you as the ranch attorney, you can assure me that the inheritance will continue to remain confidential. Is that also correct?"

"Yes, to the best of my ability."

"You've probably figured out by now that I have decided to accept the ranch. Before I leave, I'll give you a check as retainer, so that you will continue to represent me."

"That's wonderful news! Jack wanted it this way, Mark, and I'm pleased to be able to help make it happen. And I'd be proud to continue to represent you and the ranch."

"Let me tell you why it's so important to me to keep the gift secret, so everyone here thinks I bought the place."

"OK."

"I don't need the money this transaction represents. I want to give much of this windfall back to the community here. That would be a great experience, and a lot of fun. I plan to do that over the next five years, the required 'hold time.'"

"If everyone finds out this was an inheritance, no matter how much I give locally, it will not seem like enough to many folks. That's just human nature."

"That's a wise observation."

"I want the Halestone Ranch to become a place that the Upton community will always look upon as a benefactor. I've already had a wonderful and profitable life. Making the community that Jack and his parents grew up in a better place would make a lot of people feel good, including me. Does this make sense to you, Alan?"

"It's a lot more than that, Mark. Just being part of this project makes me feel good. How do you plan to do this?"

"You and I will decide that as we go along. I see that Upton has a 4-H club. I was a member in high school. One of my first projects will be to get acquainted with the 4-H leader and see how the ranch could help his kids. Maybe some new equipment, maybe even an intern program at the ranch? Who knows? It will be fun to find out how we can help them, and others, as we go along."

"Mark, you'll be a welcome sight around there as you carry out that kind of plan."

"Well, as I've told you, I really like Wyoming. I like spending time on a ranch. I'm in my upper 60s and have the time to be away from home periodically and fly out here. My wife is actively engaged in leadership of a national collegiate women's organization, and I no longer have my office, so this will be a good project for me."

"Regarding the short term, I want to keep my ranch ownership confidential until I'm back out next week. I'll let you know when I'm ready to let it be known. First, I want to meet Patti Malik and Judd Turner."

"Let me know if you need help setting up the meetings."

"I will, thank you. And, one more question about Randy Gotch."

"OK."

"Do you know him well?"

"No, I don't, Mark. Met him a few times. You said on the phone that you had been to his office. What did you think of him?"

"Well, he sure has a snazzy office. His furniture, even his suit, give the impression of being expensive. He was friendly enough, but surely wanted to tell me as little as possible about Halestone Ranch. He didn't even inquire why I was asking questions, which I found odd. Would you recommend I keep him?"

Alan shuffled in his chair and moved some files around on his desk before answering.

"Mark, I'll say that I don't know him well enough to recommend him. I suggest you interview some others in that business after you get settled in."

It was clear that he wasn't any more comfortable around Gotch than I was. With that, I told him I was ready to sign. We completed that process, and I said I would be back the following week.

As I left his office, I looked at my watch. 10:30 a.m., the time I became a Wyoming ranch owner. I can't decide how I feel about that. Time to go back to Illinois and sort out my thoughts. Off to the airport.

Two Months Earlier
Lackland Air Force Base, San Antonio, Texas

Ben Whitman and his son, Dan, arrived at the base after a long drive from Upton. They were picking up a dog Dan was adopting. A black Lab recently retired from military duty.

Ever since Dan watched a trained military dog save a soldier's life in a war movie, he had been wanting to apply to adopt one of these retired heroes. Typically, they had been trained to detect drugs, bombs and buried humans. Ben looked up the process on a website, and saw that most of the dogs ended up with their handlers. He encouraged Dan to apply anyway.

Almost a year later, Dan got a letter from the airbase accepting his application. He would be getting a black Lab named "Finder." His dad laughed about the name, said only the military would use that name for a search dog.

After passing through security, Ben and Dan were taken to the kennel, introduced to Finder, and they all got along well.

Finder had been de-programmed after being taken off active duty. He rode quietly during the trip home to Upton.

Rockford, Illinois
Monday, October 1

Tomorrow, I want to visit the ranch and meet the three employees. The more I consider it, the more I think it best to tell them the ranch has a new owner. Time to call Attorney Creston.

"Alan, I've decided to disclose my ownership. I want to meet with Judd, Zach and Patti tomorrow. I'm flying out in the morning. Please call Judd and tell him I would like to meet with the three of them in the ranch house at 2 p.m. tomorrow. I would appreciate it if you would restrict your comments about me. Tell them I'll explain more when we meet."

"OK. I'll call him and set it up, Mark."

Poplar Grove Airport
Tuesday, October 2
7:30 a.m.

Central Iowa forecasts indicate some low ceilings along the way, so I'll file IFR for the trip. I file for 8,000 feet, receive ATC clearance and depart on runway 30 on the same route I'd taken many times.

Clear skies, at least for first part of the trip, but at Fort Dodge, a low cloud cover blankets the area and much of the next 30 miles. I recall back in the days when I flew only VFR and sometimes worried about visibility ahead. I'll always believe an IFR ticket is the best life insurance a pilot can have.

Visibility is clear down to ground level at Ainsworth. After refueling, I fly VFR to Mondell Field Airport again, where Tuff Air has reserved a hangar for three days, and my rental car is waiting.

I never stop appreciating the good ground visibility of a high-wing airplane. Instead of looking ahead of the wing on a low-wing aircraft, I can look straight down. It's a lot easier to study ground features. At 200 miles per hour, the trip goes fast. By gaining an hour, I'm on the ground by 11:30.

As I get on Highway 16 to Upton, I wonder how the upcoming meeting with the employees will go. I'm sure they are all apprehensive, wondering what comes next. I've decided to tell Judd and Patti that I've already met Zach.

Finder has adjusted well to his new home in Upton. Dan doesn't like that Finder always has to be on a leash outdoors, and has been after his dad to drive out in the grasslands and let Finder run free for a change.

Ben promises to talk to his friend Zach, and arrange to take Finder out on the Halestone Ranch so he can run free.

CHAPTER NINE

Halestone Ranch
Tuesday afternoon, October 2

I arrived at the ranch a few minutes before two. I had seen the buildings from the air. Up close, they looked in even better shape. Everything looked well cared for and the paint looked good.

I recognized Zach's pickup by the ranch house. Next to it had to be Judd's new F-250 Zach had described. It sure was top of the line with chrome everywhere. Couldn't miss it. The third was probably Patti's, a tired-looking Honda.

They all met me as I stepped onto the large, covered porch. Judd was a trim 30-something, about 5'10", looked to be in good shape, with a smile. Patti was attractive, obviously took pride in her hair and appearance, wore ranch clothes, but my first impression was that she looked a little tired, maybe stressed, and her smile was forced. I wondered what made her look so worried, then it dawned on me that she didn't know if she was still going to have a job.

After the introductions, Judd suggested we sit around the kitchen table to talk.

"Well, this may come as a surprise to you, especially you, Zach, since when we talked last week I didn't mention I was considering buying it and, frankly, I wasn't even sure I wanted to, but I now own Halestone Ranch."

All three of their faces registered surprise, maybe shock. Judd seemed to be the most surprised, perhaps even stunned.

"My first goal is to get rid of any tension and uncertainty on your part, so I want you to keep doing what you've been doing, and for the next 90 days I want to learn the ranch, and everything about it."

I told them Zach had filled me in on the history of the ranch during the Hale years of ownership.

"You may have heard me flying over the ranch last Tuesday. I got a good look at it from the air.

"I know this is a lot to process and you have all sorts of questions and concerns, including who the heck I am."

Zach and Patti managed close-mouthed smiles.

After giving them a one-minute version of my life, I added, "I will not be moving to Wyoming. I'll be coming out on a regular basis."

"Today and tomorrow, I want to spend time with each of you and hear your story. This afternoon, Judd, I would like to see at least part of the herd, learn about your vet service, your feed supply for the rest of the year, and what your expenses will be the next 90 days. Let me know if there are any unpaid bills that should be taken care of."

After asking Zach to fill me in on the machinery and irrigation equipment tomorrow morning, and for Patti to walk me through her job tomorrow afternoon, I was ready for Judd to show me around.

Judd said, "Zach can come with me to gas up the ATVs and we'll be ready to go, Mr. Willand."

"Mark, please. Call me Mark."

As the two men walked toward what looked to be a machine shed, I noticed Judd pulling out his cell phone and making a call.

Judd, me, and two Polaris ATVs

An ATV has become a necessity on most ranches. Some call it a mechanical horse. It can go just about anywhere that a horse can go.

Before we took off, Judd on his ATV and I on Zach's, Judd explained the ranch layout: six fenced pastures, all named. We were starting out from the Home Pasture, which is where the ranch buildings and house are located.

At the first gate he said we were entering the South Pasture. Angus cows and calves were scattered, and quite a few were along the banks of the Bison River. It's more of a stream this time of year; we drove across it and the water was no more than about eight inches deep. I'm sure it runs much bigger during the spring runoff. It's a big asset to the ranch.

"All the irrigated hay ground is in this pasture," Judd explained. "We draw water from the river, and we have two wells for when the river has very little flow. We usually grow more hay than we need, and the rest is sold to neighbors."

The growing season is over, and round bales are neatly stacked in one corner of the pasture.

We rode into what he said was the West Pasture. Quite a few Angus cows and calves were all over the low hillsides. We rode to a gate and entered the North Pasture, which is used mainly for summer grazing. Judd said by rotating the pastures, the herd can live off the land most years, using the hay only during the winter. During the years that I had come to the ranch south of here, we had moved that herd the same way, to a summer pasture.

"Judd, from the air I noticed on the plat map a finger of Halestone Ranch that extends well to the north, above the rest of the ranch. Is it any good for grazing?"

"No, sir. The terrain is so rough, with a lot of trees, that if cattle get in there we can't get them out. It was fenced off years ago for that reason. Jack told me his grandfather didn't pay much for it, and, as it turned out, it wasn't worth much; not good for much of anything. Antelope hunters used to go back in there, but don't anymore. They found few deer or antelope in that area."

I nodded and thought about my flyover and the lane that had looked like hunters had been using it, but didn't bring it up. "According to the map," I added, "it's about three miles long, and between one-half and three-quarters of a mile wide, so about 1,400 acres that aren't good for anything."

"That sounds about right, yes."

No matter where we were that afternoon, we scared up antelope and a few white-tail deer. Fences don't stop either of them, they just jump over. There must be hundreds of antelope on the ranch. Judd mentioned that some of the same hunters have come to the ranch every fall for many years, and paid Jack for access.

We crossed into the East Pasture, with the bulk of the cattle herd scattered along the river bank. The calves looked in great shape.

Finally, we had circled back to the Home Pasture, at the buildings. Judd showed me the stables, with a half-dozen horses outside.

Back at the machine shed, I crawled off the ATV and stretched. I asked him about the cow herd. He said about 280 calves would be shipped shortly. I asked him what size cow herd he and Jack had maintained, and he said the number stayed right around 300. I asked him about his feed situation for the winter. He said they were in good shape with hay.

"Well, Judd, it seems like you've been doing a good job running things. Tomorrow morning, please call all your suppliers, including the vet, and the bank you use for checking. Tell them I now own the ranch and that I'll be stopping in soon to get acquainted. I've already met the CPA, and I'll spend more time with him to review the ranch tax returns and payroll.

Zach and Patti reappeared as Judd and I walked toward my car.

"I was just telling Judd that I'll be contacting all of the ranch suppliers, so if there's anyone you think I should be talking with, please let me know. I was also just telling him that I'll be meeting with the CPA to look over the ranch payroll. With all of my businesses, I've believed the people making these businesses run should be paid accordingly."

Another couple of close-mouthed smiles, perhaps a bit brighter this time, from Zach and Patti.

"Where do you all live?"

"Zach and Patti have apartments in Upton," Judd offered. When Jack hired me, he let me stay in the bunkhouse, and I never left. In the fall when hunters arrive, I share the bunkhouse with them."

"Alright then, I'm going to call it a day. Zach, I'll be out in the morning for the machinery and irrigation tour. Give some thought to what equipment needs to be replaced."

"Will do, sir. I'll see you tomorrow."

"And Patti, we'll talk about what, if anything, needs replacing. Starting with my next trip, I plan to use a bedroom here in the house, so maybe we can decide tomorrow which room I should use.

"One more thing: I want the name of the high school Vo-Ag teacher, and if any of you know who the local 4-H leader is, please let me know that, too. Thanks, everybody."

I left the ranch and drove back to the motel. It's been a full afternoon. The ranch appears to be in excellent shape. I sat on the deck outside my room and thought about Judd. The last thing I had asked him before I left was about his life prior to arriving at Halestone. All he said was that he had gone to school around Missoula and worked on ranches there before Jack hired him. That was the extent of the story of his life before he arrived here. I had been tempted to ask him for some references at that moment, but decided it was too soon to do that.

I sat looking at the open country around Upton, and felt better about owning the ranch. It was a mild September afternoon and the warmth of the sun lulled me to sleep. I didn't wake up till dinner.

Halestone Ranch machine shed
Wednesday, October 3

Zach was in the shed when I arrived. While there's a lot I don't yet know about how I'll run Halestone, it seems to me I've got to keep this man on the ranch. Luke and Jack Hale trusted him. What better references could I have?

"Zach, folks that have known you a long time speak highly of you. I've been with you a few times, and I see why you are liked and respected. I want you to stay on the ranch. I want you to be part of its future. I think you will really like the plans I have for this place."

No response, again, except for that close-mouthed grin.

"Can you assure me you will stay for the next 90 days, while I make those plans? By that time I'll be able to tell you what your part of that plan will be."

"Sure, I'll stay," said Zach. "This has been my home base for a long time. Jack wanted to keep the ranch in one piece. If that's your plan for the future, I'd like to be part of it. Besides that, I haven't eaten this good in years. Patti is a great cook."

"Ha! Well, OK. Now show me your machinery."

For the next couple hours we looked at the equipment, talked about the condition of each. It had been years since I was an IH dealer, so I wanted him to make the decisions regarding the ranch machinery.

As we looked at the Hesston windrower that had a lot of hours on it, Zach described their hay sales to neighboring ranches. It was obvious the Halestone Ranch makes a lot of money from hay. The ranch has enough level acreage and water to grow a lot of hay acreage.

Zach volunteered, "Sir, I think we we could add acreage without much more expense, and the neighbors want more bales if we had them to sell."

"Have you discussed this with Judd?"

"Well, sir, uh, Judd wasn't interested in talking about it."

I'm getting the impression that the two of them don't communicate very well.

I told him to look into a replacement of the windrower for next season, probably a bigger one, and during the next 90 days we would decide if more hay acreage is to be added.

The New Holland baler is a late model, as well as the CaseIH tractors and the other equipment. The ranch has an ancient road grader which Zach has maintained well enough to use it to repair the ranch roads when they get washouts.

The shop area of the machine shed was immaculate, with tools either stored or wall-mounted. It was obvious that Zach takes pride in his workplace.

This big, shy man seems to have many talents.

Halestone Ranch house
Wednesday, 4 p.m.

Patti came to the door as I drove up to the house. She looked less stressed than when we met yesterday.

The ranch house is a single-story brick ranch. It seemed to be in good condition.

"Everything works OK," Patti says. "The kitchen must have been updated a few years ago, because the appliances are newer."

"Good. Tell me about your typical day."

"Sure. I come out from town about seven, fix their breakfast, then prepare lunch. In the afternoon, I make up something for their evening meal, leave it in the refrigerator for them, and go back to town mid-afternoon. Judd reduced my wages after Jack died, and said I could work a shorter day. The last few months that Jack was still alive, I stayed till early evening to fix him an evening meal and make sure he was comfortable."

"Are you getting along alright with less wages?"

"Mr. Willand, I work three nights a week at a restaurant in town. With both jobs, I manage."

"Patti, I know I'm a lot older, but please call me Mark."

She smiled. I saw a glimmer of teeth in that one. Progress.

"Tell me about your life, where you grew up, what jobs you've had, what you enjoy doing."

"I was raised in LaCrosse, Wisconsin. My dad worked for a large construction company, and helped me get me a summer job in their office during high school. After I graduated, they hired me full time, and I got really good doing bookkeeping entries with the computer."

"I was in my early 20s when Chuck Malik got hired on one of our construction jobs. He started hanging around my office a lot. He was older and my dad told me to stay away from him. Of course, I didn't listen, and started riding with Chuck on his Harley. After a year, we got married, then he got a job here in Upton. All I could find was a waitressing job.

"Chuck started drinking too much, and on our way home from the Sturgis motorcycle rally, where he'd had more than one too many, we ended up in a ditch. My knee was broken, and we didn't have insurance. I should have gone back for therapy after the cast was taken off, but couldn't afford it."

"Does your knee still bother you?"

"Oh, yeah. All the time. Anyway, by then Chuck had lost his job, and wanted to go to Colorado to work. I was still working as a waitress despite the pain. Dad was helping me, financially and with advice, and told me to file for divorce. So he is long gone, and when Jack offered me a job, I was grateful. I really hated it when he died. He was a kind man."

"I've never heard anything different."

"That's my story," Patti continued. "I just turned 30, and would like to continue here on the ranch, if possible. My dad is willing to continue helping me with my medical bills from the knee operation, but I told him I want to be on my own again."

"That's admirable, both your dad's willingness to help, and your desire to be on your own." I told her I wanted her to stay during the 90 days that I'm putting together a plan for the future of the ranch.

"You mentioned your bookkeeping experience. Would you be interested in doing some of the ranch's bookkeeping on a trial basis?"

"Well, sure, but my days, and nights, are pretty full right now."

"Sure, I understand. If you don't mind, how much do you make from the waitressing job?"

It was so little that I told her I would increase her wages by that amount so she could quit that job and do some bookwork for me. She seemed to really appreciate that, which is what I thought the gathering of moisture in her eyes was from.

"Are you OK, Patti?" I asked after a moment as the tears leaked down her cheeks.

She reached for a tissue box on her desk and dabbed her eyes. Sniffling, she said, "I want you to know how much I appreciate this. It's life-changing for me. But," she hesitated, "I need to tell you something."

What could this be about?

"OK. Sure. What is it?"

She used another tissue. "I've, well ... there's no other way to say this, I guess. I've gotten addicted to the medication I take for my knee pain. Oxy. Oxycodone. It kills the pain, but it messes with my brain and

I crave it, pain or no pain."

I had read about this kind of addiction in the papers, but nobody I know has an issue with it. That I know of, anyway.

Patti was looking at me nervously. This wasn't a conversation I was expecting.

"That sounds serious, Patti. Are you, I mean, did a doctor prescribe the pills?"

Her eyes fell. "At first, yes, but as my addiction grew, the doctor told me I'd reached the limit on what he could give me."

She used another tissue before continuing.

"So I found other sources. It turns out there's plenty of it out there, if you can afford it."

"And that's why you were working the extra job?"

She nodded. "That's where some of the money went. The rest was to help with food and rent."

"But, anyway, the reason I'm bringing this up now, is that I'm trying to kick this habit. I need to kick it. I'm not an addict. That's not who I am. I'm not a druggie, and have never been one. But, like I said, that stuff changes your brain."

I studied her for a moment.

"Patti, I don't really know what to say other than this: How can I help?"

New tears formed as she sniffled and dabbed her eyes. "My doctor told me it's early enough in my addiction that I should be able to get off of it with just a few days of treatment. He wants me to go to a clinic in Gillette, and I'm sorry, sir, but I need to ask you for the time off. I love this job and the new role you're giving me, and I hope you won't decide to fire me, but I have to get myself clean."

It didn't seem as if I had much choice. I liked Patti. She appears to be a serious young woman who could fit into the long-range plans I'm forming for Halestone Ranch.

"Patti, I'm not going to fire you. Take as many days as you need to get through this. Your paycheck will not be affected. Speaking of money, how will you pay for the rehab?"

"My dad. My dad said he'll help me figure it out."

"You're a lucky daughter. Let me know when you're leaving and when it's possible, when you'll be back at the ranch. Zach and Judd can fend for themselves for a while. I'll just tell them you're taking some time off, but I won't say why. And this will be the last time you and I will need to talk about it. OK?"

She managed a bit of a smile and nodded, dabbing at the tears pooled in her eyes.

"Thank you, Mr. —" she stopped herself. "Thank you, Mark. I don't have the words to tell you how much this means."

"You're welcome, Patti. Go and get well. Now," I said rising, "let's get back to work. Show me the sleeping quarters."

Patti showed me Jack's bedroom. She had cleaned it and polished the furniture. I told her that's where I would be staying, starting with my next trip.

Before leaving the ranch, I called Randy Gotch and made an appointment to see him again the following morning. After that, I'll head to the airport and back to Illinois.

CHAPTER TEN

Patti Malik's apartment, Upton
Thursday, October 4
3 a.m.

She woke up in the middle of the night thinking about her conversation with Mark. A feeling she hadn't had recently, relief, settled in. It was partly because her role at the ranch had been expanded, but mostly because she had found the courage to confess her opioid problem.

There wasn't enough courage left over, though, to tell him about the hush money she'd been taking from Judd. She feared that would be a tipping point for Mark, and he'd decide to cut her loose.

Not that she had much to hush about. She hadn't noticed any 'irregularities,' except the airplane that buzzed the ranch that one night when she was still working late.

Patti feels she would be disloyal to Mark if she kept taking Judd's money, especially with her raise and expanded duties. Patti decides that she will tell Judd she's out. No more hush money. She'll also tell him she won't say anything to Mark about the money if he won't.

Judd won't like it, but she doesn't answer to him anymore. Mark Willand is her boss now, and more than that, he's giving her a chance to get clean.

Randy Gotch's CPA office, Newcastle
9 a.m.

"Thanks for seeing me again, Randy. I meant to ask you last time: Were you born and raised here?

"No, my folks lived in Montana, and that's where I grew up. I bought this practice from an accountant that wanted to retire. That was about 10 years ago."

"I see. I was remembering the first time I came to Newcastle. It was almost 20 years ago. Every year, I've spent time with a rancher friend south of here. I got thrown in 2000 while we were moving his herd to summer pasture. Broke my wrist. The hour's ride from the ranch to the clinic here in Newcastle seemed like forever, with a bone pushing through. But the clinic here was great."

"Ouch. That sounds nasty."

"Yeah, I still have the scar," I said, holding up my wrist, "and lately arthritis has been a regular visitor. Anyway, let's get down to business. Did Judd Turner call you about me and the ranch?"

"Yes."

"So you know I now own Halestone Ranch."

"Yes. Congratulations."

I wasn't sure he meant it. "I'll be coming out regularly. Judd told me you prepare the ranch payroll. Right away, I would like you to increase Ms. Malik's pay by $35 each week. What bank are you using for the payroll?"

He told me, and I advised him that I planned to start doing accounts payable myself, during my next trip to the ranch.

Leaving his office, I had the same thoughts as when I last visited. Beautiful furniture, some expensive artwork on the walls — *is that one an authentic Remington?* — and he again is wearing an expensive suit. In a town with a population of under 4,000, it didn't seem to fit.

Also, I thought he would encourage me to continue having him do the ranch tax returns. Yet he didn't even mention it.

Strange!

Tuff Air had my plane out and at the pumps, ready for me when I got there at 10 o'clock. The weather report was clear all the way, so I filed a flight plan and departed for Illinois.

En route, I thought about this trip, and the one before. Since the attorney first called me September 18, my attention has been entirely devoted to this ranch. My ranch! I never thought I'd get to say those words. These past 16 days have changed my life. It would be easy for me to block out everything else and spend every waking moment on running the ranch, but I think I had better moderate that and not try to go to Upton every week. Already, I've had to skip a museum board meeting, canceled a dentist appointment, and missed a visitation I should have attended. I'm going to stay home for a while. Maybe October 16 should be the next time. I'll meet with the various suppliers, and interview some other accountants.

Same day
7 p.m.
Ben Whitman's home

Dan had been training Finder during the two months since they brought him home and simultaneously bugging his dad to drive them to the country where Finder could run free.

"Remember, Dad," he nudged, "the sergeant who had Finder said we should exercise him that way every so often."

Ben smiled to himself at his son's persistence, and also at what a big difference Finder had made in Dan's life. He thought about an old, rarely used road northwest of Upton on Highway 16 toward Moorcraft. That area was part of Thunder Bay National Grassland, which is federal land, a good spot to run Finder. Dan didn't have football practice on the following Thursday, so they decided to go after school that day.

At home in Rockford
Friday, October 5

My vow of moderation isn't even 24 hours old, and I'm making notes about who I should see on the next trip to Upton. Randy Gotch probably won't make the list. The more I think about him, the more I'm uncomfortable with him. And I can't shake the feeling he's hiding something. There are several other CPAs listed in the Newcastle Chamber of Commerce listing. I'll visit at least one of them.

I'm sure everyone in Upton knows by now that the ranch has a new owner. I need to see the suppliers, and probably drop by KASL Radio and the Weston County Gazette. They're probably searching Google and LinkedIn to find about me anyway, so I might as well see them in person and make sure they have their facts right.

Barbara is excited about the ranch. She sees the possibilities of education funds for our grandchildren and their children. I've described my plans to give back much of the ranch proceeds to the community, and she really likes that. And she likes that I'm busy. She's not worried anymore about what I will do with my time since retiring.

CHAPTER ELEVEN

The Willand home in Rockford
Thursday, October 11
8 p.m.

My cell phone vibrates. The screen shows an unfamiliar number, but it's a 307area code. A Wyoming number. I answer it.

"Mr Willand, this is Sheriff Wirth with the Weston County Sheriff's Office. Judd Turner gave me your phone number. Are you the new owner of Halestone Ranch?

"Yes, I am, as of two weeks ago."

"I'm actually calling from your ranch. Two hours ago, an Upton resident called 911 and reported a body had been found in a remote part of your property. Have you had any other calls about this?"

"A body? No, no, this is the first I'm hearing of it." My mind raced. "Was it a hunting accident?"

"No, no sir, this appears to have been a homicide."

"A homicide? My gosh! Please give me more details. Do you know whose body it is — was?"

"Not yet. A dog found it. A fella named Ben Whitman lives in Upton. His son, Dan, adopted a retired military dog that was trained to sniff out buried humans in cave-ins, etcetera. They went out Route 16 to an old dirt road on National Grassland property to let the dog run free for exercise. That was this afternoon. The dog took off down the road like a rocket. When they caught up to him, he had crossed onto your property, about at the far north end of your ranch, and was digging. Mr. Willand, he uncovered an arm."

"Oh, my ... "

"Before he could dig deeper," the sheriff continued, "they put him back in their Jeep and called us. It's a crime scene now, we've got it roped off, and the medical examiner has released the body for autopsy.

"The M.E. described the victim as an Hispanic male, about age 40. As best she can tell, she thinks he's been in the ground about two or three months. That's all we know right now. We may get lucky with fingerprints, or maybe DNA will tell us who he was."

My head was spinning. My ranch ownership just became more complicated. I finally managed, "Sheriff, is there anything our people on the ranch can do to help you?"

"No sir, we just needed you to be aware that we closed off that part of your property for the time being. When will you be out again?"

"I plan to come out next Tuesday for several days."

"I will want to talk to you while you're here. I'll give you my phone number, and you can call me when you get in."

I hung up, sat back, and tried to assimilate what had just happened. A peaceful ranch near a quiet community is now a crime scene, and it was my ranch!

I thought about that day just over two weeks ago, when Todd Davig and I flew over the ranch. He had pointed out that finger of land at the north tip of the ranch. That's where the sheriff said the body had been found.

Why was the body buried on Halestone Ranch? Did the killer decide to dispose of the body on BLM land, thinking nobody every traveled that old road? He didn't know or care that he had crossed onto private ranch land?

Will we ever know why he was killed to begin with? Maybe the sheriff's department will know more when they get the M.E.'s results.

So many questions.

I called Judd, told him what the sheriff had said. I asked him if Zach and Patti knew, and he said he would call them. I told him I would be out on Tuesday.

Poplar Grove Airport — the Willand Hangar
Tuesday, October 16
7:30 a.m.

Low ceilings are forecast throughout central Iowa, so it's definitely an IFR flight. I filed a flight plan for 6,000 feet. It's a beautiful fall day here in Illinois, and as I pull the 210 out of the hangar I think about how owning Halestone Ranch has helped me keep my piloting skills sharp. Before Alan Creston's first phone call, I looked for an excuse to fly somewhere. I've always felt that a pilot should get in the air once weekly or close to that, to stay proficient.

Now I don't need to make up excuses. In fact, it would be hard for me to make up these excuses. A ranch, a murder mystery; I have plenty of reasons.

After completing the pre-flight I get the IFR clearance and depart on 30, climb to altitude and begin my trip across the Midwest at 200 miles per hour. After all these years of flying, I still look forward to being up here. Today, I'm looking down at the fall harvest that's well underway. Experience tells me that if there's a dust cloud behind a combine, it's cutting beans, as opposed to the "cleaner" combine in corn.

There was a time I had considered trading for a Cessna 310 twin. As I compared it to this Cessna 210 with one engine, I found that both have about the same airspeed, both have six seats, but the twin burns more fuel and costs more to maintain. I decided to stay with the 210, and I'm glad I did.

As I approached Fort Dodge, the cloud cover down below started forming, and within a few miles I'm looking down on a blanket of white. There's a unique feeling of isolation, of being separated from the ground below, and in a different world up here by myself.

Thirty minutes later, the cloud cover is gone, and I'm landing at Ainsworth again for fuel. The 210 could continue to Newcastle without stopping, but I need the pit stop, even if the plane doesn't.

On the ground in Newcastle, the staff at Tuff Air greets me and takes care of my plane, I pick up a rental car and during lunch at Mc-

Donald's, I call the sheriff's office. I'm connected to Sheriff Wirth, who says he wants to come to meet me and talk.

As the sheriff walks in, I see a serious, sharply-dressed man in full uniform. Big man, kind of what you'd expect in this country. I'd guess he's around 50. I stand and signal to him and reach out to shake his hand. It's big and meaty, what you'd expect for a big man, and it had unlikely seen lotion in quite a while, if ever. He greets me with an easy smile, and sits down across the table from me.

"Mr. Willand, thanks for calling. I've got quite a bit more information since we last talked, and I want to keep you informed about what happened on your property."

"Please call me Mark, Sheriff. What have you got?"

"His name. Ethan Alvarez. His fingerprints were in the data base as of five years ago when he was arrested in Missoula, Montana, for possession of cocaine. Cause of death was two small caliber bullets in his head, fired from very close range. At this point, we have no idea who killed him, or why he was buried on your property, but it seems likely the killing was drug-related."

"Have drugs been a problem in this area, Sheriff?"

"I'd call it an increasing problem. We've had more busts the past year than previously. Cocaine, mainly, but other things, too. As seems to be the case pretty much everywhere else, opioids are a big problem."

"Do you think this man was running drugs into this part of Wyoming, or specifically to the Upton area?"

"That would be my guess. But the connection between that and this killing is just speculation."

"Sheriff, thanks for letting me know this. I'll tell my folks at the ranch what you've told me. As long as you're here, can I tell you about my involvement in Halestone Ranch?"

"Please do."

I gave him the elevator version of my life up until this point, and wanted to let him know that I have good intentions with Halestone Ranch.

"When I heard about Jack Hale's death, the thought of owning a ranch intrigued me. Now that I own it, I'm interested in doing things for the Upton community. I plan to meet the 4-H leader this week, and see what I could do to help them. That'll be a start."

The sheriff nodded and said, "Well, I sure did like Jack. I can't think of anyone who didn't. Alan Creston told me a little about you, and I'm glad the ranch is in good hands. I'm sure we'll see a lot of each other, hopefully under much more pleasant circumstances."

We parted company then. My lunch finished, I decided it was time to visit the bank that has our ranch's credit line.

CHAPTER TWELVE

October 16
Tuesday afternoon

Now it's time to pay attention to the ranch's checking account and loan. I'll need the attorney's help on this, and tap Alan Creston's number into my cell phone.

"Alan, this is Mark Willand. I'm back in town, and want to talk to the bank about the ranch account. Can you provide me with proof of ownership so I can see them today?"

"Sure. I'll have it ready for you when you come in. Give me a half-hour to print it. And, Mark," he paused, "I assume you know about the body found on your ranch? It was in the paper."

"Yes, horrible. Of all the things I could have imagined happening in my first weeks of ranch ownership, a murder wasn't one of them."

"Have you spoken with the sheriff?"

"Yes, Sheriff Wirth called me last week, and I met with him a little while ago. I was impressed. Seems like a serious, likable guy. Is that your opinion?"

"Yes, he's a good man. I voted for him both times he's run for the office. Did he have any opinions about the murder?"

"Well, he only said the dead guy had a record involving drug peddling, so it isn't much of a leap to think he may have been selling here in Weston County, but the sheriff really didn't know, or didn't say."

"They sure picked a strange place to bury the body."

"What do you mean?'

"I mean there are lots of remote places easier to get to."

"That's true."

"Stop in shortly and I'll have your documents."

My next call was to the First National Bank of Newcastle. I told the receptionist I was the new owner of Halestone Ranch, and would like to meet with the individual handling the ranch account in an hour, if that person was available. She asked me to hold, came back on shortly, and said Tom Westedt would be expecting me.

First National Bank
3:00 p.m.

The bank looked like how a bank ought to look. It was a sturdy two-story building that had probably been built 100 years ago, and built to last. I could imagine it having been chiseled out of a huge block of sandstone that some prehistoric geological event dropped on that street corner. The lobby was a two-story echoey cavern with polished marble floors, and walls lined with granite. Three teller cages were behind decorative grills made of thick steel bars. Behind that barrier was an impressive vault, with a two-foot thick steel door, opened and showing another steel cage inside the vault. Everything about it said the depositors' money was safe here. I wondered if it had ever been robbed.

I told the receptionist I had an appointment with Tom Westedt, and as soon as she called him, he came out to greet me. Probably 55, well-dressed in a conservative suit. He certainly doesn't share a tailor with Randy Gotch.

Tom invited me to his office, a large space with wood-paneled walls and a window looking out on the street. It looked like a bank executive's office. Appropriately fancy, not lavish. On the door, "Thomas Westedt, Vice-President" was printed in gold-colored lettering.

"Please have a seat, Mr. Willand, and may I begin with congratulations on acquiring the Halestone. It sure is a beauty."

"Thank you, and please call me Mark. I'm thrilled to have Halestone and I promise I'll keep it, as you say, 'a beauty.'"

Westedt smiled. "How may I help you?"

"Tom, did Judd Turner call you regarding my ownership of the ranch?"

"No, but Randy Gotch did."

"Oh. Do you know Gotch well?"

"Not as a personal friend, only from occasional meetings. He works with several of our ranch clients. Why do you ask?"

"Tom, I was a bank director for 14 years back in Illinois. The officers knew a great deal about their clients and the services they used. They sure knew a lot about the businesses I operated, and that was their job. Given that, I bet you do the same. Would you recommend that I keep Gotch as the ranch accountant?"

He hesitated too long before answering. He cleared his throat and said, "Gotch certainly seems competent, as far as the bank is concerned. I'll say this: If you have concerns, or just want to shop around as part of your due diligence, there are other good offices in Newcastle, and I'd be happy to give you some names."

"I would like that, thank you."

Westedt pulled out a scratch pad and quickly wrote two names and phone numbers.

"Perfect, thank you. How long have you had the ranch account?"

"I'd say it's been well over a decade. No, close to two, now that I think about it. Luke and Jack came in together, and I worked with them from the start. They were good people, good customers. It sure wasn't fair what happened to Jack, but I guess that's the way life is sometimes. But I'm glad you came in, and speaking for all of us here, I hope we can begin a new, long relationship with you."

"I don't see why not, Tom. I think continuity in this case probably makes sense. I brought along a copy of the new ownership documents for you. And here's a copy of my current personal credit history, and my business career and other interests are listed on my LinkedIn page. Is there anything else you need in order to provide me with information about the ranch account?"

"No, this is all we need. What information would you like?"

"I'm going to keep your copy machine humming for a while," I smiled. "I'd like two sets of the monthly checking account statements for each of the last 12 months; two copies of the loan agreement, along with the current amount drawn; a list of who has authorized access to both, and who is authorized to sign checks. I would like to pick these up tomorrow morning."

"I'll have them ready for you at 8:30 a.m. Will that work?

"Perfect. Also, Tom, are you acquainted with Alan Creston?"

"Oh sure, I've worked with Alan numerous times."

"Would you recommend I retain Alan as our ranch attorney?"

"Absolutely. I've always respected his office."

What a contrast to how he answered the same basic question I asked about Randy Gotch.

"Good. I'll do that. You can call Alan with any questions you have about my ownership."

I rose to leave and shook hands with Tom, feeling good about the meeting and about keeping the ranch accounts at First National.

"I'll see you tomorrow morning," I said.

I decided to stay in Newcastle overnight and got a room at the Black Hills Lodge. Then I tapped in Patti Malik's cell number and told her I would be staying at the ranch for a few days starting tomorrow. She said my room was ready and waiting.

Next, I called Alan, and we agreed to meet for dinner. He suggested the restaurant in the lodge, Open Range.

Open Range Burgers and Beer
Intersection of US 16 and US 85
6 p.m.

Alan and I were seated in a booth that looked as if the benches were built out of used lumber from a ranch, and the table was against a wall that had corrugated steel as wainscoting, the kind of metal you'd see on the roof of a ranch shed. Hanging above us were old saddle bags, a lariat, and some antique sheep shears. Remnants of ranching country. The whole place was done up that way; "Old Ranch Chic," I guess, but with modern touches. The bar top was polished granite, and there had to be more than a dozen taps behind it, with beer names I'd never seen.

"Alan, I'd like to thank you for being so helpful since you first called me. I spent time with Tom Westedt this afternoon."

"Tom's a good man. He's not only a good banker, he does a lot of good things in the community."

"He speaks highly of you, too, Alan. I'd like you to continue as the ranch attorney, if you want to."

"Sure. Of course. I would like that. You talked earlier about doing a lot for the Upton community. There would be legal work involved, and it would be fun to be part of that."

"I'm going by the bank in the morning to pick up copies of the last 12 months' bank statements and the loan agreement. I'll drop off one copy at your office in a few days. Please take a close look at all of it. Call me if you see anything I should be concerned about."

"Of course."

"I would expect the bank will want a new agreement signed for the line of credit. Or, it may not want to continue it due to an out-of-state owner. What do you think?"

"Tom will tell you if they want to make changes. Do you want to keep the line of credit?"

"I would rather not make any changes during the next 90 days while I sort everything out. If the bank wants to change anything, I'll let you know before I agree. My attorney back home has always encouraged me to give him too much information rather than not enough, and let him decide if he needs to be involved."

"That's a good way to do it."

Our waiter brought our food. I had ordered meat loaf, and Alan had something called a Stuffed Cow Burger. It was one of the biggest cheeseburgers I'd seen. I ordered one of those beers I'd never heard of, a Rusty Beaver Wheat, and Alan decided to experiment with a Black Hills Brown.

Alan raised his bottle, "A toast, to you and Halestone Ranch."

We clinked bottles and each took a sip.

"Sorry to bring this up over dinner, Alan, but what about the body that was discovered on the ranch? Do I have any liability there?"

Alan took a few seconds to swallow his bite of Stuffed Cow. "I don't know anymore than what I read in the paper, but I can't see why you would, Mark."

"It has to be just coincidence that the body was buried on my land. I'm sure Judd and Zach would have noticed if something odd was happening up there. By the way, that reminds me, were there long-term employment agreements between the ranch and the three employees?"

"No."

"And, you may not, or cannot, answer this, but I'll ask anyway: Were any of the three given anything in the will?"

"They were not."

It surprised me that Zach hadn't been rewarded in some way by Jack for his long service. "During the next few days, I'd appreciate your opinion as to whether I should do something for any of them. I believe you, more than anyone, would know if they went out of their way to help Jack during his final months." I didn't mention Patti's time off for rehab. That seemed to be irrelevant to this conversation.

"I'll do that, and email you my thoughts."

My meat loaf was delicious, and I took a final swallow of the Rusty Beaver. It was good.

"Here's my last question for today, Alan. If the bank wants a new financial statement in order to continue the line of credit, do you think it'll accept a statement showing only the Halestone Trust financials, or will it try to include my personal holdings? I may not use this credit line, but would like to keep it in place for the time being."

"I don't know the answer to that, Mark. I suggest you ask Tom Westedt when you pick up your papers tomorrow."

Wednesday morning
October 17

It's 8:30 and I'm back at First National Bank. Tom Westedt invites me back to his office.

"Coffee, Mark?"

"No thanks, Tom, I just had my caffeine quota with breakfast."

"I hear ya, I have a limit, too. Here's the information you asked for, Mark. There are two copies of everything."

"Perfect, thank you. Tom, my plan is to make no changes at the ranch for 90 days. By then, I should have an accurate assessment of the place. Because of change of ownership, does First National need a new agreement signed?"

"Yes, if you wish to maintain the same credit line. I've put a new credit application in this envelope for you to complete."

"I assume you want it prepared as my personal financial statement, which will include the assets and liabilities of the Halestone Ranch trust. I'll not attempt to draw against the current credit line until you have approved my application. At this point, I don't anticipate any additional draw this year."

"Thanks. I appreciate that information."

"What is the current checking account balance?"

Tom tapped his keyboard and took a quick look at his computer screen. "$364,200."

"Who is authorized to write checks against that account?"

"When Jack's illness started affecting him, he gave Judd joint authorization, meaning Judd prepared the checks for suppliers, and both he and Jack co-signed. Toward the end, Jack's signature was virtually a scribble, and he had nearly lost the ability to speak, but I got the feeling that he was aware of what he was signing."

"Just as I was going to contact Alan Creston about the need for a new co-signer, I was told you were now the owner. I'm glad you've come in so we can determine how you want the account protected, but also make sure suppliers get paid. Randy Gotch, as you know, does your payroll, and he has solo authorization, but let's deal with Judd first."

"Tom, what do you recommend? I don't want the checking account accessible by any single individual, and I'll only be here part-time. I have no reason to distrust Judd. But 300 K is a lot of money. I don't want it exposed."

"Certainly. In the old days, you could set a limit, and Judd would have to have your written authorization to exceed that. But in today's electronic accounts, that no longer works. Why don't you co-sign all checks with him? He can prepare them and either hold them till you come out, or mail them to you. You co-sign them and mail them to the suppliers. Most bills have 30 days to pay."

"That's a good idea. I'll see him today and tell him. Just to be safe, I'd like you to look at any checks coming in that have already been written before today, but not yet cleared. Everything written from this date on must have both signatures."

"Yes, I'll put a flag on your account so everyone knows to watch for those checks."

"Thanks. Now, let's talk about Mr. Gotch. You said he's authorized to write payroll checks without a co-signature."

"Yes, but we can set that up as you want it."

"For now, how about if we just establish a total available limit of 90 days payroll? By then, I'll know if I want to retain him, and that will limit total exposure."

"Good idea, Mark. I'll set up that limit right away."

As I left his office, I felt comfortable with Tom Westedt, and thought my team of trusted advisors, currently made up of Tom and Alan, was taking shape.

My confidence in Randy Gotch is waning. I'm not planning to see him this trip. He doesn't need to know about the limit I've placed on his check writing. I still need to ask him about the LLC that Jack had asked Alan about, but that will be on a future trip. If there ever had been an LLC discussion, I assume it would have originated with Gotch.

CHAPTER THIRTEEN

Wednesday, October 17
9 a.m.

It now seems obvious I will need to come to Wyoming about twice a month. It's time to decide what airport to use. There are two possibilities and one long shot.

Mondell Field at Newcastle has an instrument approach, and overnight hangar as well as fuel at Tuff Air. If I were to ever need repairs, they have a full-service shop. Its 4,000-foot runway is ideal for the 210. I wouldn't need to stop at Ainsworth for fuel. I could leave an old pickup in the parking lot instead of renting a car every trip. Distance to the ranch is about 35 miles.

Upton Municipal Airport has a similar paved runway, about the same length. Fuel is available, and I found out with a phone call that they have a hangar for rent. I could leave the old pickup in the hangar when I'm not here, and would only be eight miles from the ranch. If I had need for service, I could stop at Newcastle en route. In the rare case where I would need an instrument approach, I could fly into Mondell Field and get a ride to the Upton hangar and the truck. However, with only 12 inches of rainfall annually, low ceilings are unlikely.

The long shot is on the ranch itself. When I flew over it with Todd Davig, we saw an open stretch on the finger of land at the north end, near where the murder victim was found. Possibly, we could take the ranch's old Cat grader and level it out. Don't know if it's long enough, or if the clearance at each end is sufficient, but it's worth a look. I want to see the murder site, anyway.

I called Judd. "I'm coming out now from Newcastle. Can you spend a couple hours with me?"

He agreed, and I left for the ranch and met Judd in the stables.

"Judd, let's drive up to the north end and look at the area where the body was found. I would like to take the same road off of Highway 16 that the killer must have used."

"Sure, we can do that. Hop in."

Climbing into Judd's new and sparkling clean Ford pickup, it was clear why so many are sold. It's nicer inside than most new cars! Leather all around, lots of room, the latest electronic gizmos. A .30-30 rifle with a scope was perched in the rear window gun rack. A rifle is a must-have in this country.

For the most part, Judd continues to impress me. He's friendly and knows livestock well. It bothers me that he won't share more about his background, but the job he does running the ranch is really the important thing right now.

We took the ranch drive to the county road, which leads to Highway 16. At that point, we took 16 north a couple miles to a barely noticeable dirt lane that turned left into the national grasslands. After a mile, we came to a small sign reading *Private Land.*

"This is where your ranch property begins, Mr. Willand."

"Mark, please."

"Mark," he grinned. "Got it."

There had been no rain since the body was found, and plenty of tracks showed ahead. We drove another hundred yards before coming to an area where all the brush and weeds had been trampled with vehicles and feet.

"This must be close to where the body was buried," I said.

Judd nodded, and pointed to a spot about 50 feet off the lane. Recently turned soil had been leveled, obviously the burial spot.

I wondered to myself how this spot could have been chosen. Was he killed here, then buried? Or was he already dead before they found this spot? Or, a worst-case scenario out of all very bad options, was he buried alive? I shuddered at the thought. Was the killer coming from the north, or from Upton or Newcastle? No doubt, the sheriff is wondering the same thing.

"Have you heard anything about the murder, Judd?"

He shook his head as he kicked at the dirt with his work boot.

"There's plenty of gossip about it in town, but I haven't seen or heard from the sheriff or his deputies since the body was found."

"I'm sure they're busy trying to figure this out. I doubt there are many homicides in Weston County."

"Nope, I don't recall hearing of any others."

"When I flew over the ranch, I spotted a clearing that I might be able to use for an airstrip. I'm guessing it's pretty close. Can you point me in that direction?"

"Sure, it's right up there a ways," he said, with his arm extended. "I can walk up there with you."

"No, I need to step it off to measure it and look at landing and takeoff clearances and the like. I'll be a while. I hope you don't mind waiting here for me."

"You're the boss."

That I am, I thought. *That I am.*

I followed a path that looked old and little-used, and after a few hundred yards I came to the clearing. As my eyes surveyed the area, I was again struck by its rugged beauty. It may not be good for grazing cows, or much of anything, but it sure is pretty to look at.

Stepping off the potential landing area, it was roughly 2,400 feet, with a clearance at both ends of at least 100 feet. Even though it was slightly covered with brush and had some rough spots, it looked like a grader could level it enough for my 210 to use.

There were other considerations, though. I'd have to build a hangar to keep the plane safe from hail, and from intruders, both the four-legged and two-legged varieties. I'd need to put up a fuel tank, and then figure out how to get it filled. As I headed back to Judd's truck, the more I thought about it, the more it made sense to rent a hangar at Upton's airport. The distance to the ranch from there would probably be no farther than taking the road back to the ranch from this clearing.

Just then, I looked down and stopped. Some faint impressions on the grass caught my eye. Light rain had fallen about two weeks ago, before the body was found. Any tracks might have been obscured somewhat, but the prairie grass was still bent over in straight lines indicating a vehicle had been here. Cars and pickups are usually five- to six-foot tracks. I stepped off the width, and it looked to be about eight feet.

And looking ahead from the center of the two tracks to the north, another line in the grass is perfectly spaced and straight.

Most vehicles don't leave a straight path when operating on a rough surface like this.

So, what made these tracks?

I turned and walked back to the south end of the clearing. There were no tracks there.

I again walked north, and after about 200 yards the tracks appeared. I continued walking north, and suddenly two sets of tracks appeared, overlapping each other several times. At the north end, one set of tracks turned back towards the south, and became the second set.

A plane, as it lands, would not touch down and leave tracks for at least a couple hundred feet. The same is true in reverse upon takeoff. Liftoff would occur a few hundred feet before the end of the runway, and any tracks to that point would end.

That was the only conclusion I could come up with. A plane had landed to the north, and departed back to the south. As rough as the surface was, I could visualize a good pilot being able to use it, assuming he had plenty of horsepower.

Maybe this is how the killer, and victim, got here!

I'll call the sheriff later with this theory. I decided not to mention it to Judd or Patti. It's just a theory.

Judd was sitting in his truck listening to music when I returned.

"Judd, thanks for bringing me out here. When I saw the clearing from the air, I wondered if it could be graded for a landing strip. It's long enough. The downside is lack of fuel, and the expense of putting up a hangar, and there's no electrical nearby. So I'll plan to rent a hangar at Upton instead, and keep an old vehicle there to come back and forth."

Judd nodded and noted, "It's pretty remote out here. Just building the hangar would be a chore."

Judd didn't have much else to say as we headed back to the

ranch. I thanked him and went to the house to talk to Patti.

Luke Hale had built the house in the '70s. It's brick, with a boot room at the entrance, a bathroom next to it. Off to one side was a big kitchen with an eating area. The table looked as if it would probably seat at least eight. The house was built back in a time when running irrigation pipes from the river required more labor, and wood fencing was being replaced with barbed wire. During busy season, Luke probably had four or five men on the payroll, all eating at the house. A big table was a must.

Down a hall at the opposite end from the kitchen, were three bedrooms and an office. In between the eating and sleeping areas was a great room, with a slightly vaulted ceiling from which a deer antler chandelier hung. Warm knotty pine lined the walls. Sofas and chairs formed a semi-circle in front of a floor-to-ceiling rock fireplace. Heads of deer and antelope decorated the walls.

Patti greeted me with a big smile. There it is! Her life probably felt more settled with the changes I helped her make and the 90-day job guarantee. I didn't ask her about rehab. That subject won't come up again, I hope.

"Mr. Willand, I think you'll like the master bedroom. I put on a new mattress pad and new sheets, and cleaned the attached bathroom. The office is just off the master."

"Patti, Mr. Willand was my father. He's not here. Please call me Mark from now on. And the bedroom looks fine."

She nodded, still smiling.

We walked into the office. I felt a bit like an intruder. There was so much of Jack Hale in here. A couple of black and white historic ranch photos were among the pictures on the walls. Some family photos, too, mostly of what I guessed were of Jack, his dad and mom. Hanging by itself on one wall was one of my favorite paintings: a cowboy standing beside his horse in a pasture, feeding it a slice of an apple with his right hand, and a pocket knife and the remainder of the apple behind his back in his left. I had a print just like it back home.

"This is pretty much as Jack left it, isn't it, Patti?"

"Yes sir, I just did some dusting and straightening. I didn't feel comfortable moving anything or throwing anything out."

"I understand. Well, I want to make use of the office, and tomorrow I'm going to clean out the desks and files. I see there are two desks. Has Judd been using the office?"

"No. He keeps everything in the bunkhouse."

"OK. Then I want you to use the other desk and get started on that office work we talked about. Do you have a laptop?"

"Yes."

"Good. I want to take the bill paying off Judd's back, and we will start doing that here in the house. Are you comfortable taking that on?"

"Absolutely."

"Today, I'd like you to stop in at the First National Bank in Newcastle. Tom Westedt will be expecting you. He will have you sign a signature card. From now on, two signatures will be required on all the ranch checks, yours and mine. I'll tell him you are coming."

"OK."

"And keep track of any expenses, such as mileage. I'll reimburse you."

Another smile.

"I'll tell Judd to bring over the files today. Please continue with the meal schedule you've been doing. I'm going back into town now, and I'll plan to stay here tomorrow night."

I found Judd in the stable where he had a horse's back leg between his, and was hammering on a shoe.

"Threw a shoe?"

"Yep," he said, after spitting a stream of tobacco juice on the ground. "Looks like she lost it on a rock. Lots of those out here."

"So I've noticed."

I told him he didn't have to handle the accounts payable any longer, that Patti and I would do that from the house, and asked him to move the files to the office in the house this afternoon.

"Also, please gather up the unpaid bills for me, and I'll take care of them."

I could tell from his expression and body language that he didn't think much of my plan. From other businesses I've bought, I've learned that no one wants to give up any of their "territory." They feel their job may be in jeopardy. Judd was just going to have to live with it.

"I see you're a bit surprised, and I'm guessing disappointed. This is not a demotion. The truth is, I want you to be freer to manage the herd, far more important to me than paying bills. All the herd records are still yours to maintain, just not the bill paying. OK?"

He gave a barely perceptible nod, but his real feelings were clear.

I saw Zach working in the shop. I stopped to tell him I would be moving into the ranch house and living there each time I came out.

"I'm heading back to Upton. I expect I won't see you till tomorrow morning." As always, he had a big smile and a great attitude.

My rental car had a Bluetooth system to which I paired my cell phone. I don't know whether talking on a handheld phone while driving is illegal in Wyoming. I doubted it, as states out in this part of the country where the population per square mile is in single digits tend to avoid laws that dictate how people behave. Except the big ones, like murder. Which reminded me to call Sheriff Wirth.

"Sheriff, I visited the site where the body was found. I might have something to add to your investigation."

"Do tell, Mr. Willand."

I told him about the tracks I found in the clearing south of the burial ground. I explained why I was convinced they were made by a plane landing and taking off. Maybe they have nothing to do with the body, but why else would a plane land on a really rough patch of ground in a remote part of my ranch?

"That's very interesting. Could be that's how the victim, and his killer, got there. That makes as much sense as somebody bringing the body in from the highway. Have your employees at the ranch mentioned seeing or hearing planes flying nearby and low?"

"No. When I first met with them, they remembered seeing me fly over the ranch one morning. That was all."

"It's sure worth another look. I'll take a deputy and go back out there. How do we find that clearing from where the body was found?"

"Continue past the grave on that same lane. It ends in a couple hundred yards. Walk farther south through the brush and you'll come up onto a bit of a plateau and the clearing after about a hundred steps."

"Thanks, Mark. You may have something here. And I'll give you some new information. I told you we had identified the victim through his fingerprints. Ethan Alvarez."

"Yes."

"Now we have a photo of him taken when he was last arrested. It's from two years ago, but recent enough. We're going to circulate it around Upton and here in Newcastle, see if anyone recognizes him.

"And we found out a little more about Mr. Alvarez. He was born in the U.S., raised in Hamilton, Montana. Arrested in Missoula for DUI once. Arrested again in Missoula for possession with intent to sell, got probation and a fine. His last known address was an apartment in Gillette, but the building manager says he's been gone from there for over six months. No credit card use, apparently he used cash for everything. Probably drug cash."

My mind raced again. "Sheriff, please keep me up to date on what you find. As you can imagine, I'm very interested. It isn't everyday that a murder victim is buried on my property."

"Ha! I hope not," the sheriff chuckled. "Talk to you later."

Something smelled, and it wasn't coming from the bottom of my boots. I had a hard time believing my ranch hands didn't hear a plane circling or landing or taking off, even at that far end of the ranch.

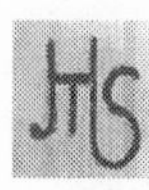

CHAPTER FOURTEEN

Newcastle
Thursday, October 18
8:30 a.m.

"Has this bank ever been robbed?"

My question stopped Tom Westedt in his tracks as he was leading me to his office. He turned, looked me up and down, and smiled.

"That's an interesting question, Mark. Why do you ask? You're not planning something, are you?"

"Oh, my lord, no!" I laughed. "It's just that this building is such a fortress, I can't imagine that robbers would even bother."

"We've been lucky, Mark. No holdups here."

As we sat in his office, I asked Tom if Patti had stopped in to sign a signature card.

"Yes, she did. She seems like a nice person."

"Since I'm going to be here only part of the time, I need someone at the ranch all the time, keeping track administratively. I'm going to give her a chance to be that person."

"I know she appreciates the confidence you've shown in her."

"Tom, I need you to do something else. Please set up a second checking account, let's call it Halestone Ranch Two. Transfer $150,000 into it from the main account. I'll be the only one authorized on the account."

Tom said he would have the account open and checks ready next time I came out.

"Great, thanks. I plan to be back out in about two weeks."

Before heading back to Upton, I stopped in at Tuff Air to make sure the 210 would be fueled and ready for my departure the following morning.

On the drive, I recall Zach telling me Ken Morris is mayor of Upton. He said it's a part-time office, and Ken is an insurance broker. Time to meet him.

Like most towns in the west, Upton was settled when the railroad was built. An extension of the Burlington and Missouri River Railroad from Newcastle was built in 1890. Upton is also at the junction of US 16 and State Highway 116. There are just over a thousand people here, a couple of churches and a handful of businesses. The Morris Agency is one of them, just off the main highway. I parked and walked into a duplex that was shared by a dentist's office. Morris's receptionist greeted me with a quick smile.

"I'm Mark Willand. I'm the new owner of Halestone Ranch. Is Mayor Morris available?"

"Hello, Mr. Willand. I'm Jean Morris, Ken's wife. Zach Talty was a classmate of Ken's, and has mentioned you. He certainly speaks highly of you. Please give me a minute and I'll get Ken for you."

A man wearing a snap-front western shirt, a rodeo belt buckle, neatly pressed dress jeans and shiny cowboy boots walked out with a big grin on his face.

"Mr. Willand, welcome to Upton! I'm glad you stopped in."

He shook my hand. Firm, but he didn't try to crush my bones, or pull me toward him. A solid handshake. No attempt to dominate. A good sign.

"Thank you, it's nice to meet you, and please call me Mark. Zach Talty works for me, and told me about you."

"You've got a good man in Zach."

"Thanks, I agree. By the way, I got a kick out of your entrance signs at the edge of town."

"Oh," he laughed, "right. 'The Best Town on Earth.'"

"Right, that's quite a bold statement."

"It goes back to the early '90s and our railroad station manager, Frank Burdick, started saying that and it caught on. Since then, all of our entrance signs have carried that slogan."

"Mayor, I would like to get your opinion on a few things. Do you have a few minutes?"

"Call me Ken, please. The only time anyone calls me mayor is when they want something. I knew Jack well. He was a close friend, and we surely do miss him. I have a feeling he would approve of your purchase of the ranch."

Ken made a good first impression. He and his wife appeared to work as a team, just as Barbara and I had done for ten years.

"Thanks, I sure hope so. I've been spending long weekends in June for nearly 20 years on a ranch south of here. Wyoming has become like a second home. Even though I'm a permanent resident of Illinois, I plan to be here quite a bit."

"Mark, as I'm sure you're aware, your ranch has been part of our community since the late 1800s. Jack's grandfather enlarged it when he bought it in the '30s. It's the largest ranch around here, and many of us here have worked there at one time or another. When I was in high school, I laid irrigation pipe for Luke for two summers. He and Jack were great to work for."

Ken had the physique of someone who had done physical work at sometime in the past, though not the recent past.

"Then you really are the right person to talk to. I want to do something significant for Upton, in memory of Jack. I plan to continue operating the ranch just as it has been, but I want to donate a part of the annual income into something that will benefit the community."

His already alert eyes brightened at that news.

"I'll be back out in two weeks. In the meantime, please think about this. It could be one big thing, or a lot of small things, or a combination of both. I plan to really enjoy the ranch, and I don't need the income to live off of. You mentioned working at the ranch. Maybe a summer internship at Halestone for teenagers that want to earn for college. Possibly Zach could teach them all about ranching. This is just one possibility. Please think big, though, not small. OK?"

"It's an incredible offer, Mark, and very generous of you. Yes, I'll come up with a list of possibilities by your next trip."

There was one other item I thought the mayor might be able to help me with.

"Ken, as mayor, I assume you are involved in overseeing Upton Municipal Airport."

"Your assumption is correct."

"I'm planning to fly out here from Illinois every other week or so for the foreseeable future, so I was looking at making your airport my base. On the charts, it says no fuel is on site. Are there no pumps on the field?"

"That's right, no pumps, but a fuel company in town carries 100 low lead, and will deliver to your hangar. Is that what you use?"

"Yes, and that could work. I can fly non-stop from my home field to here. I'll also need a hangar, and I understand there's one available. I'd like to take a look at it. How can I find it?"

"There's just one that's empty, and you can find it at the north end of the row."

I drove out to the field. The runway, listed as 3,700 feet, looks in good shape. The empty hangar was right where the mayor said it was. It's old, but has a decent door, so it will be OK for my 210.

I had one more item of business in Upton, and needed some advice. Judd had said he'd be at a bull auction today, so I called Zach.

"How ya doin', Mark?" answered Zach. He had apparently either recognized my number, or had put me in his contacts.

"I'm having a great day, Zach, thanks. I'll be heading back to the ranch pretty soon, but I wanted to buy a used pickup here in Upton. Where should I go?"

He chuckled and said, "Well, as you look around our little town, you'll see there aren't a lot of choices. There's a Ford dealer in Gillette that has a satellite lot right on 16 just before you leave town headed this direction. I've had some good experiences there when I've needed parts for my 150. Jack did business with a Chevy dealer in Newcastle."

I clicked off and drove to the lot. The selection was meager, but I picked out a clean five-year-old F-250. I told them I'd pick it up tomorrow and bring a check.

The Buckskin Bar was busy as I stopped in to pick up a burger to take back to the ranch. A rectangular building with wood plank floors scuffed up by years of boot traffic, unpainted plywood walls with a couple of neon beer signs and a big screen TV attached, a pool table, a bar and some tables and booths, it had the look of a place where everyone knows each other. On the wall above the cash register was a notice to customers reading *No Workin' During Drinkin' Hours!* It appeared everyone was paying heed.

It was late afternoon when I pulled into the ranch yard. Patti's car was gone and the house was quiet. As I munched on my dinner, I started looking through some of Jack's recent files, but quickly decided I'd had enough for one day, and headed for the porch as sunset arrived.

There's a solitude about ranch country at dusk that's sort of surreal. I first experienced it at my friend's ranch. Through the day, cows can be heard calling their calves. Meadowlarks and other songbirds are everywhere, and are rarely quiet. Sound travels a long way in this open country, and the occasional sounds of machinery carry on the wind.

At sunset, though, nearly all sounds seem to disappear, and that's when I feel the magic of this place called Wyoming. This state has the smallest population of all 50, with only six humans per square mile. That has a lot to do with my feeling of peace and quiet.

Sitting here on the porch, looking out at the open country, I realize how very fortunate I am to own Halestone Ranch. What an incredible impact the ranch has already had on my life, and all since Alan Creston's call just 30 days ago. I have no idea what surprises the next 30 days will bring, but I look forward to whatever they are. This is going to be a great, if unexpected, chapter in my life.

Newcastle Airport
Friday, October 19
8 a.m.

Tuff Air has my 210 parked in front of the flight office. The forecast shows low ceilings throughout much of Iowa, with tops at 5,000 feet. I've filed IFR for 7,000. Upper winds are almost on my tail, so I'll fly nonstop if the winds continue out of the west.

In the air and level at 7,000 feet, I think about the last few days, and what got done.

1. I saw the murder site, and discovered the plane tracks.
2. Arranged for my bedroom and office at the ranch house.
3. Put Patti in charge of mail (and ticked off Judd at the same time).
4. Talked to the sheriff about tracks left by a plane, he advised me about the murder victim.
5. Set up second bank account for my sole signature.
6. Met the Upton Mayor.
7. Rented a hangar at Upton Airport.
8. Bought a pickup truck.

I feel certain that I should keep Zach and Patti. They both have great attitudes and seem to like working here. It's hard to nail down how I feel about Judd. He's a good cattleman and knows that business well. It's just hard to get to know him. The jury's out on that one.

CHAPTER FIFTEEN

Rockford, Illinois
Saturday, October 20
10 a.m.

Since returning home, I've been catching up on yard work. All of the excitement of the past month has left me way behind in getting my lawn and garden put to bed for the winter. I'm about half-finished mowing the back yard when I feel my cell phone vibrate in my pocket.

Disengaging the mower and turning it off, I see a 307 number on my screen.

"Mr. Willand, this is Sheriff Wirth again."

"Sheriff, I'd like to say it's good to hear from you, but I worry you have more bad news. No offense."

"No, no, and none taken. I am not generally the purveyor of good news. Nature of the job. I'm just calling to see if you can offer some help in our investigation.

"Sure," I said, relieved. "What can I do?"

"That tip you gave me about evidence of a plane landing and taking off from your ranch was valuable. I know you are a pilot, and I thought you'd be interested in what we've discovered since then."

"I can't wait to hear it."

"A detective called from the Ciudad Juarez, Mexico, police department. That's right across the border from El Paso. They arrested a mechanic at their local airport. He was caught with a large quantity of cocaine. He gave them quite a confession."

"Does it involve my ranch?"

"I'll get to that. He and a friend apparently were being paid by a Columbian drug cartel. This guy was familiar with the various planes hangared on his airport. The cartel was paying him to steal certain models of planes that owners didn't use very often, lowering the risk the owner would notice it was missing. When he picked one, he would go to the hangar after work, remove the tail number, install decals with a bogus tail number, and leave the hangar door unlocked. The service shop always kept a duplicate ignition key so it could service the planes. The day of the theft, he would make a copy of the key and leave it in the ignition.

"That night, then, his pilot buddy would arrive, load the cocaine and take off. Their first choice was to steal late model Cessna Turbo 182s. Have you ever owned one?"

"I have. That turbo model can hold a lot of fuel and has a range of about 900 miles. It can land short, and can take off in 1,000 feet."

"And, I've learned," added the sheriff, "it sells well in Europe."

"Ah, I'm beginning to see the picture."

"Right," the sheriff continued, "so here's what these two were being paid to do. Steal a late model plane, use it to deliver a batch of cocaine to someplace in Wyoming. Then the pilot would deliver the plane to a pre-arranged airport in Canada, collect cash for the plane, and the buyer would then move it on to Europe to another buyer. They did that two or three times a year.

"The pilot hasn't been arrested yet, but it shouldn't be long. The mechanic gave up his name. He also identified the Wyoming drop-off point as a private field near Upton."

"I'm guessing that private field is the strip on my ranch."

"Yep, there's a better than even chance of that. There are no other private fields around Upton registered. We don't know how they picked your location. It's not much of a stretch for us to surmise that the body found on your ranch is somehow connected to the cocaine delivery."

"I was afraid of that, but this new information is unsettling."

"I sure get that, Mr. Willand. Here's my question: Do you think those tracks on your ranch could have been from a 182?"

I thought about the wheelbase on a 182.

"They could be, Sheriff. If you measure the width of the tracks and let me know, I'll confirm that."

He said he would, then said he had another question.

"The mechanic didn't know where the pilot got the fuel for the rest of the trip to Canada. He did know that the stolen planes would always be delivered to a buyer at the airport in Steinbach, Manitoba, which he said has an identifier of CKK7. Any idea where he would have fueled up after departing your ranch before heading north?"

I had walked inside the house while the sheriff was talking. In my office, I pulled out my Wyoming sectional.

"Well, let me see, Sheriff. I'm opening an FAA sectional chart for that area. Here we go. There's an airport in Lusk that has 24-hour pumps that can be activated by credit card."

"That's south about 90 miles, though," countered the sheriff. "Do you think he'd go south that far before heading to Canada?"

"No, I'm thinking he filled up before he landed on my ranch. There's no one at the Lusk field after dark. He could have used a stolen credit card, continued from there to Upton, dropped off the cocaine and then flown straight to Manitoba. I see here that it's about a 700-mile flight, so he'd have plenty of fuel."

He was quiet for a moment.

"That's interesting, Mr. Willand, very interesting. The Mexican police hope to arrest the pilot soon. I told their detective that he may have been the killer of the man at your ranch. Could be a long shot, but maybe Ethan Alvarez was holding back some of the cash from earlier cocaine shipments, and the pilot found out about it."

"Sheriff, I keep wondering why they started using the ranch for a drop-off point. Do you think the dead guy had customers around Upton? Maybe one of them suggested the remote spot on my ranch."

"Well that would make sense. Alvarez had a snake head tattooed on the back of his hand. We have that picture along with a mug shot and will keep showing them around Upton and Newcastle, see if anyone recognizes him. Mark, you've been very helpful. Thanks again."

After we disconnected, I headed back to finish the mowing, thinking about the murder. Who killed him and why?

When I returned from the ranch yesterday, I brought Jack Hale's files with me, going back five years. Checks written over the past two years were signed by Judd Turner. Routine bills were paid each month.

One recurring invoice seemed odd. Three times over the past year, Judd had written checks to GT Gelbvieh Representatives, LLC.

I had to Google Gelbvieh as I'd never heard the word. An extensive and elaborate website appeared with everything you could want to know about the Gelbvieh breed of cattle. As I read, I learned the Gelbvieh originated in Germany and is a reddish-gold-colored, fast-growing, large-framed, muscular animal, with a quiet temperament that started showing up in the US about 50 years ago. Not the actual animals, but semen, which was shipped over here used to crossbreed with Angus cattle, primarily. The results were apparently desirable, because the American Gelbvieh Association has over 1,000 members with 45,000 head "active and registered."

No results came up for "Gelbvieh Representatives, LLC," however. I looked again at the three checks Judd had written for a total of $20,000, made out to this Gelbvieh LLC. I wondered what those checks had bought. When Judd and I had toured the ranch, all of the cattle looked typically Angus. No Gelbvieh-looking animals. Odd, but explainable, perhaps.

I put those checks aside and made a note to ask Judd about them on my next trip.

Not long after, another red flag popped up. A bill from the local Ford dealer was for a $2,500 transmission repair on a Ford pickup. I recall Zach telling me the ranch had always owned Chevy trucks because of Jack's friendship with the Chevy dealer. This invoice had been paid over a year ago, and Judd's new pickup was less than a year old. I wondered if this repair job had been done on Judd's old pickup. I can't imagine Jack would have authorized this payment, but he'd turned all finances over to Judd almost two years ago.

Looks like I'd better go back out next week for a few days. I'll leave Thursday.

CHAPTER SIXTEEN

Monday, October 22

My cell phone is vibrating and it's a non-Wyoming number I don't recognize, so I ignore it. Moments later, a voice mail pops up.

"Mr. Willand," the recorded voice says, "this is Deputy Harry Reynolds at the Pueblo County Sheriff's Office, in Pueblo, Colorado. We are told you own the Halestone Ranch in Wyoming. We would like to talk to you regarding some cattle of yours. Please call me."

Pueblo, Colorado? Some of my cattle? What on earth could this be about?

I called. The deputy explained that a slaughterhouse had been raided nearby, and some hides were discovered with the Halestone brand. The brand didn't show up in Colorado records, but a wide search found it was registered to our ranch.

He asked if we had shipped any calves in mid-August. That was the date the slaughterhouse received them.

This didn't make any sense to me. Halestone Ranch was a cow-calf operation. The cows would be bred in the fall and they'd calve in the spring. When the calves are two to three months old, they'd be given their shots, branded, and castrated. Once they were about seven months old, usually in September or October, they'd be sold to feedyards where they'd be fattened up for three to six months, then sold to packing houses. Why would Halestone calves be in a slaughterhouse?

I told him I would call my ranch manager, and then call him back. I called Judd.

"Judd, what was the earliest you shipped calves this fall?" He said they all went at one time, during the first week of September.

"Was your count short when you shipped?"

"Yeah, come to think of it, we were a half-dozen or more short from what we expected to ship, but it happened around the same time

Jack died, and everything was such a mess. I didn't get around to looking into it. Why? What's going on?"

I explained that a Colorado sheriff had found a batch of hides with our brand at a slaughterhouse that had been raided. Their records showed receipt of the calves during August. The place had been closed down for buying stolen cattle.

"Well, I wouldn't know anything about that. I'll ask Zach what he knows."

I clicked off and said to myself that if anybody knows about shenanigans on the ranch, it's Judd, not Zach.

I called the deputy back, told him our count was short about half a dozen, and we had shipped none before September. He said that matched what other ranchers with missing cattle had said. He said the slaughterhouse was obviously buying rustled cattle. He suggested I send him a statement regarding our loss, so that we would have a claim in the event there were funds recovered from the sale of the business to pay for our calves.

"How many hides did you find with our brand?

"Eight."

I thanked him, clicked off, and sat there thinking about this newest incident. Who took those calves, and how did they get them off the ranch? There's only one good access road, and a cattle truck doesn't move quietly. Just one more thing I need to talk to the ranch foreman about when I get there Thursday.

CHAPTER SEVENTEEN

Poplar Grove Airport
Thursday, October 25
7 a.m.

It's 50 degrees, sunny, and fall is here. The forecast is clear for the trip to Upton. I'll file a VFR flight plan. Six hours non-stop is out of the question, though. Nature will call long before that, so I'll refuel and get coffee at LeMars, Iowa.

I recall a Barbra Streisand movie back in the '70s titled *On a Clear Day You Can See Forever*. It had nothing to do with flying, but as I'm crossing the Mississippi into eastern Iowa, the title is a good description for today's visibility. It's a beautiful day.

After the pit stop in LeMars, my heading took me just south of Rapid City, and I was close enough to see part of Mount Rushmore. I've never been there. It's only about a 90-minute drive from the ranch along US 16 over to Custer and then north on US 385, so I'll make a point of driving over when things at the ranch calm down.

It's about 12 when I land at Upton Municipal. I park in front of my newly-rented hangar and call the fuel dealer in Upton. By the time I get the hangar door open and pull my "new" Ford pickup out, the fuel truck has already arrived.

"Howdy," said the driver as he stepped down from the cab.

"You must be Johnny," I smiled.

He looked at me funny. "Uh, no, no sir, my name is Gareth."

"I meant Johnny, as in 'Johnny on the spot,'" I chuckled.

"Oh," he smiled, "I get it. Yes sir, we're just down the road a bit. You caught me at a good time."

Gareth refuels the 210 and helps me push it in the hangar.

Before leaving, I sat in the truck thinking about what I wanted to accomplish today. Then I called Randy Gotch. He was in, and I asked him if I could come by his office in Newcastle. We agreed on a 2 p.m. meeting, which gave me enough time to grab a sandwich to eat along the way. I called Judd and said I would like to get together at the ranch later in the afternoon. He said he would be there.

"Randy, this is the first time I've owned cattle. Am I right that they can be depreciated if they are breeding stock?"

He said yes.

"I see in the bank statements that the ranch spent $20,000 during the past year with Gelbvieh Representatives, LLC. I assume that was for breeding stock. Are you depreciating that amount on the tax return?

If Gotch was surprised by my question, he didn't let on.

"Let me go back through last year's return and take a look. I'll let you know."

"Good. Thank you. I have another question. A Pueblo, Colorado, sheriff's deputy called me about hides with our brand that were found when a slaughterhouse was raided. The business documents indicated they had obtained the stock in mid-August. I called Judd and he said he had sold no cattle before mid-September. Looks like the stock were stolen from our ranch. The deputy is sending me photos and a statement from the sheriff's office. Will that be sufficient to declare a loss on the tax return?"

"Yes," he said. "That should do it. Judd called me about this, after you called him."

Why did Judd call him about that? That seems odd. Or maybe I'm just being paranoid about the people who I don't yet trust. In Gotch's case, I've about decided to have someone else do the ranch tax returns and payroll.

Back at the ranch, Patti greeted me warmly. Somehow she appeared different since I saw her last. She seemed more cheerful.

Sitting at our desks in the office, she explained that checks for recent bills were ready for my signature. She gave me a stack of unopened mail and a few phone messages.

I called Judd, asked him to come to the office.

"Judd, is there anything you need? Do you have enough hay for the winter?"

"Yep, we are in good shape there."

"Great. What else is new?"

"Well, let's see, I ordered some new well equipment for the hayfields. Zach will install it. I guess that's about it since you were here last."

"You know, Judd, I've been trying to figure out how the cattle rustlers got those calves off the ranch and transported to Pueblo. There don't seem to be a lot of ways that could happen, but I certainly don't know all the access points, yet. What do you think happened?"

He thought for a moment. "Well, assuming they were stolen, the rustlers mighta brought a truck to the west border of the ranch. Pretty isolated over there. If they had a horse and rounded up the calves in the dark, they coulda got away without anybody seeing anything."

"You said 'assuming they were stolen,' Judd. What else do you think could have happened?"

"Oh, I don't know. Predators. Or maybe they got out and took off."

"Predators? Well, there'd be eight carcasses somewhere on the ranch, and not eight hides in Pueblo, right?"

He nodded.

"And are there spots where the fence needs fixing?"

He looked down and shook his head.

"OK, so let's stick with them being stolen. Have you seen any vehicle tracks that looked strange?"

"No, but it rained in late August so the tracks would have been washed out."

"Yeah, I suppose so."

I opened a file folder on my desk.

"Let's move on to something else. Over the past year, you issued three checks to Gelbvieh Representatives, LLC. Tell me about those purchases."

For a moment he seemed surprised by the question, but he quickly recovered and explained that Jack had asked him to explore the benefits of cross-breeding Gelbvieh bulls with the ranch stock. Jack had heard the mix would improve the herd, and was becoming popular throughout the West. So after that conversation, he bought several Gelbvieh bulls.

"Wonderful! That makes sense. I've done a little research into the Gelbvieh breed and it backs up what Jack heard. When can I take a look at them?"

"Well, they're scattered with the herd, but I suppose we could try on horseback. I actually haven't seen them since before Jack's funeral."

Judd added that some of this breed had been rustled in Colorado, probably because they bring good money. We agreed to look for them during the next couple of days. I said I would ride with him so I could see more of the ranch.

I found Zach in the machine shed, working on the windrower. As always, he had a big smile, and welcomed me back. I asked him if he had decided about replacing it, and he said he would like to go to the dealership with me and talk about a new one. We decided to go tomorrow afternoon.

I was apparently becoming a regular at the Buckskin Bar. As soon as I walked in for dinner, the bartender said ,"Welcome back, Mr. Willand!"

"Well, thank you! I've only been in here a few times. How you remember my name? Do you know everyone that comes in the door?"

He laughed, "No, I'm not gifted in that way, but it's a small town. My sister works as a secretary in the mayor's office, and told me you had rented a hangar. And my brother-in-law works at the Ford dealer, and told me you bought a truck there."

He also volunteered that Jack Hale used to stop in for a beer before he became ill, and Judd Turner comes in regularly.

"Matter of fact, Judd was just in a few days ago having dinner with your CPA."

"Randy Gotch?"

"Yeah, they come in together a lot."

I had no idea Judd and Randy were such good friends. I'm starting to think that the local bar is the best newsroom in the town.

I settled in a corner booth, ordered dinner, and sat thinking about Judd and Randy. They've been the only ones who don't seem happy to see me every time I come. I wonder why.

Then I thought about the conversation I had with Alan Creston when I first met him, and Jack's comment about an LLC Randy had been after him to sign. Could that have anything to do with the Gelbvieh Representatives, LLC?

I thought back to Judd's comments earlier today. Sounded like he might have trouble locating the Gelbvieh bulls he had bought. Had they been rustled, too? Did they even exist?

All of a sudden, I had a headache. I'm no detective, even though Sheriff Wirth said I had helped him find clues at the ranch murder site. Something's off here. I decided to finish my meal and call it a day.

CHAPTER EIGHTEEN

Halestone Ranch
Friday, October 26

Judd was still away at the bull auction in Gillette, which made me wonder how many bulls we had, or as I was beginning to suspect, didn't have. If we have 250 cows, we should have about 10 bulls to get all of the cows serviced. I'll have a better idea of what we have when Judd and I ride the ranch in the next day or so.

Patti cooked up a hearty breakfast, something I'm not accustomed to. I'll be packing on some ranch pounds if I'm not careful. Zach talked windrowers with me. He said he has no favorite brand.

He knew from our first visit that I had been an IH and CaseIH dealer in past years, and Titan Equipment was the CaseIH dealer in Rapid City. I looked up their website and found six windrowers in inventory. One was a 2017 with only two hours on it.

"They'll probably be most motivated to sell that one over the others because of age, Zach. How's it look to you?"

Zach zoomed in on the photo and looked at the specs. "It looks like it's the right size for us. Whaddya think they want for it?"

"Let's go find out. I have to run down to Newcastle this morning. How about meeting me there for lunch, and we'll drive on to Rapid City this afternoon?"

"Yes sir, sounds good."

It was a crisp morning as I walked to my pickup. A film of dew, almost frost, coated the windshield. As I circled out of the ranch yard, I called the sheriff and asked if he was available. He said to stop in.

This really is beautiful country, I thought, on the drive down to Newcastle through the Thunder Basin National Grassland. Sweeping vistas of rolling hills, dotted with grazing cattle and occasional herds of antelope, and hardly a tree in sight.

Sheriff Wirth is very measured in his responses, probably a product of his training and experience in talking to victims and perpetrators of crimes big and small. Mostly small out here. But he couldn't hide the surprise on his face when I told him, "Sheriff, it seems we've had another crime at the ranch."

"Don't tell me another body has been found."

"No, nothing quite that dire." I told him about the Pueblo phone calls and the hides they had found with our brand. "The rogue slaughterhouse bought these calves a month before we sold our calves. Someone took them off the ranch a month before we sold ours."

Before saying anything, he opened his desk drawer and removed a can of Copenhagen snuff. He took a pinch from the can and tucked it behind his lower lip. I remembered our neighbor's hired man doing that many years ago when we were baling hay. I'd noticed Judd chewed, but had no idea what brand.

"I didn't know Copenhagen was still around."

"Oh yeah, it's still popular. Has different flavors. I'm using it to help quit smoking." He picked up a Styrofoam coffee cup and spit. That's one habit I'm glad I never picked up.

"How many calves did you lose?"

"Eight hides were found at the slaughterhouse. You know, this is all new to me, but I'm surprised that these 500 or 600 pound calves would be slaughtered. They'd be more valuable after they were fed out."

"No question, but without a bill of sale from the ranch, a feeder wouldn't buy them. This slaughterhouse apparently didn't care. Dog food, maybe. So you think this happened in, when? September?"

"No, that's when my ranch manager, Judd, says we shipped. So this would have been before, probably in August. He thinks they may have been grabbed at night, on the west border of the ranch. It's pretty isolated there."

The sheriff thought about that.

"I've only been out there a few times, and yeah, it sure is isolated. We haven't had any recent reports of cattle stolen. I hope it was a one-time hit, but it usually isn't. And if they feel it's an easy target, they'll come again."

Now it was my turn to think. *I wonder if there's a way to remotely monitor what's going on out there. That's a lot of ground to cover, though.*

"By the way," the sheriff went on, "we found out something else about Alvarez, the dead guy. One of our deputies has been showing bartenders around the county the picture of the snake tattoo photo. One remembers seeing it when he was serving drinks. When the deputy showed the mug shot, the bartender said that was the guy who had the tattoo. Apparently the tattoo guy had been in the bar more than once during the past year. He also said he was usually with someone."

"Did he say who?"

"Nope, and he didn't recall anything else. We're going to try to find out who it was, or who they were."

"Sheriff, on another subject: I'm no Sam Spade and don't want to be." The look on his face stopped me.

"Well, you may be too young for that reference, but let's just say I don't pretend to be a detective. I have some concerns about my ranch manager. I would like to find out more about Judd's background history, and he won't talk about it. Jack Hale's attorney told me Jack was in a pinch and hired him without checking any references.

"I'm relying on Judd to run the ranch because I'm only here part-time. Can you help me find someone to check his background? Maybe a private detective?"

The sheriff nodded and scooted forward in his chair. He flipped through his Rolodex and pulled out a card.

"Yes. Here it is. I was in the Marines with a guy that became a good friend, He worked his way up to sheriff in Billings. Got shot in the knee and received a disability pension. Now he's a private detective, and a good one. His name is Gene Graf. Do you want his number?"

"Yes, please."

"I'll call him if you want me to and give him a heads up."

"I'd appreciate that."

"I'll tell him you will be calling, and why."

One hour later

"Gene, this is Mark Willand calling from Upton, Wyoming. Did Sheriff Wirth call you about me?"

"Yes, he did, Mark. He ranks you pretty high. Says you aren't a bad amateur detective yourself. Tell me how I can help."

I gave him a quick version of my story and how Judd was hired. I added, "Judd appears knowledgeable about cattle, said he had been a ranch foreman on a previous job in Montana, and had worked on other ranches near Missoula. Judd is a good-looking, pleasant enough guy, in his mid-30s, single, and does seem to know the job of ranch manager.

"Here's my concern. He is extremely tight-lipped about his past. Doesn't want to talk about family, schooling, anything in depth about past jobs. Just clams up. The two other employees at the ranch tell me the same thing. He doesn't talk to them about his past, either."

"Not a crime, certainly," Graf interjected, "but it sure makes you think he's trying to hide something."

"Exactly. Now to my suspicions: He has an almost-new Ford crew cab pickup, probably in the $60,000 range. Yet I'm told he came to town in an old pickup that barely ran, and I see in the files that he paid for a couple thousand dollars of repairs out of the ranch checkbook. So I wonder how he could afford an expensive pickup."

"Makes me wonder, too, but quite often I find these kinds of mysteries are easily explained."

"Well, that would be fine, Gene, if he would just open up and explain. But that isn't all. According to the ranch files, Judd wrote checks to Gelbvieh Representatives, LLC, for $20,000 over the past year, which he says were for bulls to cross-breed the ranch Angus. He says Jack Hale instructed him to do that. Yet when I have asked him to show me the bulls, he claims he isn't sure where they are on the ranch. I've suggested we saddle up and ride out to look for them. He said he would do that with me, but keeps putting me off."

Graf was silent. I took a look at the phone to see if we were still connected. "Still with me, Gene?"

"Yep, just jotting down some notes. Keep going."

"OK. There's one more incident, on top of the others, that led to me looking for your help. Last week, the sheriff's department in Pueblo County, Colorado, called. They said they had busted a slaughterhouse near there that was buying rustled beef. They found eight hides with my ranch's brand. The slaughterhouse records indicated they had bought the calves in August. Yet Judd tells me we sold our calves all at once, in mid-September. I'm wondering how the calves were stolen without our employees seeing anything."

"I can't imagine it would be easy, that's for sure, but you do have a big ranch, Mark."

"Gene, it comes down to trust. If I'm going to have Judd continue to manage the place, I've got to trust him. Right now, I don't. Maybe I'm imagining things because he doesn't talk about himself, but I need to know. I'd like to employ you to look into his background, find out if he's been in any trouble, and what past employers thought of him. Can you investigate him without him knowing about it?"

"Yes. I assume you can give me his Social Security number from payroll records, a recent photograph, his truck license number, and any credit card numbers you may have?"

"Sure. I have a picture of him with Jack from less than a year ago I can scan and email to you. I'll get the rest to you, too. What else?"

"Here's my address. Got a pen?"

"Yep, fire away."

He gives me his address and adds, "I'll need a $1,500 retainer. That will cover three days. After that, it's $500 per day and any expenses incurred, including travel. Are you agreeable to that?"

"Yes. I'll also send you my cell phone number, ranch address, and my Illinois home address. Don't send any mail to the ranch address, as Judd has access to my office there."

"I'll start as soon as I get your check."

Rapid City, South Dakota
Titan Equipment, Inc.
Same day
1 p.m.

Zach and I were shown the 2017 windrower we had seen on their website. We experienced sticker shock when the salesman told us the price: $155,000!

"We don't want to spend that much," Zach jumped in. "We don't need that big a machine for our irrigated hay acreage."

The salesman nodded and looked at me for a response.

"Zach knows far better than I what equipment the ranch should have. I'm good with whatever he says."

The salesman said they were about to bring in a smaller five-year-old windrower that had been traded for a larger one. Zach asked him to call when he could see it.

I was pleased that Zach took the lead during this conversation. He treated it like he would if he was the owner spending his own money. That's why I wanted to come with him today, to see how he would handle this decision. I get more impressed with him every day.

Zach dropped me off at the airport where I had left my pickup. I pre-flighted the 210, buttoned up the hangar with the Ford inside and was in the air toward Rockford by 3:30 p.m.

This has been an interesting trip!

CHAPTER NINETEEN

Randy Gotch's office
Monday, October 29

"Do you have an appointment to see Mr. Gotch?" the receptionist asked as Judd Turner walked in the door.

"I do not," as he breezed past her and into Gotch's office before she had a chance to do anything.

"Randy, what the heck's going on? What happened to your LLC plan? You said I was going to get 10% of the ranch, but this guy from Illinois says he owns it now, and sure is acting like it."

Randy slowly looked up from his laptop, clearly annoyed at Judd's interruption. "Hale wouldn't sign the LLC. I had no idea the attorney had the estate authority to sell it to Willand."

"You said I'd get a $5,000 credit for each drug drop at the ranch. I know of three, for sure, maybe there's been more. After they found the dead guy, the cops — and Willand — have been all over the place up there. I'm not going to cover for any more landings there. When do I get my $15,000 cash instead of the ownership you promised?"

"I didn't promise you anything, Turner," Gotch's tone growing scornful. "I told you if we got control of the ranch after Hale's death, you would get your share. That didn't happen. You aren't getting a dime from me. Besides, from what Willand tells me, you've already gotten money out of the ranch. He asked about a tax write-off for eight head of Halestone cattle that were traced to a shady Pueblo slaughterhouse. I'm guessing you set that up. And what about the $20,000 that you paid out for Gelbvieh breeding stock? Willand wants to know if he can depreciate them on the ranch tax return. Do they even exist? He says the two of you are going to ride out and take a look at them. Am I guessing right that this Gelbvieh LLC he says the checks were paid to is a phony account you set up?"

Judd's face reddened.

"I think you'd better start figuring out how to get out of those jams, pal, and forget about owning part of that ranch or getting any money out of me. Now get out of my office!"

Judd Turner rose slowly and glared at Gotch for a long moment, before storming out of the office. In the parking lot, he slammed a fist on his dash, feeling that Gotch had cheated him, and was getting away with it. Even though Judd knew about Gotch's drug connection, he also knew Gotch was aware of his rustling and the Gelbvieh scam.

It was a standoff. He spun gravel out of the parking lot.

Upton Airport
Tuesday, November 6
Noon

My 210 landed after a rough ride from Poplar Grove. Skies had been clear but at 6,500 feet VFR, the headwinds were almost 40 knots. When I dropped down to 4,500, the headwinds were only 20 knots, but the ride was rough. I needed to stop at Ainsworth for coffee and a rest.

On the ground at Upton, I fueled up and pushed the plane into its hangar. Climbing into my pickup, I wondered what kind of challenges this visit was going to produce. I had to chuckle as I thought back to my plan to visit Mount Rushmore when things calmed down. The way things have been going, I'll never get there.

The ride to the ranch in the smooth luxury of the 250 was a welcome change from the beating I took in the 210. Patti was cheerful as usual, and made me lunch. She had checks ready for me to sign, and there was a phone message from Upton Mayor Morris, asking for a call.

"Mr. Mayor, this is Mark Willand. I'm back at the ranch. I have a message to call you."

"Mark, nobody in all of Big, Wonderful Wyoming calls me that," he chuckled, "but it's fun to hear it. Do you have time to stop in soon? I have some ideas regarding your ranch sponsoring some activities for

Upton."

We agreed on a time and at three o'clock, I walked into his office. Ken said he and the local 4-H leader had talked. Aaron Rhodes was Upton High School's assistant principal, and four years earlier had formed a 4-H club.

"The community hadn't had one, Mark, for a number of years. I suppose there was a bit of a dry spell for kids who wanted to join. Aaron has done a lot with the club, and it has about 20 members. It's called the Upton Hoofbeats 4-H Club."

He went on. "Here is what we suggest, and I'll remind you that you told me to 'think big.'"

"Indeed I did, yes."

"Well, here goes: Your ranch would become sponsor of the club. You could provide a meeting room at the ranch, you could provide well-trained horses for riding classes. A summer internship for students could be available for members that Aaron and your man Zach would choose. Zach would conduct sessions on operation of farm equipment. The reason Zach's name came up is because Aaron has known him for a long time, and thinks Zach would enjoy being involved."

"I suspect he would. Please continue."

"Here's what Aaron thinks the club members have to bring to the table: a willingness to do whatever Zach and Aaron require. That includes some dirty work, like cleaning and maintaining the stables, maintaining the saddles and equipment provided, pitching in to help Zach whenever he needs it, like when he is laying irrigation pipe."

I make a mental note of checking the ranch's insurance coverage, as what Ken's describing could expose some liability issues.

"This would be a start," Ken concluded, "and whenever Aaron thinks there should be any additions or changes to the program, they would require Zach's approval and yours."

"Ken, let me talk to Zach and I'll get back to you. This sounds like a well thought-out proposal."

We left it at that. I'll talk to Zach tomorrow.

Wednesday morning
November 7

It's another big ranch breakfast: eggs, biscuits and gravy. It's delicious, but I'm not used to eating this much. Luckily, Zach is young and doesn't leave much on the table. He, Judd and Patti are at the table with me when I bring up the 4-H project. I told them I was planning to sponsor the club as a memorial to Jack, and then walked them through Aaron Rhode's plan.

Zach was quick to respond.

"I think it's a great idea. Many folks around Upton have worked here on the ranch part-time through the years. I'll bet some of them are parents of the 4-H kids. I've known Aaron since high school, and I would like to work with him on this."

I looked over to Judd. From the scowl on his face, I could probably have guessed what he was thinking when I asked for his opinion.

He didn't say anything for a moment, just stared at his coffee cup. Then he shot down the plan.

"These kids will be a pain in the neck. My guess is they'll break machinery, mess up the horses, get hurt, and make my job harder. I've never been in 4-H. I thought those blue jackets looked stupid."

I momentarily thought about telling him that FFA members, not 4-H members, wore "those stupid blue jackets," but quickly decided it wasn't worth it.

"Judd, "I said, "I'm disappointed you don't like the idea, but it's happening. As long as Zach is willing to be involved and work with the 4-H leader and the kids, this project shouldn't affect you. I've heard so many people tell me they liked and respected Jack and his dad. I plan to memorialize them with this project, and maybe with some others."

I decided to deny him the opportunity to respond. I walked into my office and closed the door. It had just become more obvious that Judd wouldn't be the ranch foreman at Halestone Ranch much longer.

Minutes later, my cell phone rang. I quickly answered after seeing it was from a 406 number. I had the feeling I was going to get the inside scoop on my Mr. Turner.

"Mr. Willand, this is Gene Graf in Billings. I've been looking into Judd Turner's background, like you asked me to. Is this a good time to talk?"

"Yes. I'm alone. Go ahead."

"OK. I was able to dig up quite a bit about your man of mystery. He was raised in Missoula. Went to high school there, played some sports, hung around with smoke jumpers a lot. He worked at a local gas station till he got fired for stealing six packs of beer. His dad got him a job at a local ranch, and he did a good job there, worked his way up to ranch foreman. The ranch owner said he was smart and worked hard, but hung out with some fellas that had been under suspicion at one time for rustling."

Well, well, I thought, *isn't that interesting?*

"The ranch owner had heard that a cattle truck had been spotted at the far end of the ranch late at night. Not long before, the owner had been riding a pasture near that area, and had counted his herd there. He told Judd about what he'd heard and asked him to ride that area and look for any tracks from a semi.

"Judd came back with a report that he found nothing suspicious. A few days later, he told the owner he was resigning to go see Wyoming, and left."

"And here he is at Halestone," I said. "Does that rancher think Judd stole his cattle?"

"Well, he sure has that suspicion, but he can't prove it. When he went out to re-count the herd in that same pasture, a gate had been left open to an adjoining pasture and the herds from both were all mixed together. He had no easy way to tell whether any cattle were missing, but he suspected that maybe Judd had been involved, and had quit after a rain shower had washed away any possible tracks."

"Interesting."

"Indeed it is. But, that's all I've come up with. Since Judd's been working on your ranch, nothing suspicious has come up about him. I don't see a benefit in spending more of your money to dig further."

"Thanks, Gene. I appreciate what you've come up with. What do I still owe you?"

"Nada. The $1,500 retainer you sent will cover it. Call me again if I can do anything more for you, and good luck."

I leaned back in my chair, thinking about what Graf had just told me. Stealing six-packs as a teenager wasn't a good sign, but doesn't necessarily mean bigger crimes are in the future. I've been looking for ways to trust him and keep him as ranch foreman. Gene Graf's findings sure haven't helped that any.

Wednesday afternoon

I found Judd repairing a saddle in the stable.

"Judd, I assume you don't want to be involved in buying the horses for the 4-H project?"

"I think it's a waste of your money, but Zach knows horses just as well as I do. Let him do it." A stream of tobacco juice into the dirt punctuated his statement.

"OK. I'll do that. Now why don't we take a ride and find the Gelbvieh breeding stock you bought?"

Judd hesitated a split second before straightening up and reaching around to his lower back.

"Well, I'd sure like to, Mark, but I pulled a muscle in my back yesterday. I leaned over at an odd angle to pick up a full five-gallon pail. I better wait a few days before I ride again."

I guess it wasn't painful enough to keep him from working on the saddle, but I left it at that.

Later, after seeing Judd's pickup pull out of the yard, I found Zach working in the shop.

"Zach, have you seen our Gelbvieh cattle lately, and do you know which pasture they are in?"

Zach stopped his repair work and looked at me as if I were speaking a foreign language.

"Mark, I'm very familiar with Gelbviehs and we don't have any."

Back in my office, I had no reason to doubt Zach, but I decided to check one more source about the Gelbviehs. I looked up the phone number of Howard Weston, the vet who had been treating our ranch herd for years.

As I dialed, I thought about the importance of a solid partnership with a veterinarian.

"Weston Veterinary, how may I help you?" a woman's voice answered.

"Yes, Dr. Weston, please."

"This is Dr. Weston."

I was momentarily speechless.

"Hello?" she said.

"Yes, yes," I sputtered, "this is Mark Willand, I own Halestone Ranch now, and it's my understanding that Dr. Weston has been working with our herd for a lot of years."

"Hello, Mr. Willand. It's nice to meet you. I am Dr. Emma Weston. You'll want to speak to the other Dr. Weston. Please hold."

The on-hold music gave me a chance to process what I'd just heard. Was she his wife? Her voice sounded young. Daughter?

"Good afternoon, Mr. Willand," a man's voice said. "This is Howard Weston."

"Hello, Doctor. I didn't know there were two Dr. Westons."

"Yes sir, Emma is my daughter. She got her DVM last year from the University of Wyoming and joined my practice."

"That's terrific! You must be very proud."

"I am, and I sure needed the help. Frankly, she saved the practice. I'm not as spry as I used to be. There are a lot of miles to cover out here, and I often found myself getting stretched pretty thin. Plus, I've been out of vet school for so darn long, and it's important to have the fresh knowledge Emma brings. She can also handle small animals, too."

"Sounds like a great partnership."

"It is, but I'm still her dad and I get an occasional eye roll from her," he chuckled. "How can I help you, Mr. Willand — and, by the way, congrats on the ranch. It's a special place."

"Thank you. I understand you've worked with Halestone Ranch stock for many years."

"Yep, I started coming to Halestone well before Luke died. He and Jack were good stewards of the animals and land. It was a pleasure to work with them. Boy, I was sure sorry to see Jack go into such a tailspin with that ALS."

"Yes, it must have been awful for him. The next time you're out here, I'd like to have a cup of coffee and get to know you better. Today, though, I'm calling to find out if the ranch has ever had any Gelbvieh stock. Do you know of any?"

"Gelbvieh? Nope. Not since I've been treating the herd. There are none there now, and I doubt there would have been any before I started working out there. The Gelbvieh breed had just started showing up in these parts that far back."

That did it.

"Thanks, Doctor Weston. I look forward to meeting you."

"Same here, and 'Doc' is what everyone calls me."

"OK, Doc, thanks for the help. Oh, one more thing, just out of curiosity: Are you related to the Weston for whom this county is named?"

He chuckled. "Yes sir, I am, indeed. Jefferson B. Weston was my great-grandpappy. He was a geologist, and he and his colleague, Frank Mondell, discovered coal deposits out here, which brought in the railroad, and the rest is history."

"Well, how about that?" I said, now knowing where the Newcastle airport name came from. "Very interesting, Doc. I'm looking forward to meeting you—to meeting both Dr. Westons!"

Some of my worst fears are being realized. Judd wrote checks for $20,000 for something, but it wasn't for breeding stock. He must have assumed that Jack was too sick to notice. He didn't count on me showing up.

The time has come to deal with him. The questionable background check, the phantom Gelbviehs, and the flat-out refusal to help with the 4-H project are plenty enough for me to let him go. I'll do it before I go home Friday. Probably give him 30 days' severance and send him on his way.

One question remains. Should I tell the sheriff that I'm terminating Turner? If I let him go and he leaves town, any investigation regarding the missing $20,000 will require the sheriff to bring him back for questioning. I'll be the one to file the complaint, and I have no way of knowing how vindictive Judd might be. Hard telling what damage he might do as a way of revenge.

Nope. I'm going to fire him and let it go at that. I don't have to recover the $20,000, he probably doesn't have it, anyway. And most of all, I don't want to be involved with him any further.

CHAPTER TWENTY

Halestone ranch house
Thursday, November 8
6:00 a.m.

Sleep hadn't come easy. I woke up several times during the night, a typical experience when I'm about to terminate an employee. With sunrise near, I decided to get outside and move around.

Zach had told me that the highest point on the ranch was in the South Pasture. It adjoined the ranch house, and was easy walking distance. It had always been called "The Hump." I headed there on foot with hopes of seeing the sunrise.

Daybreak is a magical time of day. The wildlife are coming alive. A mourning dove first with its gentle and rhythmic "coo, coo-coo," then the bellows of cattle complaining about some thing or another.

I climbed to the high point of The Hump just before 6:40 and, right on cue, the sun blazed over the eastern horizon.

The surrounding hills take on brilliant colors of pink and violet, which last only moments before vanishing in the daytime brightness.

Breakfast with my crew was quieter than usual. Maybe it was just me, knowing what the morning would bring, that cast a pall over the table. As we pushed back from the table, I asked Judd to join me in the office.

Terminating an employee is never easy. I try to make it a learning experience. For me, at least. I don't expect the person across from me is in much of a mood to learn.

"Judd, it's been obvious since we first met that you resent my ownership of the ranch. Would you like to tell me why?"

He didn't make eye contact, seemingly preoccupied with the

stitching on the boot perched on his crossed leg.

"Everything has changed since Jack died," he finally said.

"I wouldn't say everything, Judd. From the first day, I assumed you would want to continue as ranch foreman. I heard no criticism from anyone about the job you do, and I felt confident that you were my man. But one of the things that has concerned me is your refusal to show me the Gelbvieh stock. Every time I bring it up, you avoid taking me to see them."

I waited for him to answer me. Still no eye contact.

"So," I continued, "as I was talking with Doc Weston, I asked him about the Gelbviehs. He says he has been treating Halestone cattle for long before you got here and there have never been Gelbvieh stock on this ranch."

Again, I gave him a chance to answer. Again, he said nothing, just kept looking at his boots.

"There's something else. You locked horns with me yesterday about the 4-H program. It's important that Upton remember Jack, and respect Halestone Ranch as a benefit to the community. Support for community efforts like 4-H can accomplish that. You've said you had high regard for Jack, and it surprises me that you are against a memorial program for him."

Judd still didn't look at me, but managed a comment. "Seems like a waste of money," he muttered.

There was no reason to draw this out.

"Well Judd, that's for me to decide, which I have. And I've also decided that we need to part company. If you will pack up and be ready to leave the ranch by noon, there will be a check for your current wages plus 30 days severance. I'll have the envelope here when you are ready to leave. But," I paused, "the severance pay is contingent upon you leaving by noon. Permanently. I wish you the best."

Judd stood up slowly, showed no emotion, did not try to defend his actions. Just walked out.

I called Zach on his cell. "Zach, Judd will be permanently leaving the ranch at noon. Please make yourself available after lunch. I want to talk to you this afternoon."

I called Patti in from the kitchen.

"Judd will be leaving at noon. He won't be here for lunch, and he won't be back."

She looked surprised, but not shocked, then said she would have lunch ready for just the three of us.

What a day. It was only nine o'clock.

During my last trip, I had picked out a horse I was comfortable with. It's important to trust a 1,200-pound animal on whose back you're riding. Toby, a 12-year-old paint, shows all the signs of good training. Zach said Jack had picked him up at an auction five years ago, and had done some of the training himself. I brush and saddle him, and ride out toward the Lower West Pasture.

I pull down my Resistol, pull up my coat collar, and duck my head into a chilly breeze. It is November and I'm surprised there hasn't been snow by now. As much as snow makes ranch work difficult, we need it. In this semi-arid clime, we need every drop of moisture we can get. Whatever the weather, though, being on a horse is a unique and special experience that I never tire of. Our bodies seem to meld as I let mine move in concert with his.

Toby took me through some of the irrigated area Zach had shown me. He barely got his legs wet crossing six inches of water in the Bison River. Zach's irrigation pipe is piled all along the banks of the river. A lot of hand labor is needed in the spring to lay out the pipe, and I can see using some of the summer interns from 4-H.

Zach also had mentioned the possibility of adding more irrigated acreage, and I can see there's at least a hundred acres that would support that. He said local ranches are always in the market for more hay than we raise now, or we could keep it for ourselves if we decided to increase the size of our herd.

I turn Toby around to head back, and just like most horses, he knows the way to the stables and is anxious to get there.

My office
1 p.m.

"Zach, I told you that my plan was to keep everything the same for 90 days. As it turns out, I couldn't do that with Judd. Among other things, he didn't like the 4-H project, and I need everyone on board to make that a success. You were instantly in support of the plan."

"Yes sir."

"More than that, I felt after our first meeting six weeks ago that you and I are on the same page. We think alike."

He smiled.

"You know this ranch better than anyone. It's a part of you. I can see that. Now, I've heard that you've said that you are content being a ranch hand and had no interest in managing the ranch. Is that still the case?"

"Well, sir ... " Zach took a moment to compose his response. "I guess the short answer is no. And here's why. As I've been working here for Luke and Jack, and then Jack, and now you, I've grown up a bit. I think I was afraid to fail, so I just wanted to do work that was safe and easy for me. But now I know I can run the ranch and do a good job of it, so I've changed my mind."

"I was hoping you'd say that. Starting today, Zach, I want you to run this place as if it were your own. I plan to raise your salary by $1,000 a month. Later in the year, I'm going to put in place a bonus for you based on the overall ranch performance each year.

"I have absolutely no doubt you can do this and do it better than anyone else. I want you to make all the day-to-day decisions, and call me whenever you want to discuss something major."

He nodded.

"A big part of your job as general manager will be the budget. I will not be looking over your shoulder, but I know this will be new to you, so I plan to retain a new CPA, someone with a lot of ranch financial experience. I'll expect him or her to work closely with you as you create a new budget, and continue working with you on all financial aspects of this place. I'll expect him or her to work with Patti on her administrative duties, including tax records and accounts payable.

"Patti will work for both of us, but you will be her boss for the day-to-day things. I want to know if you are comfortable with this arrangement. If you have doubts, say so."

Zach looked a little apprehensive, but mostly excited. He had leaned forward as if he didn't want to miss a word.

"Mark," he said, "no one has ever showed so much confidence in my work as you just have. I love this place. It's home to me. I would need to keep an eye on everything, so I would like to move into the bunkhouse from my apartment in town. If I can do that, I'll do the best I can at running this place."

I stood up and walked around to his side of the desk. "So let me shake hands with the new manager of Halestone Ranch."

I called Patti into the office to join us, and filled her in on the changes. She greeted the news with a smile, and told Zach she was happy for him. I told her that on my next trip out, I had plans for additional responsibilities for her, and that Zach may need more help. I also explained that her income would go up upon my next visit.

They both walked out of the office smiling. I felt I had a team I could fully trust.

CHAPTER TWENTY-ONE

Rockford, Illinois
Home office

Sitting here reflecting on my recent past, it's hard to believe all that's happened. Less than two months ago, I was spending my time writing a book about agriculture and polishing the 210 in my hangar.

Now, I spend most of my time thinking about the ranch: future changes; who to see and what to do on the next trip; how much I truly love being on that land. I'll go back out November 19 for three days.

My thoughts are interrupted by the clatter of my cell phone vibrating across the top of my desk. I see it's Sheriff Wirth. I answer with only a slight sense of dread, outweighed by anticipation.

"Good morning, Sheriff. Good to hear from you. I'm hoping everything is OK."

"Well, time will tell, I suppose, but I'm not calling with any dire news, Mark. I need some information."

"Of course, how may I help?"

I know you fired Turner. Can you tell me why you let him go?"

"Sure. From the moment I acquired the ranch, he seemed to resent me having it. You may recall I hired your friend Gene Graf to look into Judd's background. Graf didn't find out a lot, but he did talk to a gas station owner who fired Judd when he was stealing beer. That didn't bother me as much as the information Graf received from Judd's former ranch employer, who suspected him of rustling cattle."

"I see."

"All this created doubt in my mind about trusting him. The last straw was when he refused to support my plan for the ranch to subsidize a 4-H club. I looked at it as a way to memorialize Jack Hale, who had helped the town a lot. Those are the reasons I got rid of him."

"Thanks for that," said the sheriff. I'll tell you why I asked. We're bringing him in for questioning this afternoon. We're not charging him with anything. Not yet, anyway. We just need to know his connection with the murder victim we found on your ranch."

"Do you think he had something to do with the murder?"

"Hard to say," replied Wirth. "Remember that our victim had a wrist tattoo of a snake?

"Yes, of course."

"As you know, we circulated that picture along with the drivers license photo of Ethan Alvarez, the deceased. We found a bartender who remembered him, and said he was with a guy Alvarez called 'Judd.' This pond of ours is pretty shallow and there aren't many 'Judds.' We want your Judd to tell us what his connection was with Alvarez."

"Thanks for telling me this, and to be clear, he isn't 'my' Judd any longer."

"Copy that," the sheriff chuckled.

"I'll be back out Monday." I said. "Can I buy lunch and hear the outcome of the questioning?"

"Sure. Let's meet at the Buckskin in Upton. I'll come up there and meet you around noon."

Upton Municipal Airport
Monday, November 19

Trip time was about the same as usual from Poplar Grove Airport, but November weather can start to include some icing in the clouds, which was in the forecast. Tops were under 7,000 midway, and clear at home, so I filed VFR at 8,500 feet. Winds were out of the northeast, so I made good time.

I hangared the plane and drove to the Buckskin Bar. Sheriff Wirth pulled in soon after I got there.

After we ordered, he told me about the discussion between his deputy and Judd Turner.

"I sat in during the interview. Judd showed no emotion when he was asked about Ethan Alvarez. He said Alvarez had looked him up, having heard that Judd was foreman at Halestone. Alvarez wanted to know if he could hunt deer at the ranch in the fall. Judd told him he would ask Jack. According to Judd, he ran into Alvarez at a bar and told him Jack said OK about hunting, but only at the north end of the ranch where there were no cattle. Judd indicated he was as surprised as anyone to hear about Alvarez's body being found at the ranch, and in the same area they had talked about."

"Sheriff, did you believe him?"

"I watched him closely. He's a cool customer. I think he had practiced his answers and knows more than he let on, but we have no proof of that. I told him not to leave town till we let him know, and he did say he had been about to move on and look for work."

The sheriff said he would keep me informed if there were new developments, and we parted company.

Next, I stopped at Todd Davig's office. He was at his desk.

"Good to see you, Mark. How are things at the Halestone?"

"Getting better, I believe, Todd. I just got into town from Rockford and haven't been to the ranch yet."

"I hear you and your ranch manager parted ways."

"Yes, the more I found out about Mr. Turner, the more I knew he wasn't going to be able to continue running my ranch."

"There's been a fair amount of gossip around town about that."

"Really?"

"Small town, Mark. Really small," he said with a slight smile.

"Well, here's a bit of news I'd like to keep quiet. I'm looking to replace my CPA, too."

He nodded.

"Are you acquainted with an accounting office here in Upton?"

"I am. The best CPA in Upton. He's also the only CPA in Upton. We are a one-horse town when it comes to that, Mark. But I like him, trust him and wouldn't hesitate to recommend him. He does my business and personal taxes. His name is Chuck Weinberg. Would you like to meet him?"

"I would, yes."

Todd is becoming a friend. He's always willing to help.

Todd made a call and set things up. I found Weinberg's office a couple of blocks away. It looked business-like, not pretentious. He certainly wasn't getting decorating tips from Randy Gotch. Chuck met me at the door and as we sat in his office getting to know each other a bit, I told him I was considering a change regarding tax preparations for Halestone Ranch. I asked him to send me a brief summary of his background, services and fees, and to send it to my home in Illinois. He promised to have it in the mail by the weekend.

"Chuck, do you happen to be friendly with Randy Gotch?"

"No sir, I know him only by reputation."

I nodded and wondered what he'd heard about Gotch's reputation, but didn't ask him, and he didn't volunteer more.

First impressions are important. Chuck made a good one.

Pulling into the ranch yard, I saw Zach coming out of the machine shed, and he met me as I parked.

"Howdy, Mark. Welcome back," he smiled.

"What's new, Zach? How's my ranch manager doing?"

"I'm doing well, thanks, and what's new is that swather Titan Equipment had told us about. It's a sound piece of machinery and I signed an order for it to be delivered."

There was just enough tentativeness in his voice that it seemed he was waiting for my approval. Instead, I smiled and said, "Zach, you are the manager of this place, not me."

I can see his confidence increasing as he realizes I trust his decisions. I believe that if you're going to give someone a job, then let them do it. I've seen what happens when a manager is always second-guessing and looking over your shoulder.

Tuesday, November 20

After breakfast, Zach and I settled in the office and talked about horses for the 4-H project. We agreed that they need to be mature and well-trained so teenagers will do OK with them. Zach said he and the 4-H leader decided six was a good number to start with. There's an auction in January near Gillette, and Zach and I will attend it together.

"Zach, there's something else we need to do quite soon. Take the old grader up north where that body was found and cut three trenches across the width of that bench that may have been used as a landing strip. Tear it up pretty good so there won't be any more planes landing, or at least making a safe landing. Make the trenches about two-feet-deep all across the field and space them about a third, half and two thirds down the strip."

"I'll get started on it in the morning," Zach said. "You know, that grader isn't much to look at, but it sure is a beast."

I nodded. I had guessed the Cat was built in the '70s. No frills, but there wasn't much that could stop it. A beast, indeed.

"How about hired hands, Zach? Do you have some in mind you can bring out here part-time as you need them?"

"Yes sir, there are two teenagers who have helped me in the past. They know their way around the ranch and I can get them out here on weekends anytime I need help. But, I'll probably be able to handle things for the next couple of months, until calving starts and we have to think about irrigating the hay."

"Zach, I plan to give Patti the added responsibility of accounting for the ranch, under your supervision. Do you approve?"

He nodded. "Sure do. Since Judd left, she has been helping me a lot. I need her help."

I told him I would be replacing Randy Gotch, but retaining Alan Creston. "But keep that under your hat till I come out next trip. I will tell Patti the same.

"One other thing: Let's take a look at the pasture records Judd kept to prevent over-grazing."

Zach explained that Judd hadn't kept any. Judd had always said he could tell when to move the cattle. I asked Zach how he planned to manage it. He said he already had files set up for each pasture.

My ranch manager.

I heard Zach and Patti's muffled voices as he walked out of the ranch house. I wondered how the two of them get along. When Judd was here, tension was often thick enough to cut with a stockman knife. Now, they both seem relaxed, and appear to be working well together. I know both have had some rough patches, including bad marriages, so I'm happy to seem them doing better.

I asked Patti to come in the office.

"Pull up a chair, Patti, let's talk about you and the ranch. How do you feel about your job here?"

"Mr. Willand," she smiled, "since you became owner, everything has changed. For the better! I love working here."

"When we first met, Patti, I told you that I would firm up my decisions regarding the ranch operation by the end of 90 days. I can tell you now that I want you to stay permanently. I want you to take over the accounting, with the understanding that Zach is ranch manager. You will need to keep Zach fully informed, as well as me. Each time I come out, I want to meet with the two of you, get updated on everything that's going on. Zach has been given the responsibility to run this place like it was his own."

She nodded vigorously and said, "I respect Zach and enjoy working with him. I'll do my best. I definitely want to stay."

"You will be the 'front door' of Halestone Ranch, and anyone visiting needs to check in with you. If they want to see Zach but you think it would be a waste of his time, tell them you'll talk to Zach and get back to them if he wants to see them.

"You should know I may hire a new auditor next trip out. They will be doing the tax return for the ranch, and you'll need to meet with them regularly and keep them informed."

"Of course."

"And if I see in 60 days that you are comfortable with these responsibilities and work well with Zach, I will double your current salary. Now," I smiled, "tell me how you feel about your new job."

She was struggling to keep her emotions in check. I could tell this job meant a lot to her.

"Oh, Mr. Willand, I ..."

"Mark, please, for the last time. Mark," I smiled.

"OK ... Mark, you've been a godsend for this ranch and for me. I never knew where I stood with Judd, but you always tell me what you expect. I have some certainty in my life. Thank you."

"OK, Patti, then that's settled."

She smiled and dabbed away a tear or two.

"We are going to do a lot for the Upton community. As you know, Luke and Jack were well-liked here, and I want part of the ranch profits to benefit Upton as a memorial to them.

"One more thing: If Randy Gotch stops in, please play dumb about any of these changes. I will replace him as our CPA when I'm out here next time. It's my intention to keep Alan Creston as the ranch attorney, and you can talk freely with him at any time."

"I will."

It has been a productive trip. I'm getting the ranch pointed in the direction I want it to go and feel more confident in Zach and Patti. Time to go back to Illinois in the morning.

Rockford, Illinois
The Willand home

Two full months into my ranch ownership, I'm finally developing a pattern. Up at 5:45, coffee and two newspapers, then an hour thinking about the ranch and what needs to be done during the next trip. That's how it looks on paper. The reality is, I think about the ranch nearly all the time. It's new and exciting and I'm all in.

On this morning, I'm thinking about manpower. Even though Zach says he has access to part-time help, I think we're short-handed. In the past, there were always two to do the work needed year-round. Luke and Jack ran the place as father and son. Then Zach was hired as Luke got older and couldn't do as much. After Luke died, Jack and Zach worked as a team until Jack weakened with ALS. Then Judd was hired. Now Zach is alone.

I"ll talk with Zach during my next trip out. We should plan to hire a number two man to help Zach year-round, particularly since we plan to expand the hay acreage.

I played with the wording for an ad in *Ranch Magazine*:

> WANTED: PERMANENT #2 MAN FOR LONG-STANDING WYOMING RANCH. MACHINERY AND LIVESTOCK EXPERIENCE NECESSARY. RESUME AND REFERRALS TO ATTORNEY ALAN CRESTON, PO BOX 530, NEWCASTLE, WY.

Today, the mailman left a package from CPA Weinberg in Upton. He explained his background thoroughly, provided referrals and also a schedule of his fees. After reading through it, I decided he was the man to replace Randy Gotch. No need to vet him any further. Davig's recommendation was good enough for me.

I called Gotch's office, and got his voice mail, which I thought was odd for a work day. In my message, I explained that I wouldn't be needing his services any longer, but that I had appreciated his help, and wanted him to forward all ranch-related documents to me promptly.

I ended the call and immediately felt better. Something about this guy never seemed right. I'm glad I don't have to deal with him anymore. I did, though, ponder the appropriateness of firing him via a voicemail, but not for very long.

CHAPTER TWENTY-TWO

Poplar Grove Airport
Rockford, Illinois
Friday, November 29

Time to go west again. Now that Judd is out of the picture, I look forward to time at the ranch without controversy.

Pulling the 210 out of the hangar, I can feel winter coming on. My hangar is insulated and never falls below 35 degrees in the winter. I don't worry about pre-heat before starting up. It's a different story in Upton where the hangar has no insulation. I'll need to get an extension cord to plug in the plane's pre-heater while I'm there.

The improved performance of an airplane in the winter always amazes me. The dense air makes a big difference in shorter takeoff roll and climb-out. The downside of winter, however, is the increased risk of icing. Nothing gets my attention more than that, and pilots who ignore icing rarely live to tell about it. I recall an early morning flight out of Kansas City Downtown back to Poplar Grove. There were no pilot reports that mentioned icing in the clouds. Yet when I reached 5,000 feet, ice appeared instantly on the wings and windshield. This 210 does not have de-icing equipment, but it does have a turbocharger, which saved the day. Even with the extra weight of the ice buildup, I could climb rapidly, and at 9,000 feet, we broke out into sunshine.

Without the turbo, our slow climb rate would have allowed time for a lot more buildup of ice before reaching the clear air — if we reached it.

One of the most striking memories of that day, however, came upon landing. Despite the sunshine at 9,000 feet, it was far too cold for the accumulated ice to melt off. Skies were clear upon arriving at Poplar Grove, and when I touched down, the ice shattered off the wings and scattered across the runway!

Today's trip, though, was in sunshine all the way, and I arrived in Upton at noon. I stopped in at the sheriff's office to see if anything new had developed about the murder.

Something had. Sheriff Wirth invited me into his office, and filled me in.

"You may recall I told you about a drug bust in Juarez."

"Yes, of course."

"Remember I told you about the airport mechanic who arranged for plane thefts from their hangars there?"

"Right. He'd watch for planes that didn't get used much, preferably Cessna 182s, then load his partner's cocaine in the plane, and leave the hangar unlocked so the plane could be stolen when no one was around."

"Mm-hmm. Then the pilot stops at your ranch, drops off the cocaine, then takes the plane to Canada and sells it there."

"Yes."

"Well, the police arrested the pilot. He was a Montana native, and for a shorter sentence, he told them about the Upton arrangement. He had been contacted by a drug dealer in Newcastle. Text messages only. They were from a blocked number, he didn't know the individual. He was given a phone number for a ranch foreman near Upton."

"Judd Turner," I interjected.

"Right, and Turner arranged for a landing strip. The pilot was told to contact Ethan Alvarez, who would take delivery of the cocaine. That arrangement was in place for several months until the dealer texted him about Alvarez's death and told him to cancel the trips."

"Sheriff, nothing I know about Judd, which isn't much, admittedly, would make me think he was a drug dealer or a murderer. A rustler, yes, but a killer? No. Do you think he was involved in some way?"

"I'm still putting the pieces together, Mark, but the pilot claims that Turner had nothing to do with the drug distribution. He was being paid only to provide a place to land. Alvarez would be waiting to take possession of the drugs.

"Here's where it gets a little foggy for me, though. The pilot says

Alvarez had bragged to him that he had been siphoning off some of the drug cash for himself before he turned it over to the Newcastle dealer."

"How did the dealer find out? From Alvarez?"

"That's the foggy part. The pilot says Alvarez never told him the dealer's name. If that's true and the dealer was responsible for killing Alvarez, then somebody else told him. Or maybe it's just math. He knew how much he was buying and how much it was being sold for.

The pilot claimed that his pay came through a drop box in Juarez. He admitted that the plane thefts were planned by his partner at the Juarez airport and himself. He says it had no connection with a drug cartel. Three planes had been stolen before the Alvarez death stopped everything. He's facing multiple counts of plane theft, drug peddling, trespassing on the ranch, and complicity with the Alvarez murder."

"What about Judd?"

"We've charged Turner with complicity to distribute drugs, unlawful use of your ranch's landing strip for drug trafficking, and being a possible accomplice in the Alvarez murder. He found a bondsman to provide his $100,000 bail."

"So that cost him $10,000?"

"Ten percent, right."

I decided now was the time to tell Wirth about my suspicions regarding the Gelbvieh cattle.

"Sheriff, there's more about Judd you should know. Over a span of 18 months, he wrote checks from the ranch account three different times to a Gelbvieh LLC. He told me it was for breeding stock. The total was $20,000, which Judd said had been approved by Jack Hale before his death. According to Judd, Jack had wanted to add the Gelbvieh strain into the herd."

"OK."

"There aren't any Gelbvieh on my ranch. Never have been. Three times I asked Judd to show me the Gelbvieh stock he had bought. He always came up with reasons not to."

The sheriff was writing something down.

"I had other reasons to want Judd off the ranch, Sheriff, and decided not to pursue the missing cattle. But now with these other charges, you might as well add this one to the pile."

Sheriff Wirth said he would start an investigation on the missing, or non-existent, Gelbvieh stock. He asked me to bring in the canceled checks for the $20,000.

By the time I got to the ranch, Patti was gone for the day. Zach's truck was in front of the bunkhouse. I was glad to see he had moved in.

Zach reminds me of "Hoss," the bigger-than-life son on the TV series *Bonanza.* Zach is built just like Hoss. Big shoulders, thick neck. A powerful man.

"How's the bunkhouse working out for you? Did Judd leave anything behind?"

He shook his head, looking around. "Nothing of any value, that I can see, Mark. He wasn't much of a housekeeper, but I've seen worse."

Zach told me about the bunkhouse as he gave me a tour. It was built almost 100 years ago out of logs from the woods nearby. There weren't a lot of trees on the ranch, but there are mature stands in several areas along the river. And several miles away, on the eastern edge of Upton, are the Black Hills which has an abundance of ponderosa pine.

The bunkhouse is split into several rooms as a result of many remodels over the years. Changes were made by Jack's grandfather to house hunters as well as ranch hands. The framed prints on the walls were yellow from age, mostly scenes of buffalo and other wildlife. A second bathroom and shower had been added between bedrooms. The kitchen was barebones, with a small gas stove, cabinets with ancient dishes, and an old-bordering-on-antique refrigerator that still worked, but looked and sounded tired. The floors were linoleum, also tired. There weren't many windows, and the log walls made the place feel solid and quiet from outside sounds.

As the floor creaked below my boots, I felt that if I listened carefully I would hear laughter and cussing, and smell roll-your-own smoke from cowboys long past. If only those walls could talk. What stories we would hear.

"Zach, let's talk about help. I'm not doubting your abilities, but I don't want you to work yourself to death. It's always been a two-man operation. I think we should advertise for a permanent number two man. If we plan to add more hay ground, you're really going to need him. Assuming we can find the right person you are totally comfortable with, what do you think?"

He nodded and with a sheepish smile, admitted that it is already harder than he thought it would be to keep up, doing everything by himself.

I showed him the "help wanted" ad I had prepared for *Ranch Magazine*. Zach liked it, so tomorrow, I'll have Patti submit it to the magazine. I'll also ask her to call Alan Creston and tell him the responses will be coming to his office, and he should hold them for me.

Saturday morning

Woke up at 5:30, made coffee, and stepped outside into the chilly air. The air is drier here than Rockford and maybe that makes it seem a bit less cold, but steam rose from the coffee cup and I could see my breath as I stood on the front porch surveying the ranch yard. Clanking sounds came from the machine shed. Zach must be at it already.

I retreated to my desk in the ranch house office to contemplate the changes that have been made. With Zach and Patti now permanent, an attorney and CPA that I'm comfortable with, and with new friends like Mayor Morris, Sheriff Wirth, Todd Davig and Tom Westedt, I'll return home tomorrow feeling things are now under control here at Halestone Ranch.

Patti arrived at seven and started preparing breakfast. When it was ready, Zach came in from the shop, shed his sturdy Carhartt outerwear in the boot room, and joined us at the table. I told them about hiring Chuck Weinberg to replace Gotch. Zach said he knows Weinberg and feels that will work out well.

We talked about the additional hay acreage planned for next year. Zach said he feels that all we'll need is additional irrigation pipe.

The new swather will be the only major equipment change.

After breakfast, Patti and I adjourned to the office.

"Patti, the computers and printer are long in the tooth. Microsoft doesn't even support our version of Windows anymore. Let's order new ones, but before you do, will you meet with Chuck Weinberg? He'll explain what software you'll need in order to be able to keep and transmit records to him, as well as what you'll need to maintain the tax return and quarterly payments."

"Will do, and I'll ask Mr. Weinberg if his office can spend some time with me to make sure I'm keeping the right records, and how to use the software."

I'm amazed how much this young woman has changed during the short period I've known her. She seems to dress with more care, and has all the appearances of being self-confident and assertive.

Late morning, I stopped at Mayor Morris's office. He poured coffee and told me how excited the 4-H club is about their new program at my ranch.

I told him about the upcoming horse auction.

"Zach and I will attend an auction in January. Our plan is to buy six horses that were trained on a ranch known to Zach and that will take back any not satisfactory to us. The 4-H leader can start bringing kids out to the ranch as soon as we have delivery of the animals, and Zach will start teaching them on caring for, and working with, ranch horses. We'll expand the program as we go along."

Morris's delight was evident. "I'll tell Aaron Rhodes of your plan so he can start deciding which members should be in the first session with the horses."

"I'm excited for the kids, Ken. I've found that working with horses teaches a lot of good things: patience, discipline, understanding, self-control, and dedication. And when you're riding a horse, all the noise in your life seems to fade into the background."

"Well said, Mark."

I nodded. "Before I go, Ken, I've been thinking about something else. The town square seems to always be busy, people walking through, some sitting on benches, having coffee or eating lunch on nice days. It seems like the central meeting place for the town. Do you put up a Christmas tree during the holidays?"

"No, we never have. It's been talked about, but there never seemed to be a surplus in the budget that would allow it."

I told him that since I first came here three months ago, everyone has been friendly and made me feel welcome. I already have some good friends, and I included him in that.

"Mayor Ken, let me do something for the community to celebrate the holidays. I'll pay for a Christmas tree, fully lighted, any size you choose. What do you think?"

His big smile showed his response.

"That would really be appreciated. I'll order it tomorrow. It's a generous gesture by Halestone Ranch!"

As I left his office, I really felt good. This will light up Upton for the holidays.

Saturday afternoon

I saddled Toby and rode up to the East Pasture. It borders our leased ground from Thunder Bay National Grassland.

Winter is almost here at Halestone, but it's sunny with no wind today. As Toby plods along at a steady pace, I scan the low hills around me in renewed amazement that all of this is mine.

It's quieter now than it was in the summer when cows could be heard calling for their calves. I scare up three antelope, and they bound away without making a sound, but a group of birds they flushed out sound a distress call as they fly off. *Grouse, maybe?*

The Bison River cuts through this part of the ranch. There is the time of year the flow rate is low, and Toby steps through it without missing a step. I've noted with some amusement that what qualifies as a river out here would be streams, or creeks back home.

Looking ahead between Toby's ears, I find myself enjoying every minute. Long after I'm gone, these rolling hills will still be here, hopefully still supporting cattle, antelope and deer. Next year, maybe we should consider inviting hunters again. Jack stopped that when he got sick.

I smiled to myself as I realized I hadn't even thought about the five-year rule I'd agreed to when accepting the ranch. I've been too busy to think about it. And it's only been two months!

It'll be time to go home again tomorrow morning. With Zach in charge, the place is in good hands.

For this moment, though, my new friend Toby and I are communing with Mother Nature, and she is gorgeous.

CHAPTER TWENTY-THREE

At home in Rockford
Tuesday, December 11
9 a.m.

The alert that I have a voice message vibrates my cell phone. I must have stepped away when the call came in. The call log showed a Wisconsin number.

"Mr. Willand" the recording began, "my name is John Roesner. Patti Malik works for you, and I am her dad. I would like to talk to you, if you will call me back."

I hope she's OK as I push the call back button.

He apologized for bothering me, and thanked me for hiring Patti, saying she really likes her job, talks about it all the time.

"The main reason I called is to tell you about her ex-husband. I believe she told you about him."

"A little, yes, she did."

"Well, Mr. Willand, I got a troubling call from her a little while ago. She said her ex has come back to town without a job, wants to borrow money from her and stay in her apartment till he gets work."

"Sounds like trouble."

"Oh yeah, and," he continued, "he wants her to help him get a job at your ranch. You need to know that Patti wants nothing to do with him, and is afraid he will ruin her job with you. I told her I would call you. She didn't want me to, but it's been a long time since I've seen her this happy and I'm doing what dads do."

"Yes you are, John. Patti is already a key part of our team at the ranch. Nothing her ex does will put her job at risk. She told me he has a temper. Is he in Upton right now?"

"No, he told her he had some kind of trouble to attend to and would be gone for several days, but then he'll be back and wants her to talk to you about a job."

I thought about that. Patti's ex couldn't know that the ad in *Ranch Magazine* was from us. It's a blind ad. He may have heard that our ranch foreman is gone. Probably thinks he can push Patti into recommending him.

"Any idea what kind of trouble he's in?"

"No sir. With him, it could be darn near anything."

"Let's see if we can get rid of him another way, John. There's a retired police captain in Billings that now does private investigating. He's done some work for me before. Can you get me some information on him? Do I remember correctly that his name is Dan?"

"Yes sir. Dan. What kind of info do you need?"

"If she has his social security number, date and place of birth, along with any recent jobs, I'm sure we can find out what he's been up to and if he's wanted by any law enforcement agencies."

He called back an hour later with much of the information I had asked for. Patti had his social security number from their earlier joint tax return. She had also written down his truck license plate number, and wondered how he could afford a late model truck.

I told John I would let him know what we found out, and that we would not let this guy ruin her life again. I called Gene Graf in Billings, gave him the information and sicced him on Dan Malik. His past police connections gave him access to records that most private investigators don't have. If he operates as quickly as he did with the Judd Turner case, I'll probably hear back in a few days.

It's been almost three weeks since I was last at the ranch. It's time to plan another trip next week.

Friday, December 14

I take a call from Gene Graf.

"I've got some interesting information for you on Mr. Malik."

"Good, let's hear it."

"He's been in and out of trouble since he was a kid. Has never held a job very long. Wherever he works, his temper gets the best of him and he ends up in a fight, then gets fired."

"An employer's dream."

"Right," he chuckled. "His last job was driving a construction truck in Cheyenne. A month ago he got a DUI. His foreman found out about it and fired him. Dan cold-cocked him, broke his nose. The foreman filed an assault and battery charge, but Dan skipped town before the police could find him. On top of that, he didn't show up for his DUI hearing, so a warrant is out for his arrest."

"Wow."

"There's more. Three months ago he bought an expensive Ram pickup. He hasn't made a single payment and a collection agency wants to talk to him."

"I'll bet."

"Mark, if his ex-wife has his cell phone number, Cheyenne Police will get his GPS location and arrest him. Her phone should have his number showing in her "recent" calls."

"As before, Gene, you sure do great work. I'll call Patti and get back to you. Can't thank you enough."

Patti was at the ranch.

"Patti, did your dad tell you he called me?"

"Yes, and I wish he hadn't. I'm so sorry. You've been really good to me, and I've already burdened you enough with my personal life."

"Nonsense, Patti, you are part of our ranch team. I want to help. I may have a solution to your problem with Dan. I understand he told you he was in some trouble. He sure is. The Cheyenne police have a warrant out for his arrest for assault and battery."

A small gasp came through my earpiece.

"Do you have his cell number?"

"Yes, it's on my phone."

"If you give it to me, the police will track him with GPS and arrest him."

She found it and gave it to me. I told her I would let her know what the outcome was. She thanked me repeatedly.

I called Graf, gave him the number. He said Patti should not tell her ex anything if he calls. As vindictive as he appears to be, he would blame her for his arrest.

I called Patti back and relayed the instructions. I suggested she just tell him he can talk to me about a job when I'm back at the ranch.

Upton Airport
Monday, December 17

Winter months provide a mixed bag of advantages and challenges, for private flying. Skies are clear more often during the winter for my trips between Poplar Grove and Upton. That's the good news.

The flip side is the turbulence. Often, the unsettled air offers up a bumpy ride, and today was one of those days. I was glad I had no passengers, because most passengers in small planes hate the feeling of being tossed around. I don't prefer it, either, but accept it as part of the convenience.

After pulling my Ford out of the hangar and pushing the 210 in, I headed for the ranch. A few miles down the road, Graf called.

"Mark, you can tell your employee Patti that she won't be seeing her ex-husband in Upton again for quite awhile. The Cheyenne PD located him, and the idiot resisted arrest. Now he's got several charges against him, so at the least, he will end up with probation, but my guess is he's going to jail."

I thanked him for again helping us solve a problem, and told him his check would be in the mail.

The moment I most look forward to on my short drive from Upton to the ranch has become when I turn off the main road and pass under the archway where a wooden sign proclaims I am entering "Halestone Ranch." Simultaneously, I feel the rumble of the Ford's tires crossing the steel cattle guard. My ranch. I'm home.

It's after one when I pull up to the ranch house. Patti whips up a late lunch for me as I tell her about Dan's arrest.

"As I get older, Mark, I'm realizing how my life is defined by the decisions I make. And that guy? He was a B.L.D."

I gave her a blank look.

"B.L.D. Bad life decision. I'm so grateful for your help."

"Live and learn, as they say, Patti. Live and learn."

Zach saw my pickup and came in to get caught up. He wanted to update me on the herd, the feed supply and his plans for increasing hay acreage.

I wanted to share an idea with him that I'd been mulling over during the past week.

"Zach, we're starting the 4-H program next spring. I've been thinking about a meeting place here on the ranch for them. Also, if you choose some summer interns from that group, it would be good to have a place for them to stay overnight occasionally."

"Well, Mark, I suppose we could do some remodeling in the bunkhouse. It would need quite a bit of work, though. You've seen it."

I nodded as I finished chewing a bite of my lunch. "I'm afraid the old bunkhouse would become a money pit if we tried to do the renovations I'd like to see. There's an old saying about throwing good money after bad, and I fear that would be the case here. How about building a new bunkhouse alongside the old one, with a meeting room for 4-H kids and sleeping rooms? The old one would still get used for something."

He thought that would be a great idea.

"There's another reason to add more space, Zach. I'd like to start advertising for hunters again, and we'll have a better chance of attracting out-of-state folks who will stay longer and spend more if we have better accommodations."

He nodded his agreement and I asked him to start designing a layout, and to recommend a builder. During my next trip here, we will meet with a couple of builders that Zach decides on, and sign a contract for spring construction."

Tuesday, December 18
6 a.m.

The weather app on my phone tells me today's sunrise will be at 7:26. As the day breaks, I step out the front door and skies are clear, it's not too cold, so looks like a perfect morning to greet the sunrise again from The Hump. Instead of walking or taking a horse, I decide to fire up an ATV. First, though, I fill up a Thermos with coffee.

As I bounce through the grass and sagebrush toward the 100-foot-high hump, which is the size of a football field, I circle and look for a pathway to the top. The north side, with it's more gradual slope, looks most promising. A lot of cow chips are scattered, evidence of cattle climbing here, and they are known for finding the path of least resistance. As I pick my path, I wonder about the cows. I know they climb up here in search of grass, but wouldn't it be something if they also went up for the view?

Winding my way to the top, I pass by outcroppings composed of dolomite, much of it washed smooth from the elements over many years. I'll bring a pick-axe with me next time and see if there are any crystals under the surface.

At the top for a second time, I marvel at the view and wait for the sun to rise. This will never get old. The ranch, my ranch, stretches for miles before my eyes. I pour a cup of coffee as the sun explodes over the Thunder Basin Grassland.

And so begins another day, filled with new possibilities as I'm living my dream of being a rancher.

After a lively breakfast with Zach and Patti as we discuss the new bunkhouse, what they have in mind for how it'll look and be furnished, Zach and I walk out to stake out its location.

As we're talking about what the dimensions might be, my

phone vibrated and I saw it was Sheriff Wirth's number. I asked him to hold on while I went into the office.

"Mark, I've got an update on the Gelbvieh case I thought you'd be interested in."

"You bet I am. What is it?"

"When I showed Judd the checks he had written for $20,000, he realized that he's really in a spot. The district attorney told him if you sign a complaint that the money was stolen, he's looking at jail time."

"But I told you, Sheriff, I'm not interested in signing a complaint."

"Oh, I know that, but Judd doesn't. He's trying to make a deal to save his hide, and said last night he would tell us who is head of the drug distribution ring here in Newcastle if we would give him immunity from that theft."

"That seems like a fair trade, doesn't it?"

"Yep. The DA will meet with him today. It's possible that this information might tell us more about who killed the guy we found on your ranch. I'll give you a call and let you know what I know."

I thanked him and clicked off. I regret that Judd has messed up his life. He could have had a future on the ranch. Judging from what Graf uncovered, though, this wasn't Judd's first rodeo, so to speak.

Wednesday, December 19

Sheriff Wirth calls.

"Mark, did you tell me a few weeks ago that you had replaced your CPA, Randy Gotch?"

"Yes, I did. He acted very distant each time I talked to him, in fact, he didn't seem to care if he had us as a client or not. I didn't get a good feeling about him, and when I asked around about him, my concerns were validated. So I made other arrangements."

"You were wise to dump him. Judd Turner sang like a canary in his meeting with me and the district attorney. Guess what?"

He continued without waiting for my response. "The drug kingpin for this part of Wyoming is," he paused for effect, "Randy Gotch."

"Well how about that. And Judd was involved in the drugs?"

"Only on the periphery, if he's to be believed. Turner claims Gotch drew up an LLC document for Jack Hale to sign. Upon Jack's death, the LLC would allow Gotch to obtain ownership of the ranch for a song. Gotch had promised Judd 10 percent ownership of the ranch, provided he arrange a landing strip at the ranch for drug drop-offs."

Things were beginning to make sense.

The sheriff continued, "After Jack's funeral, when it became known that you were the new owner of the ranch, Judd confronted Gotch about the 10 percent promise, and Gotch told him Hale had refused to sign the LLC. Judd demanded $15,000 cash for the broken promise, and Gotch refused. That's why Judd is now willing to testify against Gotch, in exchange for immunity regarding the $20,000 he stole from your ranch account."

What a plot! I was amazed. No wonder Gotch and Turner appeared so unhappy when I became owner of the ranch.

"Sheriff, have you confronted Gotch with this?"

"No. We're going to pick him up this afternoon and bring him in for a little chat. The only evidence we have is Judd's statement, so we can't arrest him yet. But we'll see what he says to contradict Judd's accusations. We already have a search warrant and will go through his office and records while we take him to my office for a chat."

"You told me the Alvarez murder was likely drug-related. Do you think Gotch was involved in that?"

"That's very possible, if he really is in the drug business as Turner claims. We'll see what he has to say about that."

After we disconnected, I thought again about Gotch's expensive office and clothing. Sounds like his CPA office might be just a front for his real job: peddling drugs. And he may also be a murderer.

Thursday, December 20

Sleep didn't come easy last night. The revelations about Judd and Gotch took up space in my mind, but not for long. Those two are no longer my problems. Once I was able to focus on all the good that has happened out here these past three months, I drifted off to sleep. This great ranch has become a huge part of my life, as have the new friends I've made.

With no debt against the land, and a cash balance that exceeds the small operating loan, it will be easy to operate profitably with good management. I feel I have that in Zach.

All this puts me in a holiday mood. As Patti, Zach and I sit around the breakfast table, I decide to show them I appreciate them.

"Zach, I have a pretty good idea how big a job you have running this place. If we succeed in finding a good number two man for you, that will help. But you still have plenty on your plate with the increased hay acreage, the 4-H project and building a new bunkhouse. That's on top of managing the herd."

Zach sipped his coffee, perhaps wondering where I'm going with this.

"You've taken great care of your old pickup, but I think you deserve something better. The ranch will buy a pickup for you to use both for ranch and personal use. I've always had good luck buying two-year-old vehicles with low mileage. You pick out what you want, and the ranch will authorize up to $35,000. I would like to see the ranch name and brand on the door, if you're OK with that."

He stood up with that big smile on his face and reached over the table to shake my hand.

"Boss, I've never had a pickup that nice. This will be about the best Christmas I've ever had."

Turning to Patti, I said, "I'm not forgetting you, Patti. During the months I've been coming out here, you've done everything possible to make my job easier. The house looks much better, and you've really organized my office. You've taken over the accounting job, and do it better than I expected. On top of that, you are a great cook! Zach and I agree on that."

She smiled.

"Patti, I'm giving you a $15,000 bonus, and if it's OK with Zach, I'd like to close the ranch for a few days around Christmas. Of course, that doesn't mean anything to Zach; until we hire another hand, he's pretty much tied down here. But if Zach can manage without you for a while, I'd like to see you take the time off."

Zach laughed, "Absolutely, and if you want to be gone longer, I'll manage. I'll probably starve, but I need to lose weight anyway."

I saw a tear. She said, "Thank you. This will be my best Christmas, too!"

"Well, let's hope it's the first of many great ones for all of us," I said. "I'm asking a lot of both of you. I'm counting on you to run this place as if it were your own. You are giving me the freedom to own a great ranch in a state I love, and still live back in Illinois where my family is."

I told them about the Upton Christmas tree, and to tell anybody asking about it that it was a gift from all of us here at Halestone Ranch.

Driving to the airport, I was ready to go home with the feeling that all is well at Halestone Ranch.

CHAPTER TWENTY-FOUR

Rockford
December 28

Our blind ad for a ranch hand appeared in the December issue of *Ranch Magazine,* and I am a little surprised we didn't get a flood of applications. Maybe my opinion that working at Halestone Ranch is a premier opportunity isn't widely shared. Or, maybe there just aren't that many people out there looking for this type of specialized work. Whatever the reason, the envelope from Alan Creston in today's mail contained only two applications.

They couldn't have contrasted more. One was from a 23-year-old rancher's son who had spent his life working on the family ranch with his father and two brothers. He had also attended the local community college for two years, majoring in agriculture. His application stated that he wants to continue ranching and, answering what would have been one of my first questions, he feels he has no future in the family operation because he is the youngest of the three brothers, and there just isn't enough work, and profit, for four families on their ranch.

Sounds interesting. He included several references.

Throughout my life as an owner of businesses, I've hired about 150 employees. I've also had to fire some of them, to my regret. As I look back, I blame myself for most of the terminations. I should have done a better job of hiring. I should have looked more closely at their past performances, asked for more references, and spent more time interviewing them. People don't change much. Often times, I hired individuals that just didn't fit the job.

Another mistake I made, more than once, unfortunately, was retaining an ill-fitting employee too long. A good example was at one of our farm equipment dealerships. He was our most talented mechanic, but he complained about everything. His negative attitude led him to even complain to customers that our equipment was built poorly. Finally, despite his talent in the shop, I realized we would be better off without him, and let him go. His co-workers immediately told me they were glad he was gone because he had made life difficult for everyone working around him.

This time, I'm going to do it differently. I'll talk to references, have Gene Graf check their backgrounds, and choose the best candidates to come to Upton and meet with both Zach and me. I want Zach to make the final decision. Our number two man needs to be someone Zach has total confidence in. Zach has never been a boss. I need to help him develop that skill.

After reading through the applications, I picked up the phone. I called the three references Mike Janson from Laramie had provided. One was a college instructor who gave Mike high marks.

"He was a good student. My class in ag economics was easy for him. He's part of a ranch family and understands the operation. I would recommend him."

My next reference call was to a neighboring rancher. He had known the Janson family a long time, and spoke highly of Mike. He also said he could understand why Mike wanted to work elsewhere.

"You know, he's a little like that Prince Harry fella over in England."

"Oh?" I said, caught by surprise. I wasn't expecting the royal family to enter the converstion. "How's that?"

"He's so far down the list he'll never become King. Young Mike doesn't have a shot at running his family's ranch unless the other two boys decide to do something else, and I know them well enough to tell ya that that ain't happening."

The last call was to another neighboring rancher on Mike's list.

"Before I tell you whether I think you should hire Mike, let me ask you a couple of questions."

"Sure," I said. "Fire away."

He first asked about the size of our ranch, and also wanted to know about my ranch foreman, how long he's been at it, how old he is, and what kind of work the number two would do.

"Here's what I'll tell you, Mr. Willand. I think highly of the entire Janson family. Mike is smart, has a good future. In all honesty, though, I don't think he's a good fit for the job you describe. It is not that he can't do it, it's this: Your foreman, Zach, is still a young man of 41. It sounds like you expect to keep him in that job for a long time. I believe that Mike would only want to be in a number two position for a couple of years, and then would leave you to become a foreman somewhere."

I thanked him for his thoughful and honest answer. I feel fortunate that I spoke with him. I moved the Janson letter to the dead file and looked at the second application.

This one was from Roy Nicholson near Douglas, Wyoming. At age 51, he has been involved in ranching all his life, on three different outfits. He moved to the second one for better pay, and to the third because he could be the foreman.

Why is he looking to leave? He answered that in his application by saying the ranch has been sold to a neighboring outfit. That foreman will be running the combined operation, and Roy has been asked to stay on as a ranch hand. He has never been impressed with how that individual managed men, so wants to move on.

He included references from the three ranches he's worked on.

I called all three. Each of them spoke highly of Roy, said he was extremely reliable, had raised a good family, and they would hire him back anytime. Roy's most recent employer who had sold to the neighbor, added to that.

"I sure can understand why Roy may want to work elsewhere. The fella who is the neighbor's foreman would be running the combined operation is a piece of work."

"May I ask what you mean by that?"

"Well, sir, I'll just say that he may be good with cattle and horses, but he doesn't know beans about managing people. We're neighbors, and there aren't any secrets. Roy knows how this fella treats his people, and I don't blame him for not wanting to get treated like that."

Rockford
Next morning

"Zach," I spoke into the phone, "I spent much of the day yesterday vetting our candidates for your number two man, and I am emailing an application from a man I'd like you to take a look at. When you get a minute, look it over and give me a call."

An hour later, Zach called. He said Roy Nicholson's application looked good to him.

"I agree, and the references spoke well of Roy. How about we have Roy come to our ranch next week when I'm out there, and we can both interview him?"

"That's a good two-hour drive. How about we wrap his visit around lunch? I can ask Patti to add a plate at the table."

I liked that. An efficient use of time, and considerate of Roy's travel.

Hearing Patti's name mentioned reminded me to make a mental note to ask her why she didn't take any time off over Christmas as we'd talked about.

I called Nicholson, told him we had his application and that I own the Halestone Ranch near Upton. He was familiar with the name, had met Jack in past years at auctions. He agreed to drive up and meet with us next Thursday.

If we like Roy, I'll have Gene Graf check his background. Possibly, we've found the right man for Zach. We'll see.

CHAPTER TWENTY-FIVE

Rockford
Wednesday January 2
8 a.m.

January is typically the coldest month for northern Illinois, so it's no surprise when I see it's 19 degrees as I arrive at Poplar Grove Airport. A stiff wind from the west will slow me down. A 15-knot headwind at 6,500 feet is forecast for much of the route. That looks like the best altitude for today.

Days like these are when I'm especially grateful for my heated hangar. I do my pre-flight in comfort, not like years ago when the old hangar had no heat. I would have to plug in the block heater a day ahead to warm the engine, and I had to do the pre-flight with gloves on.

It's cold in Upton in January, too, often in single digits at night, so I'm going to have to rough it again in that unheated hangar out there.

After I pull the plane out and put the SUV in the hangar, I taxi out. Today's surface wind is out of the southeast, so I depart on runway 12 and head west. It's clear all the way to Upton, and as I climb out, I open a VFR flight plan.

Ainsworth is becoming a regular stop for me on the way west, for fuel and comfort. Before leaving there for Upton, I call Zach and ask him to arrange a late lunch meeting with him and Patti.

It was a far more eventful lunch than I anticipated.

"Mark," Patti began, "something happened last week that Zach and I took care of, but you should know about it."

"OK," I said, putting down my sandwich and taking a drink. "What happened?"

Patti looked at Zach before continuing. "Mark, Zach protected me last week. I'm grateful for that. A guy in an old pickup drove up to the house, knocked on the door and said he wanted to apply for a job. He was a mess. Scraggly beard, looked like he had slept in his clothes.

"I told him the manager was gone. I shouldn't have said that. When I said we weren't hiring, he said he wanted to use the restroom. I told him I wasn't comfortable with that, and when I started to close the door, he jammed his foot in it to keep it open, said I wasn't being friendly, and started to push his way in. He really had me scared."

"Oh my, are you OK?" I asked.

"I am, thanks to Zach. All of a sudden a big hand grabbed this guy's shoulder from behind, spun him around and asked him what was going on. I told Zach he had been trying to force his way in.

"Zach told the guy he had 60 seconds to get off the ranch or he would tie him up and call the sheriff. The guy ran to his truck and left. I'm really grateful, Zach."

Zach looked at his hands for a moment, then looked up. "Nobody pushes you around. I won't let that happen."

I studied them. There's a connection I hadn't sensed before.

"I look at this as a wake-up call," I said. "Patti, you are by yourself a lot here. Please buy a can of mace and keep it close to the front door. Zach, is there a security business in Upton, or in Newcastle?"

"Yes sir, there's one in Upton. I know the guy who runs it."

"Good. Please have him install an entrance alarm, so when a vehicle enters the front gate an alarm sounds in the machine shed and house, maybe in the ranch yard, too. That way, you'll both know when someone comes on the property. Zach, do you have a handgun?"

"I've got a .38 in the pickup's glove box."

"Good. I hope you don't need to use it."

"I've got a .22 pistol," Patti offered. "It's in my purse."

Zach and I both looked at her, startled.

"What?" Patti broke the silence. "A girl can't have a gun? My dad gave it to me. He said I probably won't kill anyone with it, but it'll sure slow them down, or scare them off."

Zach and I looked at each other and smiled.

"Good," I said, chuckling and shaking my head a bit at Patti's surprise admission. "If either of you think of other methods of protection, go ahead and get them."

That afternoon, the three of us talked for an hour about the new bunkhouse. As I'd requested, Zach had sketched a layout diagram of the interior. It included a great room in the middle with an efficiency kitchen and fireplace at the far end, space for two folding tables that would seat eight at each, and enough room for a conference setup seating at least 20. On each side of the great room, a door would lead to the living quarters. Space for four bunk beds and a wash basin and enclosed toilet. This would be the boys' side.

The opposite side of the great room would be set up the same, and would be the girls' bunkhouse. These arrangements would be for the 4-H program. Hunters could use both sides.

I asked both of them to continue thinking about the design and we'll finalize it on my next trip out.

Thursday 9 a.m.

Zach and I were in my office when I saw through the window a good looking Chevy Silverado pickup pulling in to the yard. It was exactly the time that Roy Nicholson and I had agreed on. I'm always impressed when people are on time, and when their truck or car is clean.

Roy looks younger than his 51 years, appears to be in good shape. About six feet and 200 pounds, he had a quick smile. A fresh haircut, well-pressed snap-button shirt and shined boots completed the first impression of an experienced and confident rancher. We sat down with coffee.

"That's a fine-looking Silverado, Roy. That extended cab is one of the great inventions for pickups, especially pickups that are used for work."

"Thank you, yes, I've had more than one newborn calf back there," he chuckled. "I just turned 100,000 miles on it last week. Just gettin' her broke in."

"Well, it doesn't show its age. You've taken good care of it."

"Yes sir, something my daddy beat into me — well, not actually beat — he was a good man. You know what I mean. From the time I was old enough to understand, he stressed the importance of caring for all of our vehicles and ranch equipment."

I nodded my agreement, mentally marking his respect for machinery as a plus.

"Roy, I'll explain Halestone Ranch to you. I've owned it since September. I live in Rockford, Illinois, and fly back and forth a lot. Zach manages the ranch, and has been working here for a lot of years. Patti Malik takes care of meals, the house and handles our bookkeeping.

"We need a permanent number two man to work with Zach. Now, I'm counting on Zach to run this place for a lot of years, and in your application you indicated you no longer want to be a foreman, so that's why we invited you to come and talk."

Roy responded, "Yes sir, I didn't mind managing the ranch I'm on, but as things are changing there, I think it's a good time for me to go back to what I enjoy most, and that's ranch work."

"Well, again, we're glad you came up here to see us," I said. Turning to Zach, I said, "Please show Roy around and let's meet back here afterwards."

An hour later they returned and we answered his questions, talked about future hay acreage expansion, the 4-H program, the Upton community, etc. I explained that he was the first we had talked to, but we felt he was very qualified and would be in touch with him shortly.

Zach offered to buy lunch at the Buckskin in Upton, which Roy accepted. Good thinking by Zach. More opportunity for him to get a feel about Roy.

Before they left, I said, "Roy, I sure do appreciate you driving all the way up here to meet with us. Why don't you pull over to the fuel tanks by the machine shed and Zach will top off your tank for you."

Roy smiled and said, "That's right kind of you, Mr. Willand, but I can't accept your offer. It was my pleasure coming here and the cost of a tank of gas is a small price to pay for the possibility of landing a job at your ranch. I do appreciate the offer, though."

That told me a lot about Roy Nicholson. After they left, I asked Patti for her first impression.

"He seems perfect for the job. He and Zach seem really comfortable with each other. None of that edge that was always present with Judd."

I told her I felt the same way.

That afternoon, we completed payment of current bills, and I told her to start accumulating documentation for the yearly tax returns. Then I called Gene Graf to give him some more business with a check-up on Roy Nicholson.

I called Sheriff Wirth and offered to buy breakfast the next morning in Newcastle, and then it's back home to Illinois.

Newcastle
January 4
8 a.m.

I like Ron Wirth. He's always glad to fill me in on incidents affecting me. At breakfast, we talk about his questioning of Randy Gotch.

"Mark, he admits nothing. When confronted with Judd Turner's comment about the LLC that Gotch allegedly tried to get Jack to sign, he said he had never heard of it, and Judd was just trying to save his own neck. He had the same reaction to Judd's accusation about Gotch heading up local drug smuggling. He said Judd, himself, probably was paid to arrange the drug drop at your ranch. He felt that Judd and the dead guy found at the ranch probably were partners in the local drug trade, and Judd had probably killed him."

"I'm not surprised. Where does all this go from here?"

The sheriff finished chewing some hash browns and washed them down with a sip of coffee before answering.

"Well, we think Gotch is lying, and we'll keep digging until we find more evidence. We're going to search for any connection between Gotch and Alvarez."

Driving back to the Upton airport, I gave Zach a call. I had said goodbye to him quickly this morning and didn't have a chance to ask him about his lunch with Roy.

"I can't find any reason to not like him, Mark. We spent a lot of time talking about herd management, and range management. He's had some irrigation experience, so I don't see that being a challenge for him. I get the sense that he's a hard worker, and really likes the work. He seems even-tempered, and has quite the sense of humor the more he loosens up. If he's hiding anything, I sure don't know what it is."

I was glad to hear that. I feel good about Roy Nicholson. Unless we get some really outstanding applications this next week, and assuming Graf finds no problems in his background, Roy may be our guy.

CHAPTER TWENTY-SIX

Rockford
Wednesday, January 9

Another job application arrived in the mail from Alan Creston. This one is far different from the first two. It's from a young man who works full-time for a small distillery in Kirby, Wyoming. Kirby is a four-hour drive from Upton, a wide spot in the road of about 100 residents, surrounded by ranches.

His cover letter says he has worked part-time at neighboring ranches for over 10 years, and wants to get away from two jobs and work at a ranch full-time. His family would like to be nearer a town with better educational opportunities, and he wants to earn a lot more than he currently is.

As I read through his resume, I find it interesting that none of his references are ranchers. He says much of his part-time ranch work has involved fixing fences, but claims he is familiar with all ranch jobs.

Unfortunately for him, I need someone who isn't just familiar with the jobs. Zach needs someone who actually has done the jobs, and this young man isn't him.

As I had anticipated, Roy Nicholson passed Gene Graf's background check. He had a clean record. Zach and Patti like him and I think it's time to call him.

"Roy, this is Mark Willand. Do you still have interest in a job at Halestone Ranch?"

"Yes sir. Definitely."

"Then we sure would like to have you move to Upton and join us." I gave him a salary figure, told him we'd provide the same medical insurance Zach and Patti have, and would pay his moving expenses. I told him he could stay in the bunkhouse till he and his family had located a home in Upton.

I also said that if everything worked out well, he would be given a 10 percent raise after six months. That would be Zach's call to make.

During his visit to the ranch last week, Roy had impressed me as a serious man of few words, but with a cheerful outlook.

I stopped talking and waited for his response.

"Mr. Willand, I don't pull up stakes very often. I don't want anyone to think I can't hold a job. I had planned to stay here for a long time, but, as you know, things changed with the ranch being sold. But it's time to move on. You and Zach were awfully nice to me. I felt at home right away. Even Patti said she was hoping to see me again. I'll be glad to work for Halestone Ranch. When would you like me to start?"

I told him February 1 would be good, and that Zach would be in touch with him. He thanked me and I ended the call, feeling we now had a solid team. When I called Zach, he felt the same.

I also asked Zach to set up a meeting with a builder for next week who can give us a quote on the new bunkhouse.

Rockford
Friday

Patti called to say a neighboring rancher had stopped to see me. She had told him I was coming out next week, and he said he would stop back. He acted like he had a bone to pick with me, in her opinion.

That piqued my curiosity. A bone to pick? I called our new CPA, Chuck Weinberg.

"Chuck, do you know Galen Gingrich?"

"Yes, I've known him for many years. He doesn't use our services, he works with an accounting firm in Newcastle."

"Then maybe you can tell me a little bit about him. He's coming to see me and I don't know why."

"Well, Mark, I can't speak to what may be on his mind. I can tell you he is the third generation owner of their ranch. I don't see him here in town much. From what I hear, he's a good rancher and is financially sound. I do know he has a home outside Scottsdale and usually spends February and March down there."

"That's a good place to be in those months," I said. I thanked him, and stored that information away for possible use when Gingrich comes to see me next week.

Monday, January 14

After an early liftoff from Poplar Grove Airport, I arrive at Upton before noon, then called Patti to let her know I would be at the ranch in time for lunch. She said Mr. Gingrich wanted to come see me this afternoon, wanted to know if that would be OK. I said yes.

I was in my office after lunch when I heard the new warning bell, indicating a vehicle had come through the entrance gate. Minutes later, the doorbell rang, and I heard the muffled voices of Patti and a man.

I headed down the hallway and met Galen Gingrich at the front entrance. A large man, slightly overweight, with a big cowboy belt buckle holding back a sizable belly. He looked the part of a rancher. Over his shoulder, I noticed a late model pickup outside.

"I'm Mark Willand, Mr. Gingrich," I said, smiling and offering my hand.

He had a rancher's hand: meaty and rough. Solid grip.

"What can I do for you?"

"Oh, I just wanted to welcome you to the neighborhood," he said, although the serious look on his face didn't seem welcoming. "And I wanted to talk to you about Upton, if you have a moment."

Patti said she had fresh coffee, so I ushered Gingrich into the kitchen and gestured to a seat at the table.

As we sat, I asked, again, "What can I do for you?"

"Mr. Willand, my place borders yours on the northwest, and I'm a little farther from town than you."

"OK," I nodded.

"I've always tried to help Upton when they have big events. I loan them a flatbed for parades, make a donation each year to their United Givers Fund, and things like that."

I nodded again.

"Since you bought this ranch, I've heard some chatter at the coffee shop about all the things the new owner of Halestone Ranch has been doing for Upton. They think your 4-H program is a big deal, then you put up a big Christmas tree, and they wonder what comes next."

I said nothing, waiting for him to continue.

"So here's the thing: Since you have made such a big splash, I think people are now expecting me to up the ante and do more."

More silence from me. I've found silence to be a great technique in negotiations, which this seemed to be, in a way.

"I'm sure these things are small potatoes to you, and you probably pay for them out of petty cash. But I'm not in a position to compete with your big money from Illinois. I have to work hard to make ends meet, and you're making me look bad."

If he was expecting a response, he didn't get one.

He went on. "What you do is probably none of my business, but I wanted to tell you how I feel."

I forced a smile, nodded, and took a sip of my coffee. I didn't like his tone, but I wanted to make a friend, not an enemy.

"Galen, thanks for stopping in. You're correct, what I do is none of your business. However, I grew up on a small dairy farm. I was a kid when my parents died, and the neighbors helped me get through that. Ever since, I've been on good terms with neighbors wherever I live. So I'm going to tell you this one time why I'm doing these things, and that I'll continue.

"Ever since I obtained this ranch, I've heard about all that Luke and Jack Hale did for the community. When I went to Mayor Morris for ideas, I decided the 4-H project and Christmas tree would be suitable memorials for the Hale family.

"Now, I'm not sure what you refer to when you talk about my 'big money from Illinois.' I had no inheritance, earned everything honestly, and I owe no one an explanation regarding what I do with it."

I continued. "Now I have a question for you: If you are struggling to keep your head above water, how can you afford to spend two months each year at your second home in Arizona?"

He looked stunned, his face reddening.

"Galen, as I said, all my life I've wanted to get along with my neighbors. I would be happy if we can be friends, not competitors. You know a lot more about ranching than I do. I'd sure like to be able to stop in at your place once in a while and learn how you operate. Would that be OK with you?"

He acted like I had thrown him a lifeline when he was in deep water. After a moment, he slowly pushed back from the table, stood up and held out his hand.

"Willand, I misjudged you. You are right, it's none of my business what you do for Upton. I was out of line. And yep, feel free to stop in anytime and I'll show you around our set-up."

We shook hands. He left. I'm not sure if he felt better, but I did.

As Patti and I watched his pickup circle and pull out of the ranch yard, she said, "Well, you sure took the wind out of his sails, Mark."

I smiled and said, "Oh, I was just trying to set him straight, but also let him know I'm not here to cause problems. I'm sure he isn't the only one who has questions about this outsider from Illinois and his intentions. I'll bet it won't be long and he'll be spreading the truth to his pals at the coffee shop."

After Patti and I adjourned to the office to go through some paperwork, I brought up her vacation and the bonus money.

"Patti, I see you didn't use the bonus to take time off over Christmas, as I thought you were going to. What happened?"

I could tell she was nervous about answering.

"We had a storm blow through, Mark, and I decided to put off my trip. And the more I thought about it, Christmas isn't a time to be alone, and it didn't seem right for Zach to fend for himself out here.

"As for the bonus, I hope you'll approve of what I'm doing with it. My mother has always talked about remodeling her kitchen, but was always scared to spend the money. I'm planning to go home next week to Wisconsin and I'm going to give her a big chunk of the bonus, with the understanding that she spend it on her kitchen. That will give me a lot bigger thrill than taking a vacation trip. She sent me money all the time when I was still married and Dan wasn't working."

I smiled and told her she has a big heart and that sounded like a great way to spend the money. She seemed relieved with my approval.

Tuesday, January 15
8 a.m.

Zach and I left the ranch headed for Gillette and the horse auction. We rode in his almost-new Ford F-250 4WD with "Halestone Ranch" and our brand emblazoned on the driver and passenger doors. He had called me last week to be certain I would approve the purchase.

"This is a beautiful truck, isn't it? I'll use my old pickup around the ranch for dirty jobs, and take good care of this one."

I'm impressed with it as much as he is. Looks like Halestone Ranch is becoming Ford Country!

The auction was well underway when we arrived. I told Zach to get the bidding number, because he was going to do the buying, not me.

We had agreed on the way over that we wanted six well-trained, mature horses for the 4-H program. We wouldn't be using them till spring, but January auction prices are traditionally low, and we had plenty of hay on hand.

I sat in the bleachers sipping on some sale barn coffee while Zach walked through the holding yard, studying animals, occasionally writing down tag numbers.

As the animals came through the ring, Zach never started the bidding. When one of his chosen tag numbers came in, he waited till just before the auctioneer dropped the gavel, knowing that bidding had peaked for that animal. He obviously knew what he was doing around an auction house.

After he had bought six, we paid and arranged for trucking. All six had been put on the block by a single owner. Before the check was submitted, Zach got the owner to agree on replacements if any of the animals were too high strung for our 4-H kids.

On the way home, Zach said, "We were lucky today. These look like good animals, and today's small crowd kept the price down. I would have rejected them if the seller had refused a replacement agreement."

We talked about riding equipment. Zach said there were enough older saddles at the ranch for all six. About all we needed were some new bridles.

He came up with an interesting idea.

"Mark, the kids will want to know the horses' names. Right now, they don't have any. What do you think of having Patti name them?"

I said it was a good idea. I chuckled to myself. It sounds to me like Zach and Patti are becoming fast friends. I'm delighted.

Back at the ranch at lunch, Zach, Patti and I talked about the new bunkhouse. They'd been going over the rough sketch Zach had made, and Patti had some suggestions.

"First, I don't think a wash basin is enough, we should add a shower to each side's bathroom."

"Good catch, Patti." I said. "I'm not sure the 4-Hers will need it, but the hunters sure will. Anything else?"

"Yes," she said. "Include sleeping quarters in-between the boys' and girls' sides for a chaperone. These are teenagers, mind you," she chuckled.

Zach and I joined her in a quick laugh.

Early afternoon, I took an ATV to my new favorite place, The Hump. There's a slight powdering of snow on the ground. A few antelope bounded across ahead of me, and I'm always amazed how they leap so high and are so light on their feet. Regular ranch fences don't hold them in. Sometimes I wonder how many there are on the ranch, because I see them wherever I go. *Hundreds? Thousands?*

I found the same path on the north slope I had used before to get to the top of the hill. Everything looks different with a coating of snow. And sounds different, too. It seems quieter.

It's only mid-afternoon, but the shadows are already growing long. Quite often when I'm back in Illinois, I think of being here, perched on this spot overlooking Halestone Ranch, and marveling at the fact that it's mine. How did I get so lucky?

Wednesday, January 16

Zach and I meet with Ron White, a builder from Upton who specializes in garages, machine sheds and small homes.

We tell him what our plans are for a bunkhouse that could serve as a meeting room and occasional sleeping quarters for 4-H teenagers, and for housing hunters in the fall. He asked a lot of good questions, and I was impressed with him. Seems to know what he's doing.

We walked him around the site, asked him to prepare a quote by the time I come back out in ten days. Zach told him we wanted it finished in time for use by mid-spring, when temperatures start going back up.

It's mid-morning when White leaves and I want to be back in Rockford before dark, so I headed to the airport. Back in the days when I had two CaseIH dealerships 150 miles apart, I would often return home after dark. As far as I am concerned, night flying is IFR, and I always filed that way. Now that I have more freedom of time, I still file IFR, but I consider it safer to fly a single engine aircraft in daylight hours.

As I reach altitude, I feel good about my time on the ranch. Everything I wanted to accomplish on this trip, and then some, is done.

And I really like the looks of our six new horses.

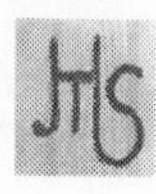

CHAPTER TWENTY-SEVEN

At home in Rockford
Monday, January 21

I'm looking out our kitchen window at four inches of new snow and, as usual, I'm thinking about the ranch. It's been over four months since the first phone call from Alan Creston. If one call can change a person's life, that one sure did.

The body found on the ranch bothers me. More precisely, the "whodunnit" bothers me. It seems there's been plenty of time to ID the killer, but maybe I've seen too many episodes of *CSI*. On my next trip, I'll ask Sheriff Wirth if any new clues have shown up.

Since coming home last Tuesday, I've caught up with friends back here that I had neglected during the many trips to Upton. I've filled them all in on the ranch, and I know some of them wonder why I bought it. They have no way of knowing it was inherited, and I don't feel comfortable telling them that. Barbara is the only here who knows.

She and I have talked several times about a trip for her to the ranch. I would like her to meet everyone I'm working with out there. Barbara has flown with me many times in the past, but winter flying is often turbulent, and she wants to wait for better flying conditions.

Today's mail delivery included a large envelope from Patti. She had enclosed a smaller envelope, unopened, with a return address from Jordan Shipley, Inc., Palo Alto, California.

Attached was her note that Mr. Shipley had called the ranch, asking for the owner. She told him the owner was not available. He then asked for a phone number to call, and she said she was not free to give that. He insisted. She didn't like his attitude, so told him if it was important, he should send a letter.

Shipley's letter indicated that he represented a client with interest in buying Halestone Ranch. He said it was urgent that I call him as soon as I received his letter.

I discarded it in my wastebasket.

Poplar Grove Airport
Monday, January 28
7 a.m.

It's 15 degrees with a low overcast. No icing is being mentioned in pilot reports, and tops are 5,000 feet, so I file a flight plan for 8,000 feet and get clearance on the ground.

Climbing into the overcast is always like walking into heavy fog. Attention must instantly switch to instruments. After flying IFR for a lot of years, I look forward to overcast skies to stay proficient.

What I really look forward to, though, is breaking out of the overcast on top, into clear skies. It's always a thrill, no matter how many times I do it. The clouds below look like a giant, white mattress.

I'd texted Patti before I took off, giving her my arrival time and letting her know I hoped the three of us could have lunch together.

It had been 60 days since I'd told Zach and Patti that I would consider pay raises by this date. During lunch, I told them I was very pleased, and their pay would be increased by 10%.

We were interrupted by the ranch's landline ringing. Patti answered, and I heard her say that Mr. Willand was not available. After listening a moment, she looked annoyed, then told the caller to hold on. She covered the phone's mouthpiece and turned to me.

"Mark, this is the same guy in California, Shipley, who sent you that letter. Now he wants your cell phone number."

I held out my hand and she gave me the phone.

"This is Mark Willand. I received your letter. I'm not interested in selling. You should delete me from your contact list."

The voice said, "Before I do that, I would like to come to Upton and tell you about my client's offer. It's quite generous. I could be there tomorrow."

"Mr. Shipley, let me make myself clear. I have no interest in an offer from any buyer." I hung up.

I walked back to the table, and could see Zach and Patti looking at me with apprehension.

"Just so you're clear," I said, "and in case anyone else asks if the ranch is for sale, I have not solicited an offer, nor will I entertain any offer for the ranch. Period."

They both looked relieved.

I recall that Shipley's return address on that envelope was Palo Alto, California, the home of Silicon Valley. I'm guessing that some tech company owner sold for a big profit and wants to buy a Wyoming ranch as a new toy. Court records would show my recent registration as owner, and Shipley probably assumed I had bought this place to flip it.

No way!

Tuesday, January 29

Zach and I met again with the builder, Ron White, for a couple of hours about the layout for the new bunkhouse. One more feature was added since our first discussion. Patti had suggested there be plumbing and electrical added for a washer and dryer. She thought the hunters would use them. White gave us his bid. I thanked him and said we would be in touch.

When he was gone, I asked Zach if he knew of any other builders he would trust to do a good job.

Zach shook his head as he finished zipping up his coat, saying, "I don't, Mark. I know Ron. He's a good man. I would rather work with him than a stranger."

Zach's judgment was good enough for me. I called White just as he returned to his office, and told him we wanted him to do the job. He promised to start as soon as spring weather arrived, and would have it completed in 30 days.

I called Sheriff Wirth and made an appointment to have breakfast. He's coming to Upton in the morning for a meeting, so we agreed to meet there. I'm curious about any progress he's made regarding Gotch and the murder.

Ranchland Diner, Upton
Tuesday morning

Oatmeal seems like a good choice for me on this cold winter morning. Sheriff Wirth went with steak and eggs.

"Mark, have you heard of any rustling in this area recently?"

I hadn't.

"Have you met your neighbor to the west, Galen Gingrich?"

I said I had, but that the subject hadn't come up.

"The spread west of Galen's reported a theft of eight to 10 head last fall. We asked Galen if he thought he'd lost any. He didn't think so, but said rustlers could enter between his land and yours without being seen."

"I agree, that area is pretty isolated, and it bothers me. I've been talking with Zach about installing a wireless motion-sensor camera. We could monitor any vehicle traffic that way."

The sheriff nodded as he cut into his steak. "Good idea. You'll probably get some interesting wildlife video, too."

"I hadn't thought about that, Sheriff, but I guess we'll get anything that moves on video. Switching topics, I was wondering if anything new has developed regarding the Alvarez murder?"

He nodded as he chewed. "This steak is sure good, Mark."

"But my oatmeal is healthier."

After swallowing and wiping his mouth, he smiled and said, "Maybe. My jury is still out on that one." Stabbing a bite of steak with his fork and holding it up at me, he added, "There are a lot of nutrients in this that you'll never find in oatmeal."

I smiled and nodded. "No argument. Now, about the murder?"

"Yep, the district attorney and I met with Turner again. We told him Gotch had denied everything and, at this point, Turner's immunity was questionable.

"Judd then said we should investigate Gotch's car lot manager, a fella named Mario Bianchi. He told us one of his friends had bought cocaine from Bianchi, and he thinks Bianchi delivers drugs that Gotch sells. Judd said he also thinks Bianchi follows Gotch's orders, and may have shot Alvarez because he was told to.

"Judd says he met Bianchi when he bought a truck from him at Gotch's recommendation. He described Bianchi as intimidating.

"We picked up Bianchi for questioning. He immediately lawyered up and shut up after we told him we suspect him of murder. We told him if he gives us the name of the drug boss we think he works for, we may go easier on him. We're waiting to hear from his lawyer."

Next stop was at the high school. 4-H leader Aaron Rhodes is also the assistant principal, and I gave him a copy of the new bunkhouse design.

"Aaron, this building is for your club to use except during hunting season in the fall. We're opening the ranch up to deer and antelope hunters again, and they'll be bunking there. The rest of the year, you can use it any way you wish."

"Mark, you can't imagine how excited the kids are about this. We have three new members who joined after they heard about how active our group is. I saw Zach at the coffee shop, and he told me about your purchase of the six horses."

"They're good-looking animals. Zach picked them out, and we bought them for one reason only: your members. Zach will help by setting up a program, with your help, for the kids to learn how to care for and ride the horses. He really is looking forward to that."

With that I left and drove into Newcastle to see Alan Creston.

Settled in a chair across a desk from Alan, I said, "There's a guy in California who keeps bugging me. He says his client wants to buy my ranch, and I keep telling him it's not for sale. Then he calls again. Do you have any thoughts as to why he's so persistent?"

"I've heard of similar situations now and then. In one case, a fellow with too much money bought a ranch near Gillette that had been in his family many years before. He thought he could come to Wyoming occasionally and play cowboy. He paid a lot more than it was worth, found out in a two-year period that he couldn't keep the help because he didn't want to pay them fairly. Sold it at a big loss."

"That probably worked out OK on his tax returns," I said. "What do you recommend I do with this fella?"

"Let's do this. Why don't I send him a letter stating that you have instructed me to write him and that you aren't going to sell, and that he might as well stop calling?"

"Good. Thanks for doing this. On another subject, did you hear that Randy Gotch is under suspicion for drug dealing? Judd Turner is also being questioned, and I'm still concerned that this is going to blow back on our ranch, seeing as they were both involved with us last year. I don't want any of this to taint Halestone."

"Yes, I've heard about it. Hard to believe that kind of stuff is going on out here, isn't it? But I don't think you have anything to worry about, Mark. I'll keep in touch with the sheriff's office to make sure."

It was early afternoon as I returned to the ranch. I'm surprised at how mild the winters are here compared to northern Illinois. Today, it's sunny and in the low 40s and the little snow that's on the ground is in danger of melting off. During lunch, I looked up Rockford's temperature. Just 20 degrees.

I saddled Toby and rode across to the west boundary. Galen Gingrich was right. This part of the ranch adjacent to his is very isolated, and the old trail that separates the two is clear enough for a cattle truck. I don't see any tracks, but if there had been a truck or other vehicles out here last fall, the tracks would likely be long gone.

I checked my cell phone. *Two bars. Good.*

As I ride back, the sun is quickly heading for the horizon behind me, and the ranch seems inordinately quiet. No deer, antelope, rabbits, birds, nothing. That surprises me.

After brushing down and feeding Toby and putting the tack away, I head for the machine shed. Zach is there, studying the service manual for the new windrower.

"That's a good-looking machine, Zach. That should do well for us for a while."

"Yes sir, not too big, not too small. It'll work just fine."

The subject changed to security for the west boundary.

"Zach, the sheriff likes the idea of securing our west border with motion-sensing video equipment. Will you do some shopping and see what's available? It needs to be sensitive enough to identify vehicles and license plates, and send you an alert on your cell phone. The sheriff said they will dispatch a deputy if you call. Don't try to go yourself. He realizes there may be some false alarms, but don't worry about that."

Zach nodded and said, "I was thinking a couple of well-placed trail cams will do the trick."

"We're thinking alike. I checked my cell phone while I was riding around over there and I had two bars, so that should be enough. Battery life will be important as you do your shopping."

"Yes sir, the models I'm familiar with run on AA batteries, and can last three to six months."

Since I acquired the ranch, Patti has maintained an apartment in Upton. Her typical daily schedule has been 7 a.m. till 3 p.m. It's only a nine-mile drive, but I have another plan.

"Patti, how would you like to live in the ranch house instead of driving back and forth to Upton? Right now, the ranch is vacant after you leave at three if Zach isn't here, and there will be times when he and Roy, once he gets here, will be away from the ranch buildings for many hours at a time. I'd feel better about having someone on the property all the time. Also, as soon as the new bunkhouse is built, the 4-H groups will be coming out. Someone really needs to be here full time.

She was delighted. "This seems like home to me anyway. I find it hard to keep the house clean, cook and get the office work done by three, so sometimes I'm here later, anyway. I'll give up my apartment on February 1, and be here full time after that."

Halestone Ranch is on its way to being more secure.

CHAPTER TWENTY-EIGHT

Upton Airport
Wednesday, February 6
Noon

Back out to Wyoming again; a fast flight on a cold winter day. Skies were clear all the way and, for a change, the ride was smooth. One thing is certain: If I wasn't a pilot, this ranch project would have been impossible. Rockford to Upton would be a 15-hour drive instead of a flight of less than five hours. No commercial flights come close to Upton, so back in September, I would have had to say no to the ranch inheritance.

After parking the 210 at its hangar, I checked my cell phone, and had a message from Sheriff Wirth asking me to call him.

"Mark, we made two arrests yesterday, and we believe both were involved in the Alvarez killing."

"That's good news, Sheriff. Is Gotch behind bars?"

"Well, he was. Last week, I told you we had questioned Mario Bianchi, the guy that runs Gotch's used car lot. He lawyered up so fast we figured he was guilty of something. We dug into his cell phone records around the time of the murder near your ranch. He had made two calls in early October that GPS showed were from an area near where the Alvarez body was found two weeks later. Both were late at night, and both were to Randy Gotch.

"That was enough to get a search warrant for Bianchi's home, and in his garage we found a pistol that ballistics says fired the bullets into Alvarez's body. We arrested him and charged him with murder. After his attorney visited him, he told us Gotch had ordered him to do it, and that Gotch was the drug boss for the Newcastle area and had found out Alvarez was skimming profits for himself.

"We arrested Gotch at his fancy office yesterday afternoon and charged him with complicity in the Alvarez murder. We also charged him with distribution of illegal drugs. He made bail, of course, but Bianchi couldn't. Gotch wouldn't put up his bail money, so Bianchi stays behind bars till the trial. Gotch is back on the street till then."

"Sheriff, I really appreciate the call. It sounds like you have a lot of evidence to put these guys away."

"Yes and no, Mark. We probably have enough to put Bianchi away, but we're going to need more on Gotch."

"I won't be surprised if you find what you need."

"Me neither. When a guy is dirty, he's generally dirty in more than one way."

I hangared the plane, plugged in the block heater, and headed to the ranch. Patti was expecting me for a late lunch. There would be a fourth plate at the table now.

As I arrived in the ranch yard, Zach and Roy walked out of the machine shed and headed for the house. The four of us sat down for our semi-regular working lunch.

"Welcome to the table, Roy," I said. "How's this first week of work going?"

He said it's going just fine. He had started looking for a home to rent in Upton, and had a couple to choose from. His wife was driving up for the weekend and deciding which to rent.

"And how are the new living arrangements, Patti?"

"Oh my gosh, this makes my job much easier. Now I've got time to stay on top of the bookkeeping, and take care of the cooking and cleaning without having to rush to and from town. I really like it."

Zach changed the subject. "Remember hearing about the dog that found the body?"

Roy's head popped up from his lunch. "Body? A human body?"

"Oh," I smiled, "I guess we didn't mention that during your interview. Yes, back in — was it October, Zach?"

"September," Zach said.

"Right. Back in September, a father and son were running their dog up on the north end of the ranch. The dog is ex-military, and it dug up a human bone from a shallow grave. It's a longer story, which we'll be happy to share with you sometime, but it appears — and this is new information from the sheriff for you two," I said, nodding to Zach and Patti, "the killer has been arrested."

"Who is it?" asked Patti.

"A fella named Mario Bianchi who worked for Randy Gotch in Newcastle. Gotch was arrested as an accessory, but he's free on bail."

Patti and Zach seemed surprised by the news.

"And was Judd involved?" asked Patti, quietly.

"Not in the murder, no, but he did allow planes to land up on the north end near where the body was found."

There was silence as they were digesting this information.

"Anyway, Zach," I said, "what were you saying?"

"I was just telling you that Dan Whitman, who owns the dog, wanted to bring it out so we could see how the dog is doing. I told him to come this afternoon so you could meet both of them."

After lunch, curious about retired military dogs, I searched the internet for information, and found that their training costs over $10,000 before they are sent into active duty. What remarkable animals they become! Here's what I found out about their retirement from the military:

- The law specifies they should be released into the care of their former handlers if possible.

- The second option is to turn them over to law-enforcement agencies that can benefit from their training.

- Third, is to give them to civilians that are capable of caring for them properly. Only a few animals each year end up in civilian care.

- Training programs instill in a war dog the deep desire for toys or something similar. The anticipation of these rewards drive the animals to succeed at their mission.

As I was reading this, Zach stuck his head in the office door and announced Dan and Finder had arrived. I walked out to the yard and met a very serious looking teenager, with his dog sitting quietly beside him on a leash. Finder was a large, black Lab, at least 80 pounds, I estimated.

I thanked Dan for the discovery Finder had made when he found the Alvarez body. I also told him the news about the arrests.

"And I was just reading about how service dogs are re-introduced to civilian life. How is Finder adjusting?"

Dan lit up with pride as he described his dog.

"When Finder was first brought to us, he was really a handful. He was jumpy and nervous until we remembered that we had been told to get a crate. As soon as he saw it he rushed inside and went to sleep. Apparently, he always had a crate when he was in the Army, and felt secure in it.

"Wherever we took him, he would go wild if he saw an abandoned toy or a baseball glove, anything that reminded him of the toys he was given while in the service.

"We had been told about the training he had been given when we picked him up at the military base in San Antonio. Apparently the training these dogs get drives them to a point where they live for the job, just like some humans. After their service is ended, they don't know how to survive without the adrenalin rush from sniffing out bombs and hearing gunfire."

He went on to say that after they brought him home, Finder would show signs of still being on duty. He wanted to smell under each door he passed. He always wanted to smell vehicle tires. He was still on alert for bombs and bodies.

"But, now Finder has been with us for nearly eight months, and he has settled down quite a bit."

Now I finally understood why the dog had located the Alvarez body. He had been trained to do that. I thanked Dan for introducing me to Finder, and asked him to visit us anytime.

After our visitors left, Zach and I took my pickup and drove to the northwest boundary of Halestone Ranch. Zach had found a sensing device that might detect rustling activity, and he wanted me to see a spot where he thought it should be installed.

The area isn't easy to get to. A ravine blocks access except for a cleared path that was used by both ranches to build and service the boundary fences.

We drove the path south alongside the fence line for the Halestone North Pasture. This looks like the only access a cattle truck could use to get near our cattle. We were able to drive all the way to the West Pasture and Lower West Pasture.

Zach described what he had in mind.

"It's called an Arlo-Go wireless mobile security camera. It will sense any large moving object. When activated, it sends a video and audio message to my cell phone. If the image shows a cattle trailer, I'll call the sheriff's office and they'll send out a deputy to take a look."

"How is the video quality at night?" I asked, thinking that most cattle rustlers work in darkness, even though it's so isolated out here that it may not make any difference.

"I checked on that, Mark, and the device takes night video that is almost as clear as daytime videos. It's battery-driven and needs no wi-fi because it transmits through the Verizon network."

We made our way back to the entrance off the main road. It looked like the device could be installed there, hidden from sight.

Zach continued. "Verizon will install and service it. Our cost would be $485 for the unit, plus $40 per month for service."

I told him it looks like a good solution.

"One thing, though, that I want to be clear about, Zach. I want you to promise to call the sheriff's office if a trailer shows up, and not go out there by yourself. I don't need to worry about you getting shot."

He smiled and agreed.

Thursday, February 7
Breakfast

The four of us spent time discussing recent decisions, including the plan for the security camera. Roy said they had lost cattle at his last place, and thought the camera was a good idea. He suggested it be programmed to send alerts to his cell phone as well as to Zach's. Good thinking.

I'm glad to see how well Roy has fit in to the group and a good working relationship already exists with him, Zach and Patti.

After breakfast, we split up. Zach and Roy prepared to deliver hay to two pastures. While they were gone, I inspected the machine shed. In the past months, I had been in it only briefly. In the Midwest, the machine shed is a vital component of a farm's success, and a lot of time is spent there maintaining equipment. In many cases, 'shed' gives the wrong impression. Many farmers have made their sheds as fancy and comfortable as many homes.

This one, though, definitely qualifies as a shed. It's an old pole-barn, probably built by Luke Hall in the '50s. It's around 30 feet high, and is maybe 100 feet deep, with a wall sectioning off a small area in the back end. I suspect Luke may have used that back area as a stable a long time ago.

The front is packed with machinery, parked neatly. Zach always keeps it well organized. An ancient Cat road grader looks to be in good shape. Most of the older equipment is IH: a 686 for irrigation pumps, a 986 with loader for round bales, and some tillage equipment. The Kubota zero-turn is for mowing the yard around the buildings. The only CaseIH equipment are the round baler and the used windrower that Zach bought from Titan in Rapid City last month.

Bale wagons, a horse trailer, and a machinery trailer filled the rest of the shed, except for a small work area, where Zach kept his tools, welder and air compressor.

I walked to the walled-off area in back, opened a smaller door and this old IH dealer couldn't believe his eyes.

Under layers of dust accumulated over I don't know how many years, were an old IH pickup, probably a 1960 or '61 model, and two International tractors.

As I brush off and blow away some of the dust, I see a Farmall Super M-TA. That's a collector's item because it was built only in 1954, and not many came off the assembly line at Rock Island, Illinois. Next to it was a 560 Diesel, with one of its rear tires flat. I stood there wondering when the last time they had been used and if any of them would be in running condition, once batteries were charged or replaced. I'll ask Zach what he knows about them.

Suddenly I thought about the Upton High School FFA. Maybe they could restore the Super M-TA. It would have definite appeal to collectors, and the FFA could make some money from it. Through the years, a lot of chapters back home have done this, and the restorations usually make the tractors look better than new. If that was too much for them to tackle, maybe they could just get both tractors and the pickup in running condition and sell them "as is" for a fundraiser. One more item to discuss with Zach.

While poking around the tractors, I thought about the huge International Harvester Collectors Club. It has 7,500 members in over 30 states and in several other countries. Numerous members in Canada. Their members restore lots of old tractors and could be a source of advice for the FFA members if they took on a project like this. They might also be a source for parts.

Back in the house, Patti and I co-signed checks for several bills, and talked about replacing some worn-out furniture.

During dinner, I asked Zach about the vintage tractors and truck. He said they had been in that same place when he started working at the ranch. He liked my thoughts on the Super M-TA and the FFA.

We talked more about the 4-H club, and Roy volunteered to

help. He said he had been a 4-H leader back when his son was young. Zach was really glad to hear that. He feels both he and Roy can help Aaron Rhodes with the club.

That night, I fell asleep thinking about those old tractors.

Upton Airport
Friday, February 8

Another good trip to the Halestone! Time to go home. It seems like staying two nights out here works best. I've been coming out almost every week, but Zach and Patti have everything well under control, so I'll skip next week.

Clear skies are forecast all the way to Rockford, with a brisk tailwind of 30 knots out of the west. Winter months often provide strong upper winds, and today is no exception. The tailwind will allow a nonstop trip home. I filed for 5,500 feet VFR and lifted off from Upton just before nine.

Flying at that altitude offers a lot of opportunity to see pretty clearly what's going on below. Depending on the time of year, it could be farmers planting or harvesting crops, and the colors change as the calendar changes. Always there, spinning in the wind, are the giant turbines. They first showed up in the Midwest in the '90s, but their numbers have exploded in the past decade or so. Once I'm above Iowa, there aren't many places where I don't see those huge blades. Iowa seems to add more every year.

Curious, I looked up the statistics on them. Wind now produces over five percent of U.S. electric power, but what really surprised me was the height of the most recent towers. They reach up 260 feet to capture more wind! Today, with clear visibility, the white blades show up in great numbers.

CHAPTER TWENTY-NINE

Rockford
Monday, February 11

For several months, I've averaged a trip to the ranch about every 10 days. With a permanent crew in place, I no longer need to go so often. I've told Zach, Patti and Roy that I have complete confidence in them. Now I have to prove that by staying away more and letting them do their jobs. I'm finding that's easier said than done.

Gazing out the kitchen window, I see new snow falling on top of old. It's a bitterly cold and windy day in Rockford. As my mind drifts again to the ranch, I remember the warm weather connection to how the entire ranch project started: the Schofield Barracks in Hawaii.

The outdoor thermometer on the patio shows 15 degrees. I plugged in Oahu on my cell phone weather app and it shows a high of 81 degrees today.

I went upstairs to Barbara's office.

"I have an idea," I began.

She smiled and said gently, "You always have ideas, Mark. One of the many reasons I married you."

"I think you'll really like this one, especially on a day like today. Let's go to Hawaii for a week. Neither of us has anything critical on our schedule and we haven't been back to the Islands for many years."

Barbara looks out the window at the blowing snow, and said, "I'm in! But are you sure you'll be able to stay away from the ranch for that long, Mark?"

I booked our flight an hour later.

Maui, Hawaii
February 18-25

Twenty-five years ago, we took the kids here; first to Oahu to see where our home was when we were stationed in the Army, and then to the island of Maui where we stayed at the Royal Lahaina Hotel.

And that's where we stayed again this trip. We've been in a lot of nice places through the years, but no place beats the Hawaiian Islands. The sweet fragrance of flowers seems to always be in the air.

Every day, I'm tempted to text Zach and see how things are going at the ranch. However, I fear he would feel I was checking up on him, so I decided to leave him alone.

That doesn't stop me from thinking about it, though. Sitting on the beach, soaking up every minute of the experience, my mind still wanders to Halestone Ranch. What a contrast of where I am, looking out onto the Pacific Ocean, to where I was sitting just a few weeks ago at the top of The Hump. I think about the bunkhouse project, the 4-H project, the old IH tractors and pickup in the machine shed, and the three great employees that run the place, and on and on as I think of all that's happened in the past six months.

Back in Rockford
Tuesday, February 26

As I push open the front door, there's a pile of mail waiting for us. The first letter I open is from Alan Creston.

He had enclosed another letter from Jordan Shipley, the pest in Palo Alto, California. It again stated that his client wanted to buy my ranch, and that the offer would be larger than I would expect. Another letter for the wastebasket.

I texted Alan, asking him to again reply to Shipley that we had no interest in selling, now or in the future.

I've thought many times about someday getting a custom-made

saddle. Through those 19 years that I helped our friend move cattle each June, the first hour in the saddle was comfortable but after that, my butt started hurting. It's similar to breaking in a pair of new shoes, except the shoes adjust to your feet. The saddle does not adjust to your butt. It's the other way around.

Today, I started thinking again about ordering one after receiving a year-end financial statement from our CPA. Cash on hand had increased from the fall cattle sale. I decided that if I was ever going to have a fitted saddle, now was the time.

After sifting through websites, I came upon a saddle-maker that will provide a template, fit form or saddle tree for fitting. I emailed "Saddle Trails Saddle" that I'd like more details on a custom saddle.

Next, I called Chuck Weinberg and asked him to meet monthly with Patti and make sure we were maintaining the right records for federal and state tax returns, and doing payroll properly. Following that call, I texted Patti that Weinberg would be coming to see her, and answer any questions she had.

Wednesday, February 27

Today's mail brought another envelope from Alan Creston. He had enclosed a clipping from the Newcastle newspaper *News Letter Journal.* The large front-page headline read:

"LOCAL CPA & CAR LOT MANAGER BOTH GUILTY"

I was shocked as I read the article.

Two murder trials concluded this week with both defendants found guilty by the juries. Mario Bianchi, manager of a Newcastle used car lot, was sentenced to 30 years imprisonment for the killing of Ethan Alvarez.

The Alvarez body was discovered last October on the Halestone Ranch near Upton. A handgun was discovered recently in Bianchi's garage, and ballistics determined it was the murder weapon. Bianchi's fingerprints were on the weapon.

Newcastle CPA Randy Gotch, defendant in the second trial, was found guilty for dealing in illegal drugs and being an accomplice in the Alvarez shooting. Incriminating evidence resulted from Bianchi testimony that Gotch paid him to kill Alvarez. Bianchi stated in his time on the witness stand, that Gotch was in charge of illegal drug distribution in the Weston County area, and apparently believed that Alvarez, whose job it was to deliver the drugs to buyers, was siphoning more than his share of the proceeds. Gotch then instructed Bianchi to kill Alvarez, for which he was paid well. He shot Alvarez and hid the body on the Halestone Ranch property, where it was found.

Bianchi's testimony against Gotch, and large cash amounts that were found in Gotch's possession, were factors in Gotch's verdict. Gotch was sentenced to 25 years for arranging the Alvarez killing and distributing drugs.

Bianchi's testimony against Gotch was in exchange for avoiding a death sentence for the Alvarez murder.

Judd Turner, another witness for the prosecution, testified that Gotch had promised him part ownership in a real estate transaction if he would arrange for light aircraft to land at night on Halestone Ranch property to make drug deliveries. Turner, at the time, was foreman of Halestone Ranch, and was given immunity from prosecution for his testimony.

End of newspaper article. And certainly the end of a normal life for Bianchi and Gotch. And who knows what will become of Judd Turner? Per his agreement with law enforcement, he must now leave Weston County and not return.

CHAPTER THIRTY

Rockford
Sunday, March 3
3 p.m.

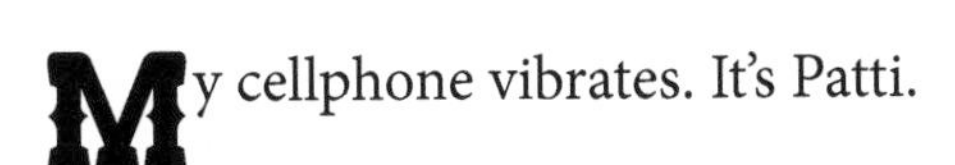

My cellphone vibrates. It's Patti.

"Mark, you should know that Zach got hurt yesterday."

"Oh, no! How is he? What happened?"

"He started riding each of the six 4-H horses to make sure they weren't too much for the kids. Yesterday, he was riding one for the first time when the outside bell rang announcing an arrival at the front gate. The bell spooked the horse, and Zach got thrown. The ground is frozen and he hit hard and broke his arm."

"Ouch! How bad of a break?"

"The doctor said it was a fracture between his elbow and wrist. He thinks it will heal quickly but they put on a cast, and he will have it for about five or six weeks."

"Patti, please tell Zach that bronc riding is not in his job description!" I said, trying to lighten the moment. "Seriously, though, I am grateful that he wasn't hurt worse."

"Me, too, Mark. He wanted me to make sure to tell you that the seller is sticking by his promise to replace any horses that aren't tame enough for the 4-Hers, and one will be delivered this week."

I told her I was planning to come out Wednesday, and to tell Zach I'm glad it wasn't more serious and to take it easy.

After the call, I realized how important a step we had taken in hiring Roy Nicholson. He's fully experienced and can take care of everything till Zach is back on his feet.

I went on Amazon and found the ideal belt buckle. It's engraved

"National Finals Rodeo" with a horse high off the ground and a rider barely holding on. I ordered it to be shipped to Zach with one-day delivery. On the gift card, I added this comment. "I'm assuming you stayed on eight seconds. Wear this with pride and get well soon. Mark."

Enroute to Upton
Wednesday, March 6

Skies are clear as I fly over the Mississippi River at Dubuque. Steam rises from the water as the cold morning air hits the warmer water. The river rarely freezes solid this far south. I've always thought the prettiest part of the Mississippi was this stretch, where the river is flanked by high bedrock bluffs. When the trees change color in the fall, it is a sight to behold on a sunny day.

The forecast for central Iowa called for 2,500 foot ceilings with tops of 4,000 feet. Winds are currently out of the north. I'm IFR at 8,000 feet, and the wind out of the north isn't slowing me down.

I could fly above the clouds before I got my IFR rating, but only if I knew I would be in clear conditions at my destination. That isn't a guessing game I'd want to be in.

It's great to be going back to the ranch after almost three weeks away. Spring calving has started, and with Zach recovering from his broken arm, I'll ride out with Roy to check on the herd.

As I land at Upton, I'm surprised at the small amount of snow on the ground. I am aware from my research, though, that March can still be a cold and snowy month, with five to 15 inches, on average.

Patti has lunch ready, and the four of us, and Zach's cast, gather at the table. Zach says he's doing fine with his cast. Then he says he has an announcement to make.

Pushing his chair back from the table and standing, he said, "I believe I'm the only person on this ranch with a championship rodeo buckle."

We all have a good laugh as he shows off the huge buckle.

"It's legit," he said. "I earned this, because I was in the saddle for way more than eight seconds before I suddenly departed. That's rodeo rules!"

He thanked me with that huge smile of his, and showed me where both Patti and Roy had signed his cast. I am delighted with the friendship that has grown among these three. He gave me a Sharpie and I added my signature.

Jack Hale had instructed Judd to buy two new Polaris Sportsman model ATVs while Jack could still ride, and they are awesome vehicles. Younger ranchers use them more than horses. Instead of going through the process of getting a horse saddled, the machines are ready to go with the turn of a key. They are noisier than horses, though.

With the meager snow on the ground, Roy and I quickly rode two pastures with the ATVs, looking for new calves. We found three in the East Pasture, just a few days old, all doing well and being well-tended to by their mothers. Crossing over to the South Pasture, we located another half-dozen, fairly new ones.

We'll take this route again in a couple days when Roy takes a load of hay out. Looks like calving is just starting, and weather conditions are good for a high survival rate.

We parked the ATVs in the machine shed, and Roy explained that he and his wife had just moved into a rental home in Upton that they really like. Neighbors had welcomed them as they arrived, and they already feel settled. I told him how glad I was that he had agreed to become part of Halestone Ranch, particularly in time to be here when Zach got hurt.

Zach wanted to talk about the new bunkhouse. We looked at the stakes the contractor had managed to drive into the frozen ground marking the outer walls, and Zach said construction would start as soon as the ground warmed up.

Chuck Weinberg's CPA Office, Upton
Thursday, March 7
9 a.m.

"Chuck," I asked, "how many ranches do you prepare tax returns for?

"Fourteen."

"How many were you doing five years ago?"

"Nine or ten. Why do you ask?"

"I'm asking because I want you to do more jobs for us, and you are obviously good at what you do because you're adding ranch clients."

"I love the work, Mark. I'm a ranch kid, grew up on one, and these folks are my favorite clients. Some were friends from before I started my practice."

"OK. Then here's what I hope you can do for me, in addition to our tax work. Please meet with Patti about once a month and set her up with the right software, filing system, and the right bookkeeping systems. I know she wants to do a good job, but she's not had much experience. I'd like you to mentor her and help her wherever you can. For instance, the 4-H program we are starting needs some extra attention to make sure the tax deductions are in line."

Chuck nodded.

"Each month when you meet with her, I want you to also spend some time with Zach. He knows the job of foreman, but being manager of the ranch is a different thing. He's never been a decision maker, and I want him to do that, not me. I've encouraged him to seek help from the county extension office regarding proper ranch management. But I want you to help him learn proper purchasing practices, how to buy salt, protein supplement, twine, etc. We are increasing our hay acreage, and he needs to learn how best to market hay to other ranchers.

"Like Patti, I know he wants to do a good job. I'd like you to help him do that. Chuck, are you comfortable taking that on?"

Chuck nodded again and said, "I'm doing something similar at another ranch that has new management. I'll be glad to work with Patti and Zach. I assume you want me to charge on an hourly basis?"

"Yes, perfect. And one more thing: Occasionally stop in unannounced. You can dream up a reason about needing to get some tax information or whatever, and while you're there, make it that month's meeting. I trust these two completely. But through the years, I've learned that absentee ownership has its risks."

"It does, and I'll be happy to help you minimize those risks."

He paused before continuing. "Mark, I assume that the jury trials of your last ranch foreman and CPA have come to your attention."

"Yes, and I'm glad that's behind us. I'm sure that with Zach and Patti taking care of Halestone Ranch, and you looking over their shoulders, nothing like that will happen again."

In the afternoon, Zach, Roy and I sat in the living room and talked for hours about the new hay acreage, the additional irrigation equipment that we need, and a schedule for branding.

"The HS branding irons and propane heater are in good shape and ready to go." offered Zach.

"I'm curious, Zach. Do you have any experience with electric branders?"

He shook his head. "We've never used one here, but I've talked with some friends who switched, and they sure like electric better. They're nice because you can heat them quickly to brand a handful of animals when you don't want to drag a propane heater out and fire it up. Just plug it in, and it's hot enough in three to five minutes," he said. "I've also heard that they make a cleaner brand, but I'm not so sure about that. Hot is hot, Mark. How clean a brand is, well, that's all in the technique."

"That's interesting," I said. "You're going to need some help. What are your thoughts on that?"

Roy volunteered that 4-H leader Aaron Rhodes has already offered to select some members that would help.

"Will that be enough?"

"Should be, once we experts teach 'em what to do," Roy smiled.

"Oh, I want to show you something," Zach said as he pulled out his cellphone and tapped it a couple of times. "Here, Mark, take a look at this."

The screen showed the app for the new security camera on the west boundary. Day or night, it would video any vehicle activity, and transmit it to both Zach's and Roy's phones.

"That's pretty amazing," I said. "It wasn't too many years ago that this sort of thing would be science fiction."

I told them I would contact Galen Gingrich and tell him we now have surveillance.

Before we adjourned, Zach wanted to be sure all four of us would be at breakfast tomorrow. He seemed a little nervous about that, and I wondered what was on his mind.

Friday, March 8
Breakfast at the ranch house

Walking toward the kitchen, I could smell the bacon before I could hear it sizzling. There aren't many aromas I can think of that I like as much. Maybe that of bread baking. Both are a treat. I grab a cup of coffee and head to the table as Patti finishes plating the eggs, bacon and hashbrowns.

Right on time, Roy came into the boot room, kicked off his work boots and hung up his coat. He said he had ridden the East Pasture again early this morning and found two more calves born overnight.

"The way it's going," he grinned, "we'll be up to our ears in calves by early next week."

As we all sat at the table, I could again sense Zach's nervousness. I didn't have to wait long to find out what it was about.

He said he's never been good at speeches, but this morning he wanted to make one. I looked at Patti and Roy, and they were smiling.

"Mark, these months since you took over the ranch have been the best I've ever had. Judd Turner made it hard to work here, and after Jack died, Patti and I were both going to quit. Then you arrived and told us you wanted us to stay on. However, we were still going to quit because of Judd. Luckily, you fired him before it came to that."

"I'm sure glad you didn't quit! Both of you," I said.

Zach continued his speech. "You gave us both a chance to prove what we could do. You listened to our ideas, let us do our jobs, and then hired Roy. He's terrific, and I'll say it with him sitting here. He knows more than I do about herd management, and since I broke my arm he's been doing everything."

Roy smiled, his ruddy face deepening with embarrassment.

"That's the first part of my speech," Zach continued. "Now, I want to say that Patti has been a good friend since she started working here when Jack was sick. In the past few months, she's become more than a friend. Lots more!" he smiled directly at Patti.

She returned the smile, blushing.

"Mark, I've asked her to marry me, and she said yes. We both hope this meets with your approval," he said. Nodding at Roy, he said, "I've already told Roy. He's part of this team, and he and his wife, Janis, have quickly become our friends, as well. They are glad for us."

I was surprised but not shocked. I am delighted because they are the future of Halestone Ranch!

"But Patti," I said, putting on a serious face, "do you really think you can put up with this big cowboy as a husband?"

Patti smiled tentatively, looked at Zach and then me, and I couldn't keep a straight face any longer.

"I sure can," she giggled. These last few months have been my best ever, the same as Zach said. You've been more of a coach to us than a boss, and Zach is the best thing that has ever happened to me."

Typically, when the four of us eat together, Roy sits across from me, and Zach sits at one end of the table, Patti at the other end. I reached for their hands, on each side of me.

"I, too, have had a great time here the last few months working with both of you. I could not be happier for you. Have you set a wedding date yet?"

Zach said they think mid-summer would work best, after calving is over, and the new hay ground is in place along with all the irrigation equipment.

Patti asked if I thought that would be OK.

"Look, you two you sure don't need my blessing, but you've got it anyway. Roy will be the one most affected by the timing. What do you think, Roy?"

He said he would have no problem getting help, if he needed it, while the newlyweds are gone. He also wished them the very best.

I sat for a moment thinking about what to say next.

"I recall Alan Creston telling me early on that the two of you were highly valued by Jack before he died. I think if Jack were still alive, he would want Halestone Ranch to pay for your wedding. So that's what we will do."

Patti and Zach look shocked, and then really pleased.

As we got up from the table, I gave Patti a quick hug and said congratulations, and I shook hands with Zach and complimented him on his speech.

Back in my office, I called the number Gingrich had given me when we first met. It went to voice mail, and I described the video security system Zach had installed between our ranches. I told him we would keep him informed of any unusual activity. I clicked off, grabbed my bag, and headed for the airport.

After a thorough pre-flight check, I'm back in the air toward Rockford. Unless something unusual pops up, I'll wait till April 2 to come back out. Zach and Roy should have a good idea about the calf crop, and spring weather should be close, although I know better than to try to predict Wyoming's weather this time of year. I look forward to more time on horseback during the next trip.

CHAPTER THIRTY-ONE

At home in Rockford
March 19
Mid-afternoon

My cellphone screen shows a call is coming from First National Bank of Newcastle.

"Mark, this is Tom Westedt. Are you in Wyoming today?"

"No, I was 10 days ago, but right now I'm at home in Rockford."

"Well, I hope all is well for you back there. This isn't the reason for my call, but I did hear about the 4-H program your ranch is starting. Some of the members' parents bank with me, and they really think you're doing something special for the kids. Just wanted you to know."

I smiled. "Thank you, Tom. I was a 4-H member a long time ago and really think a lot of the organization. It's fun to be able to do this."

"Head, Heart, Hands, and Health, right?"

"Oh, so you were a member, too?"

"Yes sir. The parents tell me you are building a meeting place for them on the ranch."

"That's right, and we are also including a bunkhouse if the 4-H leader wants to have overnight programs. That will also double for sleeping quarters when hunters come out in the fall."

"Well, Mark, you've sure done a lot for Upton in the short time you've had Halestone Ranch. I just wanted you to know your efforts are being noticed and appreciated."

"Thank you, but you said that's not why you called."

"Right. We received a strange letter from a Shipley Financial Services indicating that you may be receiving a loan from them, and they want to know what our history has been with you, as well as what we have currently on loan to you. We will not answer the letter, of course, but I thought you should know about it."

I could feel the heat rise in my head and my pulse begin to race.

"Tom, I can't believe this. I've requested no loan. If I ever need more, I'll come to you. This guy Shipley keeps trying to buy Halestone Ranch from me for a client of his. He has called me, written me, written Alan Creston, and we've told him repeatedly the ranch is not for sale. Why would he contact you?"

"I suppose he probably thinks one of our office staff will slip up and give him information, and if you have large loans he may try to convince you to sell and pay them off. But he's got to be a little stupid to think we would give out customer information."

I thanked him for calling, and asked him to scan and email the Shipley letter to me.

I am so angry I could spit. This guy is driving me nuts. I called Gene Graf to see if he can help put an end to this.

"Gene, this is Mark Willand. I've got another project for you. A guy named Jordan Shipley is some kind of a middle man for high net worth clients in Palo Alto, California. He keeps calling and writing, saying that his client wants to buy my ranch, and his client always gets what he wants. I've told him, repeatedly, in no uncertain terms, I'm not selling.

"Now he has taken it too far. Somehow, he found out where I bank, and wrote them asking for information on my business with them. My banker called me, said they're ignoring the letter, and he sent me a copy. I'm forwarding it to you. I want to stop this. Please dig up what you can about Shipley. I need some way to get rid of him."

Graf said he had some suggestions. I listened.

"I can get his Social Security number, find any lawsuits that may be filed against him, and his indebtedness. I may be able to find out who his main clients are, and then come up with the same information on them. If you confront him with any of this and tell him you will put it on Facebook if he bothers you again, this should shut him down."

I give my head a quick shake in admiration."Wow, Gene, how can you come up with this stuff?"

"That's my secret. Proprietary information," he chuckled. "But I will tell you this much. The FBI is always busting hackers who are really sophisticated. The feds give them a choice of going to prison or becoming informants for the Bureau. They always choose door number two. Anytime the Bureau wants to hack into potential criminal activities, these people do it. Do you want me to proceed in that direction?"

"Yes, I sure do."

Graf said he would get back to me. He's been a big help before. I expect he will be again.

Today I got an email response from the saddle maker I contacted. What a shock! Buying a custom-made saddle wasn't going to be an easy process. They wanted measurements and answers to a whole list of questions about options. I decided to try all the saddles we have at the ranch before I decide whether to order one. Maybe there is one that fits me well enough. If not, I'll see about answering all their questions.

As I looked at recent bank statements, I noticed the payment for the six horses we bought at the auction for the 4-H program. I recall somewhere hearing the term "Equine Therapy." I typed it into Google and one of the articles that popped up focused on its applications for troubled youth. The article says proof abounds that involvement with horses can be therapy for everyone. Teenagers, in particular, tend to bond well with horses as they groom, feed and care for the animals. They learn to anticipate the horse's needs, and these skills get translated into better person-to-person relationships.

I called Aaron Rhodes, the Upton 4-H leader.

"Aaron, this is Mark Willand. I believe Ken Morris told you that we bought six horses for your 4-H group."

"Yes, he sure did, Mr. Willand, and I told the kids. They're really excited. Some of our members are ranch youngsters and have grown up around horses. But the others really want to learn how to ride. I plan to assign them to a specific animal so they can learn to care for and groom them, in exchange for riding lessons. Roy Nicholson from your ranch has volunteered to be in charge of that."

I was happy to hear Roy had reached out to Aaron.

"You know, Mr. Willand, two of our members are quite, well, shy I guess is the right word for it. I'm hoping their involvement with the animals will do them a lot of good."

"I hope so, too, Aaron. You should know that the new building should be ready in early May and it will be yours to use except for during hunting season in the fall. Also, I'll be back out April 2 for several days, and if you would like to bring your members out after school we'll introduce them to the horses."

He said they would like that, so I'll ask Zach to set up the visit. I want to be there so I can meet the group.

March 22, 2 p.m.
Phone call from Gene Graf

"Mark, I've got some information for you on Jordan Shipley."

"Great. Go ahead."

He gave me his Social Security number, details on a pending lawsuit against him for investment fraud, and information on a pending investigation pertaining to misrepresentation of a real estate property that he sold for one of his clients.

Graf continued by giving me the names of two of Shipley's largest clients, both with pending lawsuits regarding fraudulent tax returns.

"Mark, my suggestion to you is to advise Shipley you will anonymously release this information on Facebook, unless he backs off and leaves you alone. My guess is that one of the clients facing tax investigations is the one that wants your ranch. He's got a ton of money. I didn't come up with information on any other Shipley clients that have large net worth."

I thanked him, and commented again that his help has become a real asset to me.

Before dialing Shipley, I spent a couple of hours processing the information Graf had dug up and made some notes about the approach I was going to take.

"Mr. Shipley," I began, "this is Mark Willand. I'm sitting here looking at the letter you sent to my bank, telling them I have requested a loan from you, and you would like them to provide details about any loans I have with them."

There was a long silence.

"Do you want to tell me when I asked for a loan from you?"

"Well, uh, I guess I was a little reckless asking them about you."

"Why did you?"

"There's nothing illegal about that request," he said defensively. "I just thought if you had a lot of debt, my client might be willing to pay it off in addition to buying your ranch."

"Do you have a pen?"

He hesitated and said, "Sure. Why?"

"Write this number down."

I read off his Social Security number.

"Hey, that's mine! Where did you get that?"

"There is an investigation underway in regards to evidence of real estate fraud by you. Does that sound familiar?"

"That's none of your business!"

"You've been convicted of investment fraud and no longer have securities licenses. Is the public fully aware of both of these?"

Shipley didn't say anything for a moment. Finally, "What's this all about, anyway?"

"I'm not done. Do these two names sound familiar?' I stated the two client names that Graf had supplied.

"Again," he said with growing agitation, "none of your business."

"These two clients of yours are both under investigation for tax evasion, which you probably didn't even know. One of them, the first one I named, is probably the one that wants to buy my ranch so badly. Apparently, his grandparents lived in Upton at one time, and I'm guessing he wants to buy my ranch because it's close to town and he wants to be a weekend cowboy."

Shipley's voice grew louder. "You can't use any of this. We'll sue you!"

"Oh, I don't think you and your clients want to have all of your dirty laundry aired in court. Don't worry, I don't plan to use it. But if you don't drop all efforts to buy my ranch, somebody who also has this information will be posting all of it on Facebook."

"You wouldn't dare!"

"You aren't in much of a position to find out if I'm bluffing. You need to tell me right now what your decision is."

"I can't speak for my client."

I said, "In that case, you have one hour to let me know his decision." I ended the call.

Forty-five minutes later, Shipley called. He said there would be no more attempts to buy my ranch.

He'll never know I couldn't sell it for almost five years, anyway.

I called the ranch house and Zach answered. I asked him how his arm is healing.

"It's doing OK, other than my skin itches like the dickens under this cast. The doctor says he'll cut it off next week."

I told him that the California guy had promised to quit bugging us about selling the ranch, and that he should tell Patti. He was glad to hear that.

CHAPTER THIRTY-TWO

Rockford
April 10

Spring has arrived. It's a sunny, warm morning in Poplar Grove. The forecast calls for clear skies all the way. I file VFR for 4,500 feet and depart on runway 30. Winds are forecast for 30 knots on the nose most of the way, so an Ainsworth fuel stop will be wise.

It has been over a month since my last trip, and the color of the landscape along my flight path is dramatically different. It has changed from the monotone of winter to the green of spring's rebirth; the difference between looking at the same photograph in black and white, and in color.

The Upton runway comes into sight around noon, and after getting the F-250 out of the hangar, I push the plane in and depart for the ranch. I had alerted Patti, and the four of us will have a lunch meeting.

As I pull the Ford into the ranch yard, I see the new bunkhouse is framed, and two carpenters are installing siding. Looks like an April completion is within reach.

At lunch, we talk about the 4-H project, and Roy said the members were coming out tomorrow to see the horses.

"What time are you expecting them? I want to be sure to be here."

"It won't be until after school gets out, which is about three, so probably 3:15, or thereabouts."

"You know," I said, "this may turn into more than just a chance for the 4-H members to learn how to work with horses."

I recounted my visit to the Rockford stables that concentrate on helping troubled kids via equine therapy.

"For that matter, riding a horse can be therapy for anyone —

I know it is for me. I was talking about this last month with Aaron Rhodes, and he told me there are a couple of his club members he hopes can benefit in that way."

Patti, smiling playfully at Zach, said, "Let's just hope they all stay on the horses."

Zach put up a mild protest, and we all had a chuckle.

"By the way," added Patti, "I'd like to talk about the names for the six animals."

"Let's hear it," I said.

"All six have distinguishing marks. One has a half-moon white mark on his forehead, another has white stockings on both front legs, all of them have some marks that set them apart."

She held up a whiteboard with six numbers, and alongside each was a description of that animal's particular marking.

"Tomorrow, I'd like to ask the 4-Hers to agree on a name for each horse. Roy has put a halter on each animal with their number showing on it. As the animal is named, I'll put it on the whiteboard. We will hang the board in the stable and before long, I think the kids will know every animal's name without looking at the board. New members can learn the names from the board. I think the kids will feel more attached to the horses this way."

Roy told her it was a great idea. Zach and I agreed.

Changing topics, Zach said he and Roy had staked out the best area for more hay acreage. I told them one of my past dealerships had sold and installed Zimmatic Center Pivots, and asked them if they were planning to install a pivot or a traveling gun.

"The new area will be 110 acres, which will work well for a pivot," Zach said. "But a pivot costs a lot more than a traveling gun. We're wondering if it's wise to spend the extra money."

I reminded them of the much greater labor requirement to operate the gun as opposed to a center pivot. I asked Zach what the downside of a pivot would be.

"Just the extra initial cost."

"Long term, the extra investment will pay off. The pivot requires almost no labor. I think you should go that direction."

Zach said he would contact B & C Contractors, the Zimmatic dealer in Buffalo, Wyoming for a quote.

"OK," I said, slapping my palms on the table. "Enough ranching talk. Let's talk about the biggest event of this year: the wedding! Have you two decided when it will be?"

A smiling Patti said, "Zach still thinks mid-July would be best. The first cutting of hay will be complete, and Roy says he can easily take care of the irrigation on the old acreage."

Zach added, "Mark, would you be able to join us here for the wedding on Saturday, July 13? We would be gone for a week, and Roy already has a 4-H member that would help him while we are gone."

"I wouldn't miss it for anything! Have you thought about the location for the wedding and reception?"

Patti and Zach looked at each other. Patti said, "We want to have it right here on the ranch. Is that OK with you, Mark?"

"Absolutely! The ranch will pay all costs, including the reception. I paused and then added, "And your honeymoon. We want to pay for your honeymoon. Have you decided where you're going?"

Zach looked like he could hardly believe his ears.

Shaking his head, he said, "Mark, we can't ask you to pay for the wedding and the honeymoon, too."

"Well, number one, you didn't ask," I smiled. "And second, you two, along with Roy, allow me to be 800 miles away and not worry about everyday ranch decisions. I'm delighted to have a part in your wedding plans."

Roy spoke up to say he would take care of everything while they were gone.

"Roy, we are all glad you are here. Zach and Patti would probably have a very short honeymoon if you weren't."

Ranch house
April 3
3 a.m.

A knock on my bedroom door jolted me out of my sleep. It was Zach.

"Mark, the camera on the west boundary just sent an alert to my cell phone. The picture shows an old pickup pulling a horse trailer, heading south alongside our ranch border. I called the sheriff's department. A deputy wasn't far away and is heading there. He'll follow the truck in to see what's going on. They told me to come to the entrance and wait there. Do you want to come along?"

On our way to the pasture, Zach's phone rang. It was Roy, saying he'd gotten the alert, and wondered what was going. It was good to know the Arlo-Go works as designed. Ten minutes later, Zach and I were at the entrance to the boundary between the two ranches. A second deputy pulled up alongside us, told us to wait there, and went to back up the other deputy.

Fifteen minutes had passed when Zach's cell rang. We were told to join them about a mile ahead.

Both squads were parked alongside a battered pickup towing a banged up and dirty horse trailer. We could hear young calves jumping around inside the trailer and bawling. Several cows were milling alongside the fence, trying to get near the trailer and their calves.

The deputies were questioning a big man, about 250 pounds, scraggly beard, acting more confused than guilty. He claimed he had been hired to pick up a dozen calves, and he had to come at night because he worked a day job. He said he didn't think he was doing anything wrong.

Zach stormed up to him. "What the hell are you doing here? I'm the ranch manager. This man," throwing his arm in my direction, "is the ranch owner. Who hired you?"

"I don't know his name. He comes into the bar where I work

outside Four Corners, and yesterday paid me $100, gave me directions and said the cattle would be bedded down for the night near here. He said I could grab the calves that someone owed him, and he would pay me another $200 when I delivered them."

A deputy handcuffed him, read him his rights, and told him he was being arrested for cattle rustling. The man appeared totally bewildered. Putting aside the thought that he had to know he was stealing, it looked to me like someone was using him to do their dirty work.

One of the deputies said he'd called the sheriff, who said he wanted to take custody of the calves until they could determine who had ordered the theft. Zach said the calves were due to be weaned, anyway, so it was OK. The deputy said they would keep us informed.

Zach and I headed back to the ranch house. It would be dawn soon.

Later the same day
3 p.m.

Sheriff Wirth was on the phone.

"Mark, the rustler fell all over himself trying to cooperate. We wired him with a microphone, and trailed him back to near Four Corners with an unmarked car. When he delivered the calves to an abandoned holding pen as instructed, the guy drove up and told him to unload the calves and he would pay him. Our deputies were listening nearby, and when they heard that, they moved in and arrested him."

The sheriff paused.

"Mark," he resumed, "I've got a surprise for you."

"Is it a good surprise?"

"Well, I'll let you be the judge of that. The man we arrested is Judd Turner."

I couldn't even speak for a moment, I was so surprised.

"Him again!" I finally managed. "I know you aren't lying, Sheriff, but I can't believe he would do that, especially after how close he came to going to prison."

"As the old saying goes, Mark, you can't cure stupid, but you can watch it self-destruct. Turner will be out of your hair. We have plenty of evidence to put him away for a long time."

"My goodness, sheriff. What about the rustler?"

Wirth said he would recommend probation and a lot of community service. Apparently the man had barely survived through the years, hardly finished grade school and never went to high school. He was two months behind on his rent, and was desperate. He says when Turner described the reason for taking the calves, he believed the story. He cooperated in arresting Turner, and the district attorney gave him a pass regarding jail time.

At dinner I told Zach and Patti what had happened. They were as surprised as I had been, and found it hard to believe that Judd would be so stupid.

"Mark," Zach said, "that video gear just paid for itself." I agreed on that. I went to bed early.

Thursday, April 4
6:00 a.m.

Sunrise will be 6:33 this morning. I saddle Toby for a ride to The Hump, and just as we reach the top, the sun starts to appear on the horizon. The hills turn red, then orange, then pink as the sun gets higher over the hills. This never gets old. It's always different.

Riding back toward the stable, thoughts from yesterday come flooding back. What could Judd have possibly been thinking? Sheriff Wirth had told him back in February that he would be given immunity if he testified against Gotch. He was told at the same time to leave Weston County permanently.

Now he's arrested, again in Weston County, and this time he'll go to prison.

I recall years ago when my nephew Charley, a state trooper, told me a story about an arrest he made. While on patrol, he stopped a motorist for speeding. When Charley bent down to look into the car, he saw a pistol on the passenger seat. He asked the driver for a gun owner's permit and license to carry. The man had neither. This stop then became a criminal arrest instead of a speeding violation.

I asked Charley why the driver hadn't thought to hide the weapon as soon as he saw the flashing lights.

"Because he was stupid. In my years in law enforcement, most lawbreakers do stupid things, not thinking about the penalties if they get caught."

I thought about the sheriff's statement about "stupid" in reference to Judd. Apparently it's a pretty common theme across all levels of law enforcement. From the time Judd got caught stealing beer and up to this.latest arrest, he kept getting involved in thefts that now will send him to prison. Maybe it isn't that the crooks don't think about what will happen if they get caught. Maybe they don't think they will.

Before breakfast, I received a text about a visitation for a good friend who died recently back in Rockford. It is scheduled for tomorrow morning. At breakfast, I told the crew that I hated to miss the 4-H visit this afternoon, but needed to return to Rockford instead.

I called Galen Gingrich and told him about the overnight arrest. He was glad to hear about the mobile camera, said he appreciated the protection that it gave his ranch as well as mine. Maybe he's warming up to me a little.

This was a short trip, but not a dull one! None of them are.

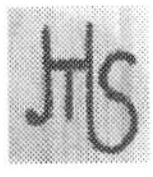

CHAPTER THIRTY-THREE

Poplar Grove Airport
Monday, April 22
10 a.m.

Heavy fog held up my departure, but it dissipated as I headed west, and by the time I crossed into Iowa, the skies were clear. Below, field work is underway wherever I look.

I arrived at the ranch in mid-afternoon and noticed the bunkhouse is now enclosed, and two carpenters are doing the interior finishing. Walking in to take a peek, I saw the center section looks complete, with kitchen installed. Bathrooms are almost done, and the two sleeping wings are being dry-walled.

Patti showed me pictures of the furniture and beds she purchased for the bunkhouse, and said they'll be delivered next week when the carpenters are finished.

"Looks like you've got it all under control, Patti. Tell me about your wedding plans."

That brought a glow to her face. "We've got the minister and caterer reserved. We've made a reservation at the Brown Palace in Denver for our honeymoon. I've never been to Denver, but Zach has, and we both want to explore the city and the area."

I found Roy in the stables. At one time, Luke and Jack Hale apparently had several horses, or at least thought they might, because the horse barn they built was large enough to accomodate our six recent additions.

Roy wanted to talk about horseshoeing.

"I think we should get a farrier out here," he said. "None of the ranch horses have been checked for a long time, and proper shoes are essential. There's a fella in Newcastle who came down to Douglas last year, and he really knows what he's doing. The animals will serve us better if they are properly shoed. Same goes for the six new horses. I think we should have him look at all of them, and Zach agrees. What do you think?"

I told him I agreed. I asked how the 4-H kids who came out to the ranch earlier in the month did with the horses.

"Oh, I think they're a pretty good group, Mark. As you know, some of them are ranch kids, so all of this is familiar. A few of them, though, haven't been around horses much, if at all, and were a little spooked by how big they are."

"Sure, that's natural. And do you think the horses are all of the right temperament?"

"Yep, I do," he smiled. "Our broncbuster and I ran them through their paces and they're ready to go."

I smiled at his reference to Zach.

"That reminds me, I was talking with a stable owner back home, and he said he always tries to match riders and horses based on size."

Roy agreed that made sense, and said he'd try to do that with the 4-H members. "A couple of them are, well, larger kids, so I'll try to put them with the biggest of the new horses."

At dinner, Zach told me the video camera on the west boundary had come into use again.

"Last Wednesday night about 11, I got another alert. The camera at our west boundary showed an old pickup had stopped near the entrance, right by the camera. There was no trailer, so I knew they couldn't be trying to steal cattle.

"After our last intruder, I put up a big *No Trespassing/Private Property* sign ahead of the camera, so that everyone would know they were on private property. Anyway, I called the sheriff's office, and they sent a deputy to meet me a half-mile nearer the highway. I got in and rode with him, and we came up right behind the pickup with our lights off.

"The deputy flipped on his headlights and flashers, and at the same time ordered the driver to exit the truck with his hands up. His loudspeaker even scared me, it was so loud."

Zach threw back his head, laughed, and continued the story.

"A teenage boy stumbled out of the truck, trying to button up his shirt, and at the same time trying to get his hands up in the air. From the passenger side, a girl about the same age jumped out, with her clothes all messed up, and put her hands over her head."

All three of us roared at that.

Zach said, "They were from Upton. He apologized for ignoring the no trespassing sign. He said three or four times they would never come here again. The girl was trying to hide her face.

"The deputy told them they could leave, and warned them next time they would be charged with trespassing. They turned around and hightailed it outta there.

"I've known the deputy since high school. We sat there for a while chuckling, and also knowing how scared we would have been in the same situation as teenagers when the flashing lights appeared out of nowhere!"

Tuesday, April 23
6 a.m.

It's a perfect spring morning for a look at the calf crop.

I saddled Toby and rode across to the North Pasture. Roy told me I would find a small herd there and a batch of new calves.

Sure enough, at least 30 calves were scampering everywhere, and their mothers were noisily trying to keep track of them. To me, the cows' moos all sounded the same, but maybe there was something unique in each one that the calves could identify as coming from their moms.

Spring flowers were in bloom wherever I looked. The rain over the weekend had helped turn everything green, and the sweet smell of the damp earth and sagebrush filled the air.

Two bulls were butting heads, each needing to prove his superiority.

Heading back for breakfast, I thought again about all that has happened since last September. I also thought about my ongoing search for a comfortable saddle. Part of my body was making it clear to me that the one I'm on is not the one.

Patti always goes all out making breakfast. She's a good cook. Gathered at the table, the four of us talk about all that's happened in the few weeks since my last visit.

Patti said the 4-H kids had a lot of fun naming the six horses, and the names are now posted on a stable wall.

Roy brought up a subject to discuss, admitting ahead of time that it was "off the wall."

"One of the kids said they had seen a buffalo on a ranch in Colorado. Some of the others started talking about that, and asked if we had any. I said no. They asked if they could start a fund-raising campaign, and buy one. They would make it an honorary member of their 4-H club. I laughed and said a buffalo would be expensive, but that I'd bring it up with the rest of you."

Zach said, "I'm not surprised the kids are curious about them. They're a huge part of our history here in Wyoming, but are a novelty now. I don't think there are any near here."

I thought about my friend's ranch south of here. "The ranch I visited for many years had a bison. There's actually a difference between bison and buffalo, and historians say there never were any buffalo in these parts, only bison. Anyway, every time I saw him, I rode close to him and thought about the history he represented. His ancestors roamed this part of the country by the thousands, heck, by the millions, before being nearly wiped out by white settlers. If you two want to come up with a program with the 4-H kids, I'm all for it. What if the ranch puts up a dollar for every dollar the kids raise, for a bison fund?"

Roy said he would talk to Aaron Rhodes.

As we were talking, Zach had been looking at his iPad. He said there were some single buffalo ads on the internet.

He whistled. "Wow. The kids are going to have to raise a lot of money. These ads show prices around $6,000."

As we moved on to other topics, Zach said he had ordered the center pivot for the new hay ground. It would be installed near the end of this month. That will double our hay acreage.

Ever since I was a kid on the farm I've looked forward to working with hay tools. As a teenager, I worked for a neighbor who did custom baling with a Case baler. It was wire-tie; he pushed and I tied. The dust eventually caused severe nosebleeds, and I had to quit.

I want to plan my future trips to the ranch so that I can run the CaseIH windrower we bought in the winter.

Upton
Tuesday Afternoon

I'm sitting in the office of Chuck Weinberg again.

"Chuck, back in March we discussed a plan for you to train Patti and Zach. Have you had a chance to start that?"

"Sure have, Mark. I had a session with both of them March 20, and another on April 10. We plan one more in May. They are both good students. Patti already knew how to use Quicken, and is learning a new records system that I started her on.

"Zach is really anxious to run your ranch properly. He asked me to find him some homework materials on business management. He knows more about good business practices than he realizes, and he wants to keep learning."

I thanked him, and headed for the ranch. During the drive, I thought about the crook the ranch used to have as a CPA. I'll always be grateful to Todd Davig for recommending that I retain Chuck. He's working out really well.

Back at the ranch, I walked to the back of the machine shed, and again looked at the two old Farmalls. Some tractors are abandoned in fields or pastures when they've outlived their usefulness, and just rust away, or animals rub on them and tear them apart. Luke and Jack did a good thing by parking these two out of the elements. The paint is in bad shape, but there doesn't appear to be much, if any, rust. As I walk around the tricycle front, there's no metal damage to speak of.

I blow off and brush away some dust and climb up to take a seat behind the wheel of the Super M-TA. The seat groans. It hasn't had any weight on it for a long time. Some of the knobs and gauges will need replacing, but the International Harvester Collectors Club is a great source of replacement parts. Sitting here, I'm more convinced than ever this will be a good project for the local FFA chapter. I'll stop by the school tomorrow morning on my way to the airport, and talk to the Vo-Ag instructor.

Upton High School
Wednesday morning

The high school office told me where I would find the Vocational Agriculture teacher.

Glen Baysinger was in his office adjoining a large shop with an overhead door. No class was in session. I told him who I was, and he recognized my name.

"Mr. Willand, I'm familiar with the 4-H project at your ranch. Aaron Rhodes told me about it, and two of my FFA members are also part of the 4-H club. That's a great thing you're doing."

I told him I had been a member of FFA and 4-H during high school.

"Let me explain why I came to see you. The ranch has a couple of old Farmalls stored in a corner of the machine shed. They haven't been running for many years. I'm a member of a large national organization, International Harvester Collectors Club. The mission of the group is to keep the IH logo alive, and help people who are restoring or collecting International tractors. Members of the organization have helped FFA members restore tractors as projects in other states."

"Yes sir, I've heard of that."

"Here's my offer: If your FFA members were to tackle the restoration of our old Super M-TA, and we could locate some IHCC members in this area who would help direct the project, I would donate the tractor and pay for the parts needed. Your members could then sell it and the chapter could keep the money."

Baysinger smiled and seemed amazed at the offer. "That's an incredibly generous gesture, Mr. Willand. I'll need to talk to the members, see what they think, and clear it with our school principal. Is it possible you could locate members of the Collector's Club who would help us? That's probably the first step, because if we don't have that expert guidance, I don't think we'll be able to do it."

I nodded my agreement. "Why don't we start there, then, and if I find someone, I'll be back in touch."

Wheels up by 10:30, and I was back in the air, en route home. Another interesting trip to the Halestone!

CHAPTER THIRTY-FOUR

Rockford
Monday, April 27

The Farmall project has been on my mind since returning last week. I got the ball rolling by calling the membership office of International Harvester Collectors Club, and asked if they had any members with Upton, Wyoming, addresses. I thought it was a long shot, but they had one. A long-timer named Helmer Ross. I dialed his number.

"Mr. Ross, my name is Mark Willand. I'm a member of International Harvester Collectors Club. I'm told that you're also a member."

"You betcha, I have been for a long time. And Helmer will do, thanks. I retired from a ranch up north and moved to the Upton area 10 years ago. I've been keeping busy restoring old IH tractors. Completed three and I'm working on another. Do you live in Upton?"

I gave him a quick version of my Rockford-Upton connection.

"Well that's a coincidence. I knew Jack Hale. I was trying to buy one of his old tractors before he took ill. I was sure sorry to hear that he had passed."

"Helmer, those old Farmalls are why I'm calling."

"Do you want to sell them?"

"Not exactly. I was a member of the Future Farmers of America when I was in high school here in Illinois. I think highly of the organization, and when I heard that Upton High School has an FFA chapter, it got me thinking. I talked to Glen Baysinger, the Vo-Ag instructor who mentors the FFA chapter. I told him I would donate our Super M-TA to his chapter, along with all necessary parts, if his kids would like to restore it as a fund-raiser. He thought it would be a great idea, if someone that is experienced in restoration would mentor the project.

"That's why I called you, Helmer. Would you have any interest in being their advisor on this?"

Helmer was quiet for a moment.

"Now, let me get this straight. Mark, was it?"

"Yes sir, Mark Willand."

"Well, Mark, did you say you would donate the tractor and all the parts?

"Yes, I did."

"That could be a lot of money if it was done right. Tires, paint, muffler, god knows whatever internal parts that may be needed? You would pay for all that?"

"Yes, and I would want it to be done properly, so the members would learn something and be proud of it. And, as you know, not many of that model were built, and the market is strong for it. It should be a good fundraiser."

"Yep, when it's done, it'll be worth good money. The M has always brought good money from collectors, but the SMTA is a lot more valuable. There were 270,000 Ms built, but only 26,924 were SMTAs."

I was impressed with his ready knowledge of the numbers.

"So, Mark, my answer is I would be glad to work on the project. I've got a good friend who helps me work on my tractors. I'm sure he will help as well."

We talked at length about IHCC and all the effort being made to keep the IH brand alive.

"You know, Helmer, I'm convinced IH is as popular as it's ever been. There's a whole new generation, heck, two generations now, of IH fans who hadn't been born yet when the company fell apart in 1984."

I told Helmer that Glen Baysinger would be calling him. I then called Glen with the news. He said their principal was in favor of the project, and he would talk to the FFA members, make sure they were willing to take on the project, and then he'd call Helmer.

I didn't mention the 560 Diesel in our shed. The Super M-TA will be a less complicated restoration. If it goes well, we can consider the 560 as a later project.

Rockford
Wednesday, April 29

The Caller ID shows my neighbor is calling.

"Mark, this is Galen Gingrich, at the ranch next door. I'd like to stop in and talk if you're available."

"I'm back in Illinois right now, Galen. The aviation museum I'm involved in here is about to have a big event, and I'm helping. I'm coming out to Upton on May sixth. Can it wait till then?"

"Well sir, let me tell you what's on my mind, and you can think about it before you come on the sixth. I'm seriously thinking about selling my place, and moving to Arizona for good. Our ranches share a lot of fence line, and I'm calling you to see if you would be interested."

This catches me by surprise. Why on earth would I want a second ranch?

"Galen, from what I saw when you invited me over, you have a great setup. Do you really want to quit ranching?"

"I've given it a lot of thought, Mark. I just turned 70, and we really like Arizona. When we packed up to come back a month ago, I hated to leave. That's when I started thinking about selling out."

"Well, I'm sure you won't have any trouble finding a buyer. Let me think about it, and if you want to get together after I come out, we can talk some more. I really doubt that I would want to grow that much bigger, but I'll give it some thought."

Galen said he wasn't going to put the ranch on the market until the summer, and that he would like to talk more when I get there in ten days. We left it at that.

Wow! Six months ago I was about to acquire a Wyoming ranch, and now someone wants me to have a second one. I see no reason to be interested in Galen's place, but it's always wise to think twice about any opportunity.

In a little over four years, the restriction on the sale of Halestone Ranch will be ending. That's a long way down the road, too far to be wondering what I'll do at that time. If land values in ranch country were going to escalate during that time, maybe buying Galen's place would make sense. But I'm also well aware that what goes up also goes down. Land values around Northern Wyoming could go down as well, during the next few years.

Would a much larger acreage be more salable, if I decide to sell out four years from now? No one can give me that answer.

I can't see any reason why I would want to take on a second place. I'll meet with Galen just to see what he's thinking regarding price.

I wonder what his acreage is? He didn't say and I didn't ask.

But I'm not interested, anyway.

Certainly the equity I have in Halestone Ranch would be more than enough to obtain a mortgage.

Anyway, I'm not interested.

CHAPTER THIRTY-FIVE

Halestone Ranch
Monday, May 6
1 p.m.

The bunkhouse is complete. The furniture Patti bought is in place, and 4-H members have already made themselves at home, posting awards on the walls that the club has received through the years.

According to Roy, the members are delighted to have their own meeting room. He's been scheduling riding lessons with several members. Aaron Rhodes is working each week with other members on various projects.

I called Galen Gingrich as promised, and we arranged to meet tomorrow at the Upton Coffee Shop.

Zach and I saddled up and rode out to see how the new Zimmatic center pivot is doing. We were almost there when Toby jumped sideways. We stopped.

Zach looked at me and spoke. "Did you hear the rattle?"

I hadn't.

He pointed to a nearby bush. A rattlesnake lay curled underneath. Zach dismounted, removed the cinch from his saddle and walked near the snake. He snapped the cinch like a whip, and the steel buckle on the end of the cinch virtually beheaded the snake. He picked up the snake and put it in his saddlebag.

I looked at him. "Wow! You've done that before!"

"Yep. Not often. We don't have many rattlers here on the ranch, but now there's one less."

"Is that a Diamondback? I asked."

"Nope, kinda looks like one, but they don't come this far north

That one's a prairie rattler."

Continuing to the pivot, we found the new seeding is already turning green as a result of the steady watering. This will almost double our hay acreage, and allow us to sell more hay to other ranches. Zach says we'll get one cutting, maybe two this year. It looks like a sound investment.

Upton Coffee Shop
Tuesday, May 7

Galen and I arrive at the same time. He again thanked me for installing the video camera, and we had a chuckle about the teenagers who got treated to a visit by Zach and the deputy sheriff.

Galen got down to business quickly. "Mark, between now and October, I want to sell my ranch."

"Yes sir, I understand that. I'll tell you again, though, that I'm not looking to take on another ranch. But, I am curious about how big of a spread you have."

"You know, it used to be big, but by today's standards it isn't. There are 6,000 acres deeded, and another 2,000 acres leased. I'm sure you know as well as I, that only about 200 head can fit on that."

I nodded.

"My neighbor to the west has expanded farther in that direction, and doesn't have any interest in my place. To me, it makes sense for you to buy it and combine our ranches. You could easily run both places as one operation."

I gave him a slight nod and took a sip of my coffee.

"Galen, I really like being involved with Halestone. I've only had it eight months, and I'm just getting it organized. It's a good size, and the two men I have are handling it well. I can't see any sense in throwing more work at them."

"Let me give you a little background so you know I didn't just pull this idea out of thin air."

"Sure," I said, "go ahead."

"Three years ago, I talked to Jack on this same subject. That was before he got sick. At that time, he had some interest in buying me out, because he said the equipment he had was enough to handle more acreage. Then he got sick, poor guy, and I gave up the whole idea of selling. Now I'm again thinking I would like to retire and stay year-round in Arizona. You, sir, would be the one who would benefit the most from buying my place."

"Besides yourself, you mean." I smiled.

He smiled back. "Yes, besides me."

"Just do this, Mark," he continued. "Think about it. If you will do that, I'll not list it with a realtor until July 1."

Then he wrote on a napkin and handed it to me. He had written the exact acreage and the price he wanted per acre. I put it in my pocket.

"OK, Galen. I'll give it some thought. But not very much. In the meantime, tell me about Arizona. Why do you like it so much?"

Galen told me all about his place in the Valley of the Sun.

"Do you plan on living there in the summer, too? I hear it gets hotter than Hades."

"Yep, year-round. We have air conditioning that'll keep us comfy and a pool I can go float in. What we don't spend staying warm in the winter, we'll spend staying cool in the summer."

I promised to keep in touch. He bought the coffee and I went back to Halestone. As I drove I thought about the offer, but I can't get very excited about more acreage. Maybe I'll talk about it with Zach on my next trip out here.

Tuesday afternoon

Glen Baysinger called.

"Mr. Willand, I talked to Helmer Ross about the Farmall, and he's interested in helping our FFA chapter restore it. Our chapter members are 100% for the project. This is the most exciting thing to happen here in quite a while. I've got a couple of graduating seniors who are jealous that they won't be able to work on it."

I smiled to myself.

"Two of the boys said their dads would probably also help. I cleared it again with my principal, who said we could go ahead on it. Are you still willing to do this?"

"Absolutely. I know you still have a couple of weeks of school remaining. We can truck the Farmall to your shop this week if you want it now."

He said that would give them time to start planning the disassembly before the school year ended. I told him Zach would let him know when it would be delivered.

Wednesday, May 8
5 a.m.

Sunrise is scheduled for 5:41. Perfect time to pour some coffee into a Thermos, saddle Toby and ride to The Hump in time to see the sun blaze over the eastern horizon again.

Riding Toby in the pre-dawn light is always a thrill. Off to my right, a mourning dove sings his sad song. A couple hundred yards ahead, two mule deer trot across my path. As I move in rhythm with Toby, I'm trying to think of the right word to describe this moment and how I feel. Then it comes to me. Serene.

The sky lightens on a clear morning and I get to the top of The Hump a few minutes early. Sipping on my coffee, I check my watch. Right at 5:41, just as advertised, the sun appears over the horizon and splashes all the amazing colors of a new morning on the hills around me. What a special place to greet the new day. Serene, indeed.

On the way back to the ranch, my mind drifts back to my discussion with Galen Gingrich. I decide that this should be a project for Zach to consider, not me.

After breakfast Zach and I inspect the new bunkhouse. We pulled up chairs to one of the meeting tables, and I explained to him that Gingrich wanted to sell. I said no more, just waited for him to respond. I've noticed that Zach never starts talking until he's had time to think. I respect that. Finally, he looked up and his eyes met mine.

"Mark, sometime back, Jack told me Gingrich had suggested we combine his ranch with Halestone. A few weeks later, he told me that he had thought it over, and decided against it. Even though we could run 200 to 250 additional cows on that acreage, there were just two of us to do the work, and it would spread us too thin. It wasn't too long after that he got sick, so the conversation never came up again."

He paused, and then asked, "What do you think about it?"

I told him I had no opinion either way, and that Gingrich wanted us to give it some thought before he listed it with a realtor July 1.

"Zach, I tell you what. I'd like you to give some careful thought to this. Assume that you own Halestone Ranch. Gingrich has approached you to buy his place, a little over 6,000 acres with 2,000 leased acres. You will need a mortgage, and you want the income from this purchase to cover the mortgage payments.

"Calculate how much you will need to invest in the brood cows, bulls, feed, maintenance, labor and all the other costs such as you have here at Halestone Ranch. Will you need more machinery? Don't leave out any potential costs of owning and operating the new location."

He nodded.

"Then, determine how much profit you can expect yearly from livestock sales, and any other sources of revenue. I'd like you to use Patti's help on this. She's a good accountant. Let her draw up a sample profit and loss statement, as well as cash flow figures. Also use our CPA Weinberg if you need his help."

"Will do."

"After you have the numbers together, you and I will go to Tom Westedt, show him what you've come up with, and see what he thinks about a loan. I am willing to consider purchase of the Gingrich place, but only if your figures support it as a good investment. You are the one putting these numbers together. The price we would then offer to pay Gingrich would be based on how large a mortgage the place would support."

"OK."

"One more thing. This should be kept entirely quiet. You can include Roy to get his input, but otherwise no one but you, Patti and the CPA should know we are considering this. I would like to see your figures within a month, and I'll schedule a trip here when you are ready for us to see the banker."

Zach felt he could be ready in a month.

Newcastle
First National Bank with Tom Westedt
11 a.m.

"Tom, within a month, Zach Talty and I may bring a proposal to you. Galen Gingrich wants to sell us his ranch. I've asked Zach to run the numbers on what it would cost to take on that ranch as part of our operation. He and my bookkeeper will see if the proceeds from the added acreage will cash flow after all expenses. If it looks feasible, and Zach is comfortable with the added work, we will both come in and let you look at it. If you will consider a mortgage based on a specific purchase price, and we can service the mortgage entirely from the new location, I will consider buying the place."

Tom smiled and said, as I knew he would, that with the huge equity I had in Halestone Ranch, a mortgage would not be a problem.

An hour later I was in the air, en route to Rockford, thinking about all that happens every trip.

CHAPTER THIRTY-SIX

Rockford
May 13
9 a.m.

Sheriff Ron Wirth is calling from Newcastle. Even though I like the man, there's always a bit of apprehension when I see his number pop up. It's never a social call.

"Good morning, Sheriff. What's happening in Weston County?"

"Oh, a little bit of everything and a whole lot of nothing, Mark. Good morning to you, too. I'm calling about Judd Turner."

"Uh-oh. What now?"

"No," he chuckled, "no new mayhem to report. Remember last month when we arrested him for trying to steal your cattle, and you said you would testify about his cash thefts when he was running Halestone Ranch? Are you still willing to testify?"

"Absolutely, if it will help prosecute him."

"It sure will. Our district attorney will be in touch in the near future. The court calendar is jammed up, so it will be the first week of September before the trial starts."

"I'll be there. You and your deputies have helped our ranch every time we call. I'll be glad to testify."

After we disconnected, I sat and thought about Judd Turner. He was good-looking, intelligent, capable, and if his attitude had been better, I would have kept him on the ranch.

Instead, his past and stupid mistakes have caught up with him, and he will likely spend a lot of time behind bars.

If the judge will allow it, I would like to talk to him after I testify, and encourage him to set goals for his time in prison. He could get an on-line college degree, choose a career and prepare himself for life after prison. He still has a lot of life ahead of him.

I've often heard the term "recidivism." I Googled the exact definition of the word:

The tendency of a convicted criminal to reoffend.

Maybe Judd can be encouraged to avoid that. Everyone needs a push in the right direction.

Rockford
May 20
3:30 p.m.

Zach is on the phone.

"Mark, Patti and I will have our recommendation regarding the Gingrich ranch ready by Friday. She has been the lead on this and, with the CPA's help, put together a lot of questions. The three of us got together several nights after work, and filled in the blanks. We will be ready to go over everything with you anytime after Friday."

"I'll come out Tuesday."

Poplar Grove Airport
Tuesday, May 28
7 a.m.

I lift off through a thin layer of fog into clear skies. Scattered showers are predicted over Iowa, mostly north of my route. I've filed IFR direct Omaha, then Ainsworth direct. I'll file VFR from Ainsworth to Upton. This will keep me south of the predicted showers.

Everything in sight is green. Corn and beans are well along, I'm at 6,000 feet today, and from this altitude visibility is great. I click on the autopilot and look down at the occasional low clouds.

Halestone Ranch
Lunch

Reading the faces and body language, I have a feeling I know what the recommendation will be regarding the purchase of the Gingrich ranch. Eagerness fills the room. During lunch, Zach explains again how the three of them worked together and with the CPA to come up with a recommendation.

After lunch they each made a presentation. Roy went first.

"Zach and I toured the Gingrich ranch. Galen stopped in one day and invited us, so we took him up on it. Mark, if we did end up with that ranch, Janis and I would like to rent the house. It's nicer than what we now have in Upton, and closer to Halestone. The distance is almost seven miles by road, but Zach and I took an ATV ride between here and the Gingrich headquarters, and the distance is about three miles as the crow flies. We think we could carve out a road between the two with the old Cat grader."

I smiled. "I'd like to see that old Cat at work," I said. "By the way," I added, "crows don't always fly in a straight line, so I hope you don't use one of them as your guide."

That gave everyone a good laugh.

"The machine shed is in good shape," Roy continued, "and after Gingrich sells his equipment, we think the building would be ideal for storage of boats, campers and trailers. There's no space like that in the area, and it could be a good revenue source. If Janis and I lived in that house, she could oversee the rentals.

"Zach asked me to evaluate our hay crop. With the new acreage under the center pivot, I'm sure we will have enough hay for the additional cattle on the Gingrich ranch."

Patti was next.

"Chuck helped me develop expense categories and profit potential for this project. Zach and Roy have filled in the blanks. We spent a lot of time on two categories. First was purchase price of the cattle for the new location. Zach and Roy both felt we could put 200 head on that land. Zach went on-line for current prices of bred heifers mixed with bred cows. That's the cost we used.

"Second, is a category we called 'Miscellaneous.' It includes items like vet bills, extra machinery repair due to additional use, fence and building repairs at the new site, and an extra lump sum for unexpected expenses.

"One source of revenue I think you should decide, Mark, is rent for the Gingrich home if Roy rented it. The other is an estimate of revenue from campers and motor homes in the machine shed over there. Do you have any thoughts on that?"

I nodded, and said, "Yes. I do. Assume Roy would pay no rent. Having him and his wife living there would be a big benefit to keep an eye on the herd and the property. Also, as Roy mentioned, Janis could oversee the rentals in the machine shed. So leave those categories both blank for the moment."

Roy turned to me.

"That would put us in the nicest home we've ever lived in, Mark."

"Roy, you've become a vital part of this team. I hope this works out."

Looking back to Patti and Zach, I asked, "Are you ready to summarize your recommendation?"

"Yes," Zach said. "Weinberg gave us a formula to use for estimating revenue from the annual sale of calves. He gave us the sale price average for the past five years. Roy and I decided to use the lowest three years' prices, and take an average of those three. That's what we gave Patti to use for income from livestock sales.

"We put in no income from hay sales, assuming we would use all of it between new and old locations. We aren't including any cost for additional machinery. What we have is enough for both places.

"We think the cost of additional labor will be small. Several of the 4-H kids will want part-time jobs with us every year. We will need them mostly during the summers.

"What we don't know, is how much the mortgage payments will be, but unless they are really big, we'll be able to turn a profit."

Zach handed me the calculations that Patti had prepared. There was a lot of detail. They had done a lot of homework.

Last week at home, I had estimated the annual mortgage payments if we gave Gingrich his asking price. Patti's calculations indicate that if we gave him his price, the mortgage payments would put the entire project in the red.

Despite the enthusiasm these three have for taking on the Gingrich ranch, I'm not sure it is a sound decision for me.

First National Bank, Newcastle
Wednesday, May 29
11 a.m.

Zach and I sat down in Tom Westedt's office and I told him that Zach, Patti and Roy had done the research on a possible purchase of the Gingrich ranch. I asked Zach to present his case to Tom.

Ten minutes later, Zach was finished.

Tom looked at me.

"Mark, what's Gingrich asking for the place?"

I gave him the acreage and the asking price. I added that, according to my estimates, we would have to buy the place at a considerably lower figure in order to break even on the operation annually. I asked him for his suggestion of a purchase price that would be low enough to provide a positive cash flow.

Tom stood up. "Why don't you two go next door for a cup of coffee, and come back in a half-hour. I'll have a figure for you then."

Zach was nervous. He barely touched his coffee, which seemed wise. Caffeine is not what his body needed at that moment.

"Doggone it, the numbers don't look good, Mark. I was really hoping this could work."

"I know you, Patti and Roy were hoping this could work. But it's good to do our due diligence, be a little patient, and not rush into a decision we may wind up regretting."

"Buyer's remorse," he said.

"Yes, exactly. Let's see what number the banker comes up with. If it isn't too far from what Gingrich wants, maybe we can make it work."

He nodded his agreement.

When we returned to Tom's office, he gave us an annual mortgage payment that left a considerable operating surplus annually, after all expenses and the mortgage. But, it was based on a purchase price of $90 less per acre than Gingrich is asking.

I thanked him, and we drove back to the ranch. I told Zach he had done a fine job of research, and that I would be making an offer to Gingrich in the near future.

Later than afternoon, I was finally able to meet the 4-H members, and I watched Roy giving riding instructions to two of them.

Inside the meeting room, Aaron Rhodes and I observed another group making plans to do a car wash in Upton to raise money for their "buffalo project." They're very enthusiastic, and their goal is to raise enough money by next spring, that with the ranch's match, will get them their mascot.

Aaron said the ranch involvement and the new clubhouse has attracted several new members. Two members have been chosen to work as interns this summer at the ranch, to help Zach and Roy.

Thursday, May 30
Homeward bound

After breakfast, Zach and I saddled up and rode out to the new hay ground. The regular watering from the center pivot continues to work its magic on the new crop.

"I think we will be able to take a first cutting off this ground in two weeks. This is the earliest we've ever cut hay."

"I'm pretty impressed by this Zimmatic," I said. "They've come a long way since the first ones I sold many years ago. These have state-of-the-art components, are much more efficient in their use of water, the application of chemicals and fertilizer, and, as we talked about, there's a big saving on labor. I'm expecting a solid return on this investment."

He pulled out his phone. "I don't think I've shown you this, Mark. This is the app that allows me to control the pivot. When I water, how long, how much water. It's pretty slick."

Amazing. I told him I would come out June 17-19, and would like to run the new windrower.

Upton
Thursday afternoon
1 p.m.

After running the pickup through a car wash, I drove to the airport, pulled the T-210 out of the hangar and put the Ford in its place.

There's a forecast for clear skies all the way to Poplar Grove Airport, and a strong tailwind above 6,000 feet. I filed VFR for 9,500 feet to take advantage of the wind.

Wheels up a little past 1:30. As I climb, I again appreciate the turbocharger. It allows me to maintain a 1,000 climb rate and reach altitude quickly. In bad weather, when I want to climb quickly to reach clear skies, the turbo is a life saver — figuratively, and potentially literally.

At 9,500 feet, I let the autopilot take over, and thought about the Gingrich project. It's risky, and I'm not sure I want that at this age. I need to take a hard look at it this weekend before I call him with a counteroffer.

CHAPTER THIRTY-SEVEN

Rockford
Monday, June 10

An invitation came in the mail today. The design was western-themed, and it said Barbara and I were invited to participate in the joyful union of Patricia Malik and Zachary Talty. The wedding will be Saturday, July 13, at Halestone Ranch, Upton, Wyoming.

I held the invitation, thinking back over the events of the past eight months, how much has happened, and how quickly it happened. I recalled meeting Zach for the first time at the motel in late September. Two weeks later at the ranch, I met Patti for the first time.

Both have been invaluable during this transition. I'm delighted they have decided to spend their lives together. The wedding also makes it more likely that they will both continue with their jobs on the ranch. That's good for them, good for Halestone, and good for me!

Two days later, my phone screen shows Galen Gingrich calling.

"Good morning, Mark. Are you in Upton or Rockford?"

"I'm here at home in Rockford, Galen. I'll be back out next week on the 17th. We've got hay under a new center pivot that'll be ready, and I'll cut it on the 18th. That's one of my favorite jobs."

He wasn't in the mood for small talk and got right to the point.

"Have you decided if you are interested in my place?"

He's anxious. We're three weeks away from his July 1 deadline. That's good for me.

"Yes, Galen, I am interested. But only if I can pay a price that will allow us to make money. I asked all three of my employees along with our CPA to do an analysis. I understand Zach and Roy visited your place on your invitation, and that helped. I've been back out and discussed it with them, as well as with our banker Tom Westedt.

"I'll make you an offer now of $120 less per acre than you asked. If you want to consider that, let's meet at the same coffee shop in Upton at eight next Wednesday morning, the 19th."

Galen took a moment to respond.

"Boy, that's an awful big hit for me to take, Mark. If I list it with a realtor next month, it'll get exposure all over the country."

"Yes. That's true. However, the realtor's fees would be substantial. You won't have that expense with our offer."

Another moment of silence.

"Well, let me think on it," he said. "Let's meet anyway, on the 19th."

After we disconnected, I called Alan Creston, gave him all the details, and asked him to draw up a contract to purchase, leaving the purchase price blank, with an October 1 closing. I told him I would pick it up at his office before noon on June 17, and he said it would be ready.

Overflying Halestone and Gingrich Ranches
Monday, June 17
11 a.m.

This is the first time I've flown over Halestone Ranch since last September. The circle of green under the new center pivot stands out prominently. I can't wait to run the windrower tomorrow.

Flying west, I can see the boundary between Halestone and the Gingrich property. I flew a tight circle around the Gingrich buildings. They all looked to be in excellent condition, which confirms what Zach and Roy told me. Most of the topography of the ranch is similar to Halestone, but with more wooded acreage on the west boundary. Less grazing land there.

It will be interesting to hear what Galen has to say Wednesday at the coffee shop. I expect him to reject my offer and list it with a realtor, and that's OK. We don't need it if it's a drag on Halestone finances.

Perfect weather made today's flight ideal. I drove down to Newcastle and stopped in briefly at Alan Creston's office to pick up the contract. I thanked Alan for the effort, but told him I didn't expect to use it because I had no interest in paying what Gingrich is asking, and I doubt he wants to take what I'm offering.

I stopped in Upton to pick up lunch for the ranch. I'd told Patti I'd bring food because she was probably busy with wedding plans.

During lunch, Patti said the wedding was going to be bigger than they expected, because she and Zach had decided to invite all the neighboring ranchers, as well as friends and relatives. RSVPs were coming in steadily. Roy had recommended a country-western trio to play at the reception, and a caterer had been booked. She said she was doing her best to keep the cost down. I told her I appreciated that, but to do it right.

After lunch. Zach and I took ATVs and rode to the new hay ground. It's ready for cutting, and I'll bring the new windrower out in the morning and get started. Zach said he would bale two days later.

At dinner Zach talked about his trip to the high school Vo-Ag department, to see the progress on the Farmall rebuild.

"Even though school is out for the summer, Baysinger has started taking our old Super M apart. Helmer Ross is supervising the teardown, and two of the Vo-Ag students are helping. They're making a list of parts they need, and one of the students put up a poster of a similar model, fully restored, as an example of what this one will look like."

Roy talked about how the 4-H riding lessons are going.

"Right now, there are three kids learning to ride, and others come out once a week and ride the South Pasture. Those six horses you and Zach bought are getting a workout. The whole club has a lot of pride in their programs here, and the clubhouse and horses have provided Aaron with everything he needs for a successful program."

Patti added a new twist to the 4-H program.

"Some of the girls in the club want to learn how to cook. Many of their mothers work and don't have the time. Aaron told me the high school doesn't teach Home Ec anymore, so this fall, I'm going to help them learn some simple dishes. I never thought I would be acting as a Home Ec teacher, but it should be fun. And one of the boys wants to join the class."

Zach smiled and said, "That's a wise boy. I spent a lot of years cooking for myself, and some lessons would have come in handy."

No one mentioned the Gingrich ranch. I haven't told them I'm meeting with Galen Wednesday.

Just before we left the dinner table, Zach announced that he had something for me.

"Do you remember the rattlesnake we killed?"

I said I sure did. I almost departed the saddle when Toby side-stepped away from the rattle.

Zach pulled out the skin. "We dried the skin and made it into a hatband. If you leave your Resistol with Patti tonight, she will replace your hatband with the skin and also the rattle. From now on you'll be wearing a Halestone rattlesnake."

This really touched me. Every trip, I become more connected with this ranch.

It's been a full day. I was ready to sleep eight hours.

Machine shed
Tuesday
7:30 a.m.

Zach and I checked over the windrower from one end to the other. He'd already serviced it and it was ready to go. I drove it out to the new hay. It felt good to be at the controls, and after trying several different rates of speed, I settled back to do one of my favorite jobs — cutting hay! The sweet smell as it's cut is one of the reasons I like this job.

I've never used a swather as modern as this one. It's quiet, smooth and lays a windrow without any effort.

The day passed quickly, and when not focusing on the task at hand, I thought about tomorrow's meeting with Galen Gingrich.

Upton Coffee Shop
Wednesday
8 a.m.

Galen is sitting in a booth drinking coffee when I walk in.

Based on our past conversations, I wasn't expecting him to talk about anything other than the sale of his ranch. Not much for small talk, this one. But right off the bat, he surprised me.

"Mark, I got an invitation to the wedding at your place."

"Good, Galen. Zach and Patti told me they were planning on inviting you."

"I bet you're happy about those two getting married."

"Absolutely. They have worked hard to keep everything going since Jack died, and I'm delighted for them, and for the ranch."

"My wife and I plan on being there."

"Good, I'll get to meet her, and you'll get to meet Barbara."

And that was the end of the chit-chat.

He had a file folder on the table in front of him. He opened it, looked at it, then looked up.

"Mark, you said last week that you were stuck on a price $120 an acre below what I asked. Is that still where you stand?"

Rather than give him an immediate yes or no answer, I said, "First of all, thanks for inviting Zach and Roy to see your place. I gave them the job of analyzing the possible purchase, and that visit helped them. A lot of time went into this project. Patti and our CPA created a series of questions, and then Zach and Roy did the research. A few weeks ago, I was back out here and we spent a day talking about it."

Galen maintained his gaze.

I continued. "That's how we came up with the $120 discount, and, yes, that's where I stand."

I took a sip of coffee as Galen continued to look at me, silently.

"Let me run this by you, Mark. I'm willing to discount $65, and include in the deal 200 head of Angus, mixed heifers and cows, all bred by a closing date of October 1."

I put my file on the table and opened it. I found Zach's estimate of what 200 cattle would cost. I subtracted that from the purchase price and calculated a new price per acre. With the cattle thrown in, Galen's $65 counteroffer was equivalent to $105. At only $15 below my starting offer, it was well above Tom Westedt's healthy cash flow target of a $90 discount, so Galen's offer would allow plenty of room for us to make mortgage payments.

I put my pen down, looked up and said, "Well, that sure gets us closer to where we need to be. Let's talk some more."

And for the next half-hour, we discussed the Angus he was including in the proposal. We talked about the acreage that is wooded on the west boundary, which has no value for grazing. He proposed that they would leave all the furniture in the house, because their Arizona home is furnished already. Hand tools in the machine shed would be left behind as well.

Finally, I thumbed through the papers in my file, took out the purchase offer, smiled and said, "Galen, you just sold your ranch!"

We filled in the final price and a closing date of October 1, and both signed. I gave Galen a check for $100,000 to secure the purchase. We shook hands, and both of us left the coffee shop happy.

Back at the ranch, Zach, Patti and Roy were all off somewhere. I had the place to myself for the first time in quite a while. I saddled Toby and headed for The Hump.

Climbing to the top, I sat for a long time thinking about all that had happened that led to my sitting up here.

Only nine months ago, Alan Creston called to tell me I was in Jack Hale's will. A lot has occurred since, including a lot of bad things, like murder, drug trafficking, cattle rustling, and embezzling.

But the good outweighs the bad.

Love blossomed and a ranch marriage is imminent.

I've got a team of three, Zach, Patti and Roy, now running the operation, and doing it really well.

With the added help of my trusted associates Alan Creston, Chuck Weinberg and Tom Westedt, I'm able to be an absentee owner.

The Upton 4-H club has a new clubhouse along with six horses to use.

The Farmall Super M-TA that Luke Hale bought in 1954 is getting a new life at the high school.

I still want to find a good home for the 560 diesel. Maybe we should donate the 560 to Helmer's IHCC Chapter 40. Let's see how the Super M project goes.

Maybe we should renovate the old International pickup for the ranch. I had one just like it as a "company car" when I was a Harvester zone manager.

Enough reminiscing for one day.

Looking out over this land, my thoughts turn to this morning's meeting with Galen. As a result of that session, Halestone Ranch will grow more than 50% and encompass over 17,000 acres with 500 head of cattle.

I shift in the saddle as Toby grazes. I am reminded I still need to find a more comfortable saddle.

I think about the stipulation in the Hale Trust that I must maintain ownership for another four years and three months. What happens then?

It's early to think about that, but I wonder if an LLC with Zach and Patti would be a good option. And maybe Roy, too, if he continues be such an asset.

Maybe a bonus buyout over five or ten years?

There's plenty of time to consider that.

Someone once said we don't own land, we just borrow it. During future generations, the land will still be here and we will be gone, replaced by others.

These deep thoughts have worked up an appetite. Time to get back to the ranch house for lunch, and then pack up for my return home to Rockford. In a month, Barbara and I will fly out for the wedding.

There's a lot more to this story.

Just not now.

THE END

JHS

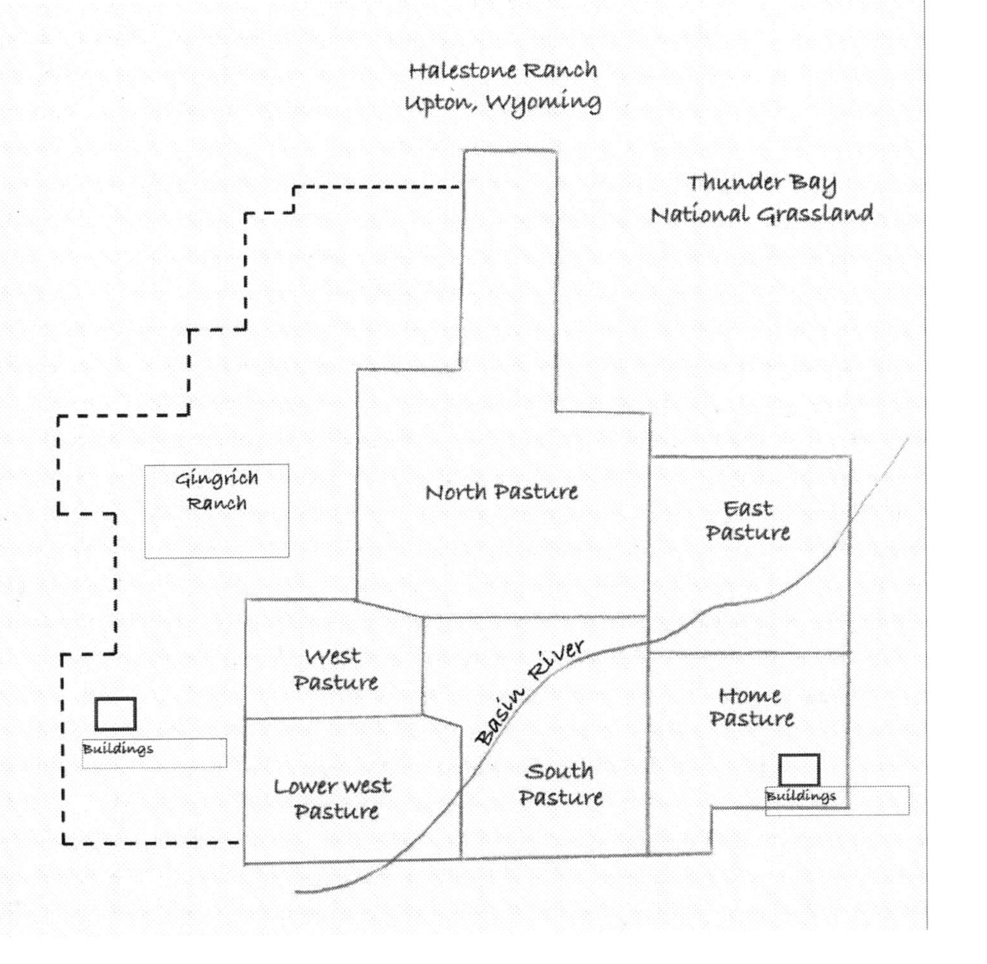
Halestone Ranch
Upton, Wyoming
Thunder Bay
National Grassland
Gingrich
Ranch
North Pasture
East
Pasture
West
Pasture
Basin River
Home
Pasture
Buildings
Lower west
Pasture
South
Pasture
Buildings

ACKNOWLEDGMENTS

To my wife, Joan, and children Jeff, Linda, and Stephen, for their constant support of my new addiction to writing.

Stephen deserves extra appreciation for designing the cover, inside artwork and the Halestone Ranch brand.

To Bob and Jean Harshbarger at the 4W Ranch for their friendship and hospitality during my many trips there. Little did I know that those experiences would lead to this book.

To International Harvester Collectors Club and its 7,500 members for their huge support of my earlier book *The Breakup*, which led to the Farmall and FFA storyline in this one. They keep the IH legend alive.

To Diane Montiel and Steve Alexander at Main Point Press, my editors and publishers, for their inspiration and guidance.

OTHER BOOKS BY PAUL WALLEM

Private Wings — My Life in Logbooks (2016)
The Breakup — What Really Happened (2019)

Made in the USA
Columbia, SC
16 June 2020